"WE'VE GOT TO GO BACK. THEY NEED US MORE THAN EVER NOW."

Merrilee looked up through her tears and cried, "No! That's not the way!" Her sharp cry split through the shell of rage engulfing Danner, and blinking, he looked down at her. "North!" she spat. "Our way lies north!" Then her voice became deadly calm. "In Gron dwells the source of the evil. The best way to kill a snake is to cut off its head. And that's what we must do—snare the viper in its nest. . . ."

New Worlds of Fantasy for You to Explore

BOOK THREE OF THE IRON TOWER TRILOGY
THE DARKEST DAY

DENNIS L. McKIERNAN

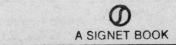

A SIGNET BOOK

NEW AMERICAN LIBRARY

SIGNET TRADEMARK REG. U.S. PAT. OFF. AND FOREIGN COUNTRIES
REGISTERED TRADEMARK—MARCA REGISTRADA
HECHO EN CHICAGO, U.S.A.

SIGNET, SIGNET CLASSIC, MENTOR, PLUME, MERIDIAN AND NAL BOOKS are published by New American Library, 1633 Broadway, New York, New York 10019

First Signet Printing, October, 1985

1 2 3 4 5 6 7 8 9

PRINTED IN THE UNITED STATES OF AMERICA

"... it is the way of our living that is testament to our spirits, and perhaps the way we die ..."

Tuckerby Underbank
February 1, 4E2019

CONTENTS

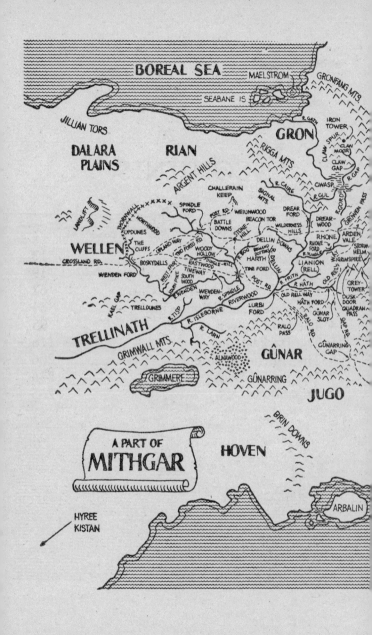

SYNOPSIS

This is the third part of The Iron Tower.

The first part, *The Dark Tide*, told of unsettled times in the Boskydells, where the Wee Folk—the Warrows—prepared for trouble. Amid rumors of Wolves and of mysterious disappearances, of War and of dark Evil looming to the far north, five young-buccan Warrows—Tuck, Danner, Hob, Tarpy, and their guide Patrel—set forth from Woody Hollow to join the Thornwalker company guarding Spindle Ford. On the way, the buccen were attacked by evil, Wolf-like Vulgs, and Hob was slain.

Surviving to carry the word that Vulgs were in the Bosky, the four remaining buccen continued on to Spindle Ford, where they took up their Thornwalker duties in Patrel's squad. Some days later, as a Kingsman came sounding the High King's call to War, Tarpy was killed during another Vulg attack.

Swearing vengeance, Tuck, Danner, and Patrel, and two squads of Warrows set forth from the Boskydells to answer the muster at Challerain Keep.

Upon arriving at the stronghold, they learned of the Dimmendark, a spectral Shadowlight to the north, where the Sun did not shine and Adon's Ban did not rule; hence, evil Modru's vile creatures

—Vulgs, Rūcks, Hlōks, Ogrus, Ghûls, Hèlsteeds—
roamed free.

The Warrows were assigned Castle-ward duties,
and Tuck became friends with Princess Laurelin,
betrothed of High King Aurion's elder son, Prince
Galen, absent from the castle on a mission into the
Dimmendark.

Tuck, Danner, and Patrel were invited to Laurelin's birthday feast. At the height of the celebration a wounded warrior came bearing news that
the dreadful pall of the Dimmendark had started
moving southward toward the Keep. The Winter
War had begun.

The next day Princess Laurelin departed Challerain Keep, heading south on the last waggon
train of refugees. She was escorted by the King's
younger son, Prince Igon, who was travelling to
Pellar to hasten the King's Host northward.

The Dimmendark soon swept over the Keep and
beyond. The spectral Shadowlight baffled eyesight:
Men saw at most two miles over open plains and
much less in forests and hill country; Elves saw
perhaps twice as far as Men; but the strange, jewel-
hued eyes of the Warrows, as if seeing by a new
color, saw farthest of all, as much as five miles.
Hence, the Warrow company was sundered, and
the buccen were assigned to various of the King's
companies to be their eyes in the Dimmendark.

At last one of Modru's evil Hordes came through
the Dimmendark and assaulted the woefully un-
dermanned Keep, overwhelming the defenders. On
the final 'Day of combat, Challerain Keep was
abandoned by the King's forces as they attempted
to break free of the Horde.

Separated from the others during the last desperate battle, Tuck eluded a Rūck patrol by taking
refuge in the ancient tomb of Othran the Seer.

Weaponless, he discovered in the sarcophagus an elden blade of Atala and a single red arrow for his bow. By happenstance, Prince Galen came to the same tomb. Alone and armed with only the Atalar Blade and the red arrow, the Man and the Warrow fled southward, striking for Stonehill to rendezvous with any other alies who might have survived.

Before reaching Stonehill, Galen and Tuck came upon the slaughtered remains of Laurelin's refugee train, ravaged by Ghûls. Neither Laurelin nor Igon was among the slain. Taking up weapons from the dead, Galen and Tuck followed the Ghûl track, hoping to overtake the Hèlsteed-borne Ghûls and somehow set the Prince and Princess free—if indeed they were captives.

Two 'Darkdays later the Man and Warrow came to the Weiunwood, the site of a three-'Day battle wherein one of Modru's Hordes had been repelled by the Weiunwood Alliance of Men, Elves, and Warrows. From the Captains of the Alliance, Galen and Tuck learned that a party of Ghûls bearing eastward had passed by some six 'Darkdays ago, later followed by a lone rider.

Continuing their pursuit, Tuck and Galen rode eastward too and came at last to the Elven strongholt of Arden Vale. Upon hearing of their mission, the Elven leader, Lord Talarin, led them to a house of healing where they found Prince Igon, wounded and feverish. In a moment of lucidity Igon confirmed that Laurelin was in fact a prisoner of the Ghûls.

In that same moment Elf Lord Gildor arrived at Arden Vale to tell Galen that Aurion Redeye was dead and that Galen was now High King of all Mithgar.

The second part, *Shadows of Doom*, told of Laurelin's capture and the journey to the Iron

Tower—Modru's strongholt in Gron—where she was thrown into a filthy lightless cell.

Meanwhile, Danner and Patrel, escaping from the ruins of Challerain Keep, made their way to Stonehill and thence to the Boskydells, where they discovered that Ghûlen ravers had invaded the Seven Dells.

Rescued from death by Merrilee, the two buccen organized the Warrows to carry the fight to the Ghûls. Using Merrilee's plan, they fought and won the Battle of Budgens and began planning a strike against the Ghûlen camp in Brackenboro.

Elsewhere, in Arden Vale, Galen, now King, torn between love and duty, chose duty: He set forth southward with Tuck and Elf Lord Gildor to rally the Host against the Horde. As Galen and his two comrades began the journey, Gildor's brother, Vanidor, and three other Lian warriors set off to the north—to Gron—to scout out Modru's strength and to attempt to rescue Laurelin.

Galen, Tuck, and Gildor happened upon the Dwarf warrior Brega, the only survivor of a clash between Dwarves and Spawn, and Brega joined the trio. It was from Brega that Galen learned that the south was beset by others of Modru's cohorts— the Rovers of Kistan and the Lakh of Hyree—hence the beleaguered Host had been unable to answer the King's muster at Challerain Keep.

The four comrades were discovered by the Ghûls and pursued to the Dusk-Door of Drimmen-deeve, where Brega—speaking the arcane Dwarven lore-words of old—caused the Door to open. As the four prepared to take refuge in the West Hall, the Monster of the Dark Mere, the Krakenward, assaulted the comrades.

And far to the north in Gron, Laurelin was taken from her cell deep in the dungeons and led to

Modru's evil sanctum high atop the Iron Tower. There she was forced to witness the torture of Vanidor, for his mission to rescue the Princess had failed and he had been captured. Modru sought to gain from the Elf information about others who may have come into Gron.

During the torture, Modru boasted that his own master, Gryphon, an evil being as prepotent as the high deity Adon, would be brought to Mithgar by the power of the Myrkenstone—a fragment of the Dragon Star. Modru also boasted that the force of the Myrkenstone was responsible for the Dimmendark.

Vanidor refused to answer Modru's questions and was slain upon the rack.

And far south at the Dusk-Door, at the moment of Vanidor's death, his twin, Lord Gildor, cried out Vanidor's name and collapsed during the Krakenward's attack. Hauling Gildor, Brega fled with Tuck and Galen into the dread-filled halls of Drimmen-deeve.

Trapped by the Krakenward and unable to re-open the Dusk-Door, the four made their way eastward through the dark caverns of Drimmen-deeve toward the distant Dawn-Gate. Ere reaching that eastern exit, they were whelmed by the Gargon, a massive, hideous, fear-casting Mandrak that came to slay them. By happenstance, the comrades managed to kill the creature and flee out through the Dawn-Gate.

The four companions—Man, Elf, Dwarf, and Warrow—strode southward away from the Quadran, and at last escaped from the Dimmendark into sunlight and came to the Larkenwald, where Coron Eiron ruled. They pressed on by Elven boat down the River Nith to the Great Escarpment and thence upon the Great River Argon, faring for the Argon Ferry far to the south, hoping to obtain aid in finding the Host.

It was during this river ride that Gildor at last remembered the rede thrust upon him by his twin at the moment of Vanidor's death. From the death rede, the comrades deduced that during a forthcoming solar eclipse Modru would somehow bring Gyphon to Mithgar, and then all of creation would be in Gyphon's power.

The four raced on to the Argon Ferry, where they discovered a defeated Host in retreat.

Following the counsel of Brega and of a Valonian Reachmarshal named Ubrik, the four galloped day and night with Ubrik to come to Gûnarring Gap. There their hopes were realized, for they found a victorious army of Harlingar, warriors of Valon. These Vanadurin had the fiery steeds needed to reach the far-distant Iron Tower ere the coming of the eclipse—ere the coming of the Darkest Day. For Galen had decided that only by launching an attack on the Iron Tower would the Alliance stand even the slimmest chance of thwarting Modru's vile plan to bring Evil Gyphon to Mithgar.

Yet as the Valonian cavalry prepared to depart from Gûnarring Gap, a mounted force of unknown origin charged down upon them from out of the pass . . .

But as *The Darkest Day* begins, we return to the Boskydells on the 'Day after the Battle of Budgens.

CHAPTER 1

THE GATHERING

It was the 'Darkday following the Battle of Budgens, and at Whitby's barn a breathless buccan scout flung himself down from his lathered blowing pony and dashed into the huge byre.

"Cap'n Patrel!" he cried. "The Ghûls! The Ghûls have burnt Budgens!"

"Wha—?" Patrel's eyes jerked up from the map lying on the rough table before the council, and he spun toward the scout as the rushing buccan skidded to a halt before him. "What did you say, Arcy? Did you say Budgens?"

"Yar, Cap'n Patrel, Budgens!" blurted Arcy, red-faced, gesturing wildly. "The Ghûls, they came—a great drove of them—lookin' for Warrows. And when they didn't find any, they put the whole town to the torch!"

Luth's clenched fist slammed down to the planking, and Merrilee's hand flew to her mouth, her eyes wide. Bitter looks fell upon the faces of some Lieutenants, while others ground their teeth in rage.

"They seek revenge for what we did to them,"

said Patrel, his voice grim. "Woe to the Warrow who falls into their hands, for death will come slowly, but agony swift."

Orbin leapt to his feet and paced in agitation. "We've got to root them out of the Seven Dells before the Bosky is destroyed! For even should we win this War, it will go hard on the survivors, and harder still if there is no place to live, no shelter!"

"Argh!" gnashed Norv, the muscles in his jaw jumping. "I say we've got to kill 'em all, or at least enough of 'em to drive 'em out, else none of us will survive, shelter or no!" Shouts of agreement rose up.

"Calm down, all of you!" barked Patrel, facing the council. Then he turned once more to the scout. "After torching Budgens, Arcy, which way did they ride?"

"South, Cap'n," replied Arcy, "back toward the Crossland Road."

Luth growled. "They've probably got back to Brackenboro. How about the patrol, Arcy, the one we sent to the ruins?"

"Ar, Lieutenant Luth, they were gone on before the Ghûls came, so Cap'n Danner and his scouts weren't delayed any," answered the buccan.

At mention of the scouting party sent to the ruins of Brackenboro, Merrilee's face took on a frown, for Danner had gone with four others south through the Dimmendark to come among the hills surrounding that devastated place to spy out the movements of the Ghûls. Merrilee was beset by doubt, for it was a dangerous mission—a mission of her own devising.

"Well," said Patrel, vexed, "until Danner gets back, we'll do nothing."

* * *

Over the next two 'Darkdays, Patrel paced the barn floor and gritted his teeth and flung himself busily into fletching arrows and often rode through the Shadowlight to the top of Whitby's Hill to look for Danner; but of the Woody Hollow buccan and his quartet of scouts, there was no sign. And when Patrel would come back to the barn and faintly shake his head no to Merrilee, both of their spirits would fall.

The damman, too, spent long hours staring through the Dimmendark for sign of Danner's band; yet, like Patrel, Merrilee would come dejected back to the Warrow headquarters and throw herself into busywork.

And secretly in both their hearts they wondered if something had gone awry: Perhaps Danner and the others had been wounded or slain . . . or worse yet, captured by the vile maggot-folk. But of these covert fears they said nought to one another, although each knew the hidden dreads harbored in the bosom of the other.

Yet late on the third 'Darkday, Danner and his squad came unannounced unto the barn. Danner was filled near to bursting with glad news, and he grabbed Merrilee up and hugged her and dizzily spun her around and set her down awhirl, and then he slapped Patrel on the back. "Paddy! Merrilee! I saw my dad! He's alive! He says my mom is fine, too! He and she and a great many other Warrows have got to the Eastwood—folks from Bryn and Midwood, Thimble and Willowdell, and some from Budgens and Woody Hollow . . . and Brackenboro, too. They're all making it into a strongholt, like Gildor told that the Weiunwood is. Dad's helping organize the resistance—got his own company of archers: Hanlo's Reya, they call themselves in the old tongue—Hanlo's Foxes. They haven't fought yet, but they'll join with us at Brackenboro when we strike."

And Danner and his scouts were drawn inside and given a warm meal and hot tea, and tears of happiness glistened in Merrilee's eyes, for the squad was safe.

"Down along the Southrill we went, till we came to the hills around Brackenboro." Danner paused long enough to fill his pipe with leaf and light it, leaning back to blow a smoke ring or two. "When the town was due west of us, into the downs we went, cautious as field mice slipping past the weasel.

"Imagine our surprise, then, when before we could reach sight of the ruins, another band of Warrows came like smoke out of the bracken to ask us who we were and what was our mission.

"When I gave 'em our names and told 'em our purpose, they said to follow them, they'd show us what we were up against. Seems that they, too, were spying on the Ghûls in Brackenboro. Those eight buccen had all lived in the 'Boro before the Dimmendark and the reavers came. But they had fled to the Eastwood and had formed companies, and had come back to scout out the Ghûls, for the Eastwooders are thinking of attack, too.

"Now we came to the hills directly surrounding Brackenboro, and we all slipped down from our ponies and stealthily crept on foot to the crests overlooking the town.

"It's a ruin, Paddy: all burnt down, but for a few buildings. And Ghûls swarm all around, and sweep in and out like a plague of locusts that comes and goes. There are a thousand or so of them—"

"A thousand!" interrupted Luth. "But we've only

got three hundred, four hundred Warrows! We can't take on nearly three times our number!"

"Aye, Luth," answered Danner, "you are right. And that's exactly what I thought at first. But I don't think it'll come to that. You see, all one thousand of the Ghûls aren't always at Brackenboro at the same time. While we were there, companies of them rode in and out, and at times there were as many as eight, nine hundred. *But at other times there were as few as one hundred.*"

As few as one hundred, thought Merrilee. *Just days ago, one hundred Ghûls would have seemed an invincible force, yet now we think once more to attack five score of these monstrous reavers, as we did in Budgens. But this time they will not be caught in a high-walled trap.*

Merrilee's attention was tugged back to the council as Danner spoke on: "And so we lay belly-down on the backslopes of the ridgetops and watched the Ghûls come and go all that 'Darkday. And as we watched, the Eastwooders spoke of the burning of the 'Boro, and how they and other Warrows had come to the woods, though they'd left many dead behind.

"And they told how they formed companies out of six hundred or so archers, and set about preparing to defend the Eastwood. But one of their Captains, back in the 'Wood, had said as how they ought not only to defend, but also ought to attack if a way could be found to kill Ghûls. And, 'Oh, by the way,' said one of the Eastwooders as we lay there on the ridgetop, 'your name is Bramblethorn . . . Are you any kin to that Captain? Hanlo is his name, Hanlo Bramblethorn.'

"Lor! I could have grabbed up that Eastwooder and kissed him right there on the spot, but the Ghûls below might have disapproved if they had seen us, and so I just lay there looking down at a ruined town teeming with relentless enemies, and I couldn't stop grinning for joy.

"I had sent some of the buccoes around to the south and some to the north, and when they finally reported back, we compared with each other what we'd seen that 'Darkday, and with what the Eastwooders had seen on other 'Days.

"And we decided then and there that the only way we can attack the enemy is by joining our two forces and falling upon Brackenboro when the Ghûlen numbers are at a low ebb. We can bring perhaps nine, ten hundred archers to bear, and if the enemy is at a hundred or so, then we can whelm them, even though they won't be penned up like they were in Budgens."

A murmur of agreement rippled through the Lieutenants.

"What do the Eastwooders say?" asked Patrel.

"They're for it," answered Danner. "We rode from Brackenboro deep into the Eastwood, and the next 'Darkday we met with their Captains and Lieutenants. That's when I saw my sire. Lor! You should have seen him start when he clapped eyes on me. Almost crushed me in a bear hug, he did. But I think his ribs creaked a bit, too.

"In council, I told them of the way to slay Ghûls, and what we'd done at Budgens. They'd heard none of it before, and it was glad news to them, for now they knew that they had a way to fight. I also told them about Challerain Keep, and that King Aurion was dead. These dire tidings only stiffened their resolve.

"Paddy, they want us to bring all our company down into the Eastwood, to join with them and lay assaults upon Brackenboro until the enemy is driven out—out of that town, out of all towns, out of the Dells, out of the Bosky."

Danner paused, then said, "My sire put his finger on it: 'There's a loose Horde up at the Keep, now,' he said, 'and soon they'll be marching south, I ween. We've got to have these Ghûls out of the Boskydells and the Thornring stoppered up tight before Modru's Swarm comes knocking on our doors; for if they come before we can shut them out, nothing will survive. All will die. Modru will see to it. The forests will be hewn down and the trees left to rot where they lie; fields will be plowed and salted; the wells, streams, lakes, and rivers, poisoned; animals, both wild and tame, will be slaughtered; and Warrows, put to the death or let slowly starve in bondage. This doom must not befall the Dells!'" Danner's countenance was drained of blood, his lips compressed in a thin line. "My sire is right. We have much to do and little time to do it in. We must strike the Ghûls, and strike now!"

The next 'Darkday, the entire company—three hundred sixty-two buccen and one damman—rode south by covert ways into the Eastwood, where they joined with the Warrows waiting there. Long did they lay out their plans, with Captains Patrel and Danner joining the four Eastwood Captains in a great council of Lieutenants. And when the plans were laid, the last question was asked by Neddy Finch, a Lieutenant from Midwood: "The only thing left to decide is when we strike, so I asks it: When?"

Hanlo Bramblethorn spoke up: "You all know how I feel in this matter—the sooner we strike, the better. Yet though my Reya are ready now, we'd best get some rest, for the fight may be long and hard, and the pursuit merciless. But this I do say, not a 'Darkday should pass without action against the Ghûls. Hence, I say we fight on the morrow." And the chestnut-haired, amber-eyed buccan sat down. Merrilee's heart hammered in her bosom, but when the vote came, she added her *aye* to all the others.

They rode from the barren Eastwood, crossing first the Southrill and then the trace running north and south, and they came at last among the Brackenboro Hills. They were six companie˜ strong: fifty-four squads, one thousand eighty-six Warrows, armed with nought but bow and arrow to go up against the spears and tulwars and Hèlsteeds of the Ghûls.

Among the Warrow companies rode the guides from Brackenboro, buccen familiar with the hills and vales around the town. And they led the squads behind the ridges and through the downs until the 'Boro was beringed by the Warrow warriors.

Long did they wait, hidden on the hillsides, and they watched as companies of Ghûls on Hèlsteeds rode along the Boro Spur, coming and going to their evil ends.

Now the Warrows crept unseen down through the bracken—unto the very edges of the ruins—and once more they waited, this time for the signal.

Ghûls rode in and Ghûls rode out, and yet still too many stayed among the ruins. Merrilee's heart hammered loudly in her ears, and she despaired that the odds would ever tumble in the Warrows' favor. And every moment that passed increased the chances of discovery. But at last more reavers seemed to be riding out than rode in, and the numbers of the remaining Ghûls began to dwindle. The Warrow strategy was simplicity itself: When the Ghûl numbers had diminished favorably, the archers would strike fast and hard, and if they overwhelmed the Ghûls remaining in Brackenboro, then the archers would lie in ambush along the Boro Spur and slay the Ghûlen companies as they each in turn came back from their foul missions. Should the odds shift in the Ghûls' favor, then the Warrows would retreat through the Shadowlight, first to the hills and then to Eastwood, covering their tracks in the snow, losing the foe in the Dimmendark. Yet though their overall scheme was simple, still they had planned their movements and signals down to the finest possible detail, with alternative plans should events turn in other ways. And now approached the moment to see if their stratagems would succeed or fall.

The numbers of Ghûls had fallen below five hundred; and still the Warrows watched. And Merrilee's heart raced, for two more Ghûlen companies prepared to set forth; and she knew that when they were gone, the signal would sound and the attack would begin. Once again she checked her arrows. She bore two full quivers, and nearby lay bundled sheaves of extra quarrels.

Now the Hèlsteeds' hooves thundered as the two companies of Ghûls set forth upon the Boro Spur, swinging west then north to join the Crossland Road. And Time seemed to step on quickened feet.

At last the companies passed beyond seeing behind the downs, but still the signal was not sounded, for the Warrows waited until the Ghûls were beyond hearing. It would not do to have the reavers hear the call to battle, or the sounds of combat.

Time passed, and Patrel kept watch upon the hill northwest of Brackenboro, and so did nearly all the Warrows; for upon that hill a lookout was posted, and he would signal when the Ghûls were beyond seeing.

At last the hooded lantern flashed—just once—and all then knew the battle was only a tick of time away.

And arrows nocked strings . . .

And hearts thudded . . .

And eyes sought out the nearest Ghûls, the nearest targets . . .

And breaths were drawn in . . .

And time seemed frozen.

And Patrel raised the silver Horn of the Reach—the Horn of Valon—to his lips, and a clarion call split the air: a call to arms, a call to War, a call to attack: *Ta, tahn! Ta, tahn! Ta, tahn!* Even as the silver notes pealed forth, a sleet of arrows hissed through the air to strike home. Warrows were up and running and setting new bolts to string, then stopping to loose the quarrels ere dashing forth once more.

Again and again the silver call belled forth, and everywhere brave hearts were lifted and bold spirits surged. Yet the Ghûls quailed to hear such notes, and Hèlsteeds reared in fright.

Hails of arrows thudded into corpse-flesh, and foe fell slain, pierced through the heart. But Ghûls rallied and mounted beasts and spurred forth upon the Wee Folk. Barbed spears and curved tulwars pierced and hacked, and some Warrows were caught unaware and slain by point, edge, and hoof, for the Hèlsteeds were trained to trample enemy underfoot. Yet though Warrows died, still the flying quarrels rained into the Ghûls.

Merrilee nocked arrow after arrow, her eyes and aim following charging Ghûl, and Tuck whispered in her mind as she methodically loosed bolt upon bolt. And where she aimed, reaver fell.

But Danner was magnificent, for his amber eyes were everywhere his arrows could reach, and he dropped Ghûls left and right. Along with a select few, Danner's was the chore to spot Ghûls coming at Warrows unknowing, and to slay the foe ere they could rend death. And only one buccan in Danner's sector fell by Ghûlen hand, and that was by a flung spear.

And almost as soon as it had begun, the battle was ended. The Ghûls had stood little chance, for the odds were five to one against them. And the Warrows had cast death from afar and did not stand to fight, but instead slipped aside as elusive as the shadows in and out of which they faded. The Warrows had been victorious, but not all the Ghûls had died, for a score or so had fled on Hèlsteeds, some down the Boro Spur, others up through the hills.

A scattered cheering broke out among the Warrow ranks but was silenced quickly, for only this skirmish had been won and not the Battle of Brackenboro, not the War of the Boskydells: the Struggles went on. And squads were assembled to trot swiftly down the Spur to set up ambush for the returning Ghûlen companies, likely now to be on alert, for the escaped foe would warn them.

The six Warrow companies lay in Shadowlighted ambuscade along the Boro Spur—three on the north side, three on the south—and this was their plan: once the returning Ghûls were deep within the trap, the companies would catch them in a deadly cross fire. And when the Ghûls were slain, if need be the companies would move up the road away from the slaughter and lay in ambush again.

But though that was their plan, no Ghûl had yet fallen victim, for none had yet returned. Long had the Warrows waited; and all about them a westerly breeze rustled through the winter-dried bracken.

"They've never stayed away this long before," said Rollo Breed, one of the Brackenboro scouts. "By now the 'Boro should be full of them again."

"Ar. Those that escaped have warned them off," gritted Hanlo. "Like as not, they'll be coming in force and we'll have to melt away before them."

Patrel looked to the hilltop with the sentinel on it and fretted, for no signal had come from the lookout that Ghûls were on the way: green meant that the returning force was small and could be ambushed, whereas red would mean retreat.

On a premonition, Patrel said, "Rollo, head up to the hilltop. Make certain that nothing untoward has befallen Chubb. I just now recall that one or two escaping Ghûls rode that way."

Rollo ran through the stirring bracken and sprang upon the back of his pony. And as the buccan spurred up the snowy hill, Danner grunted, "Good idea." They watched the scout as he disappeared among the winter-dried fern brakes.

Long they peered, both along the road and up the hill. Yet nought did they see. Then Hanlo raised his hand and barked, "Hist! I hear . . . something." And before any could say aught, the elder Bramble-thorn dropped to the ground and laid his ear to the earth. "Hooves! Many hooves! Like thunder they come!" he cried.

At that moment Rollo and his pony burst back through the bracken. "Cap'n! The Ghûls! The Ghûls are coming!" Rollo leapt down at Patrel's side, breathless words tumbling past one another in the scout's urgency to get them all out. "Chubb is dead, slain by Ghûl spear, and a dead reaver lies nearby, but I found the tracks of *two* Hèlsteeds. Chubb got one Ghûl, but the other got him. Chubb's

lamps were shattered, so I couldn't signal you when
I saw the Ghûls down on the Boro Spur. Ghûls
come on Hèlsteeds: hundreds ... and fast. And
three miles or so behind comes another bunch:
five, six times as many. We've got to get away!
Now! They are too many!"

"Too late!" spat Hanlo, setting an arrow to string.
"Here they come!" And bursting 'round a bend in
the Boro Spur hammered five hundred Hèlsteeds,
howling Ghûls on their backs, Ghûls yawling for
revenge.

Patrel glanced at Danner for his advice, but that
young buccan, just like his sire Hanlo, set arrow to
bow, preparing for battle.

"Wait!" cried Merrilee. "Rollo is right! We can't
stand and fight them! They are too many, and an
even greater force follows these! Signal the retreat, Patrel, and most of us will live to fight again!"

Patrel looked sharply at Merrilee and then at the
charging Ghûls, now less than a half mile away,
the Hèlsteeds' driving pace rapidly closing the
distance.

Withdraw! Withdraw! Withdraw! The silent hand
signal flashed up and down the Warrow ranks on
either side of the road, as Patrel gave the order to
retreat. And buccen began to slip quietly back into
the Shadowlighted fern brakes, moving with the
legendary stealth of the Wee Folk.

But then the foetid scent of the charging Hèlsteeds
was borne by the wind unto Rollo's pony, being
led through the brake, and the small steed plunged
and reared and screamed in fear at this foul stink.
The animal jerked the reins from Rollo's hand and
bolted in fright through the bracken and onto the
road, fleeing eastward down the Spur.

At sight of the stampeding pony, the Ghûls

harshly checked their 'Steeds to churn about while
some stalked forward, their dull, flat, dead black
eyes trying to pierce the rustling bracken alongside the Spur; it had not occurred to the Ghûls
that an ambush could have lain along their path,
for they had thought instead that their foe now
occupied the ruins of Brackenboro.

A Ghûl in the fore uttered harsh barks and howls,
and the Hèlsteed force split in twain: half rode
into the bracken to the left, half to the right. And
now they were alert and wary, their spears lowered at the ready, tulwars in hand. The Hèlsteeds
breasted through the rattling fern brakes, surging,
lunging apace, while before them—as yet unseen—
the Warrows faded back among the shadows.

Yet Hèlsteed is swifter than Warrow on foot,
and suddenly there came a Ghûl yawl, cut short in
mid howl by swift arrow; even so, fleeting Warrows
on the north side of the Boro Spur had been discovered, and at nearly the same time Hèlsteeds
stumbled across pockets of Warrows on the south
side, too. Chilling yowls split the air, and there
came the raucous blats of Rūckish horns, answered
by the hiss of deadly quarrels as Warrows paused
to loose arrows at the questing foe ere fading onward through the bracken.

Now the Ghûls knew their enemy, but despite
the fact that the corpse-foe had been whelmed in
Brackenboro, they as yet held the Wee Folk in
contempt, and charged the Hèlsteeds through the
winter-dried fern brakes. *Swish! Swash!* rattled the
bracken at the passage of the Hèlspawn, while
hidden Warrows fled among the shielding growth.

But the balance between the reavers and the
archers began to shift, for the close-set bracken
was a two-edged sword: not only did it shield the
Wee Folk, but it also hid the Ghûls, and Warrows

could not see to loose their arrows. And Ghûls burst forth upon buccen, and spears dipped to take their toll, or slashing tulwars rived redly, and Warrows were trampled under cloven hooves. Thus did Regin Burk die, and Alvy Willoby, and Neddy Finch, and many others, for now the spear and blade and driving 'Steed were favored in the shock of sudden onslaught, and Warrows fell by the tens and twenties as they fled through the brakes and up the hill slopes.

Danner and Patrel and Merrilee ran among the bracken, and to right and left Hèlsteeds crashed by unseen. Now and again the trio would glimpse other Warrows flitting through the Shadowlight, but for the most part they saw no one else, though howls of Ghûls and blat of horns and grunts of Hèlsteeds and hammer of cloven hooves were all about them, as well as the grim cry of Death.

Merrilee's breath came in harsh gasps as she dodged among the brittle ferns with Danner and Patrel at her side, and racing blood pounded in her ears. North and up over the hills they had tried to flee, but always it seemed they heard Ghûls that way, and so they were driven east, back toward the ruins of Brackenboro. And Merrilee felt as if she were being *herded* by cruel hounds. East they went, and east some more, flying before blind pursuit. At last, after endless running, they were driven from the rattling brakes to come in among the charred spars of the ravaged 'Boro, and they fled along streets littered with the corpses of Ghûls the Warrows had slain earlier. They heard the clatter of cloven hooves sounding on the cobbles around the corner ahead, and the trio crouched in hiding amid tumbled rubble alongside a blackened wall.

"We've got to get out of here," panted Danner.

"The Ghûls'll come, some already are here, and we've got to be away before then."

Patrel squinted at the hills above, his breath blowing in and out. "Our ponies are yon, beyond the near downs, yet Ghûls hunt the slopes between there and here. Perhaps we can—"

Patrel's words were chopped short by a hideous howl as a Ghûl on Hèlsteed rounded the broken wall and saw the trio.

Thuun . . . shthock! Danner's loosed arrow struck the reaver in the breast, and the foe pitched dead from the saddle. But a lifeless foot was stirrup-caught, and the Hèlsteed grunted and squealed in terror at this dragging thing and plunged away bucking. Yet though the Ghûl was dead, his last howl had brought others running, and three more Spawn on Hèlsteeds galloped around the corner, cloven hooves ringing on the cobblestones.

Ssthack! Sssthok! Thock! Flying death hissed through the air to fell two of the reavers. The third hauled his Hèlsteed back and over too sharply, and the creature crashed to the icy cobbles. And as the Ghûl rose to his feet, *Th-th-thock!* three arrows slammed into him, any one of which would have slain him, and he fell slaughtered as his 'Steed scrambled up and bolted.

But now the three Warrows heard the hammer of more cloven hooves upon the pave, and other Ghûls burst 'round the edge.

Taa-tahn! Taa-tahn! The silver call of the Horn of Valon split the air as Patrel set the rune-marked bugle to his lips and blew. And the Ghûls checked their Hèlsteeds and quailed back from the pure, bell-like call, for the notes drove fear deep into the corpse-foe. Danner and Merrilee loosed hissing death upon the milling Ghûls, and two fell slain while the remaining five spurred forward, howling in anger.

Calmly, Merrilee continued to pluck arrows from her quiver and set them to bow, and her bolts flew at the oncoming foe. Danner's quarrels, too, and now Patrel's sissed in deadly flight through the air. And the Ghûls charged at the Warrows, barbed lances lowered to spit these three; cloven hooves rang on the cobble as on the Hèlsteeds came.

But bolts sped true to pierce Ghûl breast and heart, and corpse-foe fell slain. 'Steeds veered wide, no longer commanded. Four Ghûls came on . . . now three . . . now two; and as the pair thundered down upon the Warrows, Danner, Patrel, and Merrilee leapt aside among the rubble, falling and rolling as the hooves hammered past. The barbed spears missed the dodging targets, though a point pierced Patrel's jacket to skitter and glance along the golden armor underneath. Danner sprang up cursing and felled one more Ghûl as the two reavers raced away. The lone survivor veered his Hèlsteed, and Merrilee's arrow thudded into the Ghûl's side and did not pierce his heart.

Now the Hèlsteed passed beyond arrow range, and the Ghûl spun his mount and checked it. He plucked the offending arrow from below his ribs and flung it away, and then he raised a brazen horn to his lips and blatted a call of assembly. Blares of nearby Rūckish horns clamantly answered from the surrounding ruins.

Calmly Danner began laying out arrows before him upon a fallen spar, where the quarrels would be within easy reach. "They've got us cornered, Paddy, Merrilee, and they'll come in numbers too great to overcome, yet we'll take as many down with us as we can."

Harsh blares and brazen blats drew nearer, and there was the clatter of cloven hooves upon the cobble pave. Now two, then eight more corpse-folk rode into sight to join the surviving Ghûl at the north end of the street. Wrawling horn blasts came from the south, as distant Ghûls hove into view, and calls from east and west sounded, too.

Merrilee set her quiver before her and put arrow to string. Her jaw was set at a grim angle, and her breathing was deep and measured. There was no hint of fear in her clear, sapphire-blue gaze.

Patrel took up the Horn of the Reach. "I'll sound it one last time. Then we'll give 'em a battle that bards would tell of ages from now if any but knew."

And amid the blats and blares of the brazen *Spaunen* horns, a pure silver clarion cry rose up into the sky and across the land as three Warrows— two buccen and a damman—prepared to fight a last battle, prepared to fight and die.

And as the call of the Horn of the Reach pealed across the land, the blatting blares of the Rückish brass fell silent, though in the distance it seemed that other horns sounded, too, as the silver echoes rang from the hills. The Ghûls paused a time, and peered uneasily about.

But at last the chief Ghûl among them raised his face to the darkling sky and howled a chilling cry. And from the west—from around the corner of the standing wall—there came the sounds of driving hooves upon the stones of Brackenboro and blasts upon belling horns.

"They're coming!" cried Patrel, facing toward the corner, his bow drawn to the full, death set to fly.

Now the hooves drummed louder—a thunder to the ear—and the pealing of horns rang clear. Then the first of many riders hove past the wall and into view:

Men upon horses!

"No!" cried Danner, knocking Patrel's arm up,

sending the arrow flying skyward over the silver-bearded horseman's head. *"It's Vidron!"*

And thundering upon coursers charging through the streets of Brackenboro came a full one thousand Men: warriors bearing the blue-and-white colors of Wellen, warriors sounding the horn calls of that western Land, warriors led by Kingsgeneral Vidron, Hrosmarshal of Valon. Squads and companies hurtled among the ruins of Brackenboro, and swords rived and lances pierced. The deadly Ghûls were utterly overwhelmed as shafts burst through their hearts and blades clove their heads from their bodies.

Amid the clash and clangor of battle, and while the hooves of steeds hammered past, and as the peals of horns split the air and lifted spirits, three Warrows—two buccen and a damman—danced about and shouted deliriously and hugged each other and cried.

"Arn, Captain Patrel, when I heard that silver horn—Elgo's horn of Sleeth's hoard—I knew 'twas you in desperate straits!" A wide grin split Field-marshal Vidron's face as he sat on a crate by the burnt-out wall where he'd come riding to find them. The reunion was like that of a grand uncle and his favorite nephews. And when Merrilee was introduced, the eyes of the veteran warrior widened in amaze. And he bowed to the damman, yet by his hearty manner he put her at her ease. Now they all sat in converse. "And so, to save your scalawag necks, I ordered the charge into Brackenboro, and no company of Guula are going to withstand a thousand horse-borne Wellenan warriors."

"But General Vidron," Merrilee quietly protested, "these are not all the Ghûls: another four hundred or so ride the downs and bracken, searching for our kindred. Warrows are now hard-pressed by the corpse-folk: The Ghûls hunt them like reya, like hounds after foxes."

"Aye, we know, lass," responded Vidron, beaming at the damman. "Some of your lads stopped us on the road and told us. Two thousand more of the Wellenen hunt the foul Wrg even now; list, you'll hear their horns." From the hills—north, south, and east—intermittently sounded the calls of the horns of Wellen.

"Two thousand more?" Patrel's eyes flew wide. "How came you by this army, Fieldmarshal? And in the Bosky, at that!"

"Why, lad, I went to Wellen and got them," answered Vidron. "And as to why, let me say this: When we broke free of the Guula at the north gate of Challerain Keep, we rode in a long arc to come at last to Stonehill—"

"Stonehill!" burst out Danner. "But we—Paddy and I—we were in Stonehill, waiting . . . three days."

"Two and a half," interjected Patrel.

"Two and a half days, then," continued Danner, "and no one came."

"When?" asked Vidron.

"Let me see," said Danner, reckoning the day while Patrel counted on his fingers. "I make it exactly two weeks past when we arrived there, early in the 'Darkday. The rest of the 'Day we stayed . . . all the next, too. Finally we left early on the third 'Darkday. And if my reckoning is right, that would make it the eighth of January." Patrel nodded in confirmation.

"Why, then," responded Vidron, "your path to Stonehill was swifter than mine." Then the Man's eyes widened in surprise. "Hola! If you left early on the eighth, you must have ridden out of one gate just as we rode in another!"

Danner and Patrel looked at one another and then at Vidron, and all three realized how close they had come to meeting together in Stonehill. And each realized, too, that the difference of but a moment in a person's life can alter the course of events forever. Why, perhaps if the Warrows had met with Vidron, the Battle of Budgens would not have occurred, or Vidron's journey to Wellen might not have taken place. Yet perhaps these things would have happened in any case, with the outcomes altered—in major or minor aspects—or . . .

Merrilee's question broke into the thoughts of the three. "General Vidron, did any Warrows ride from Challerain Keep with you? Perhaps Tuck . . ." Her voice trailed off, her eyes anxious.

"Ah, but no, lass," answered Vidron, shaking his head sadly. "When we broke free, not a Waldan was among us."

Merrilee looked away from the Hrosmarshal, and her shoulders sagged in despair. Silence reigned among the four for long moments, though the hills cast occasional horn calls to their ears, and the clatter of hooves rattled on the cobblestones of Brackenboro.

At last Vidron cleared his throat and spoke: "Of the five thousand defenders at Challerain Keep, I had thought that only sixty-three of us survived that last battle—sixty-two Men and one Elf, Lord Gildor. But now I find that Danner and Patrel cheated Death, too, bringing the tally up to sixty-five. And so there is yet hope—though slim it is— that others also survived the ordeal and live on . . . perhaps your Tuck." Vidron reached out and drew Merrilee next to him. The young damman sat with the Man and leaned her head against the warrior's side, and tears trickled down her face, yet she made no sound.

After a long pause Vidron picked up the thread of his tale: "On the second 'Darkday after we rode into Stonehill, a horseman came from the south. An ex-soldier he was, named Jarek. His cottage is in the Alnawood in Gûnar. His tale was chilling, though it explains much. Yet it leaves as many questions behind as it answers.

"It seems that Jarek was on his way to Valon, only to find that the Gûnarring Gap had been seized by a force of swarthy warriors—perhaps from the south: Chabba, Hurn, Hyree, or Kistan, he did not know the which of it. Ai! But Fortune favored him, turning her smiling face his way, and he was not discovered by the foe.

"And Jarek turned north, riding for Challerain Keep, bearing the word to Aurion . . . or if not to the High King, then to the Kingsmen.

"Across Ralo Pass he came and down into the Riverwood. Near the ruins of Luren, at the ford across the River Isleborne, he came through the Black Wall and into the cursed Dimmendark.

"Again Fortune favored him, for no Spawn did he meet while riding through the Shadowlight up along the Post Road, though at the bridge spanning the Bog River, he did hear the distant howling of 'Wolves,' though I deem it was Vulgs instead.

"At last Jarek came to Stonehill, and there he found us—the pitiful remnants of Aurion's northern might. And he told me his tale.

"Ai, but it was dire news, for I then knew why no word came from the south, and why the Host did not come to Challerain Keep: They fight an invading army in the south . . . likely our ancient enemies from Hyree or Kistan or both—for, ages past, they were in league with Modru, during the Great War."

"But that means the Host will not come," protested Patrel. "At least not for a while. Who, then, will fight the Horde? Who will keep them from the Bosky?"

"The Thornwall will thwart the Horde," said Danner, "if we can get it stoppered up again. But we've got to slay the Ghûls, too, or drive 'em out."

"We must slay them." Merrilee's voice was low.

"Vengeance?" asked Vidron.

"Nay," answered Merrilee, "though to some vengeance would taste sweet. No, not revenge, but instead this: We must close the Thornwall now, to keep the Horde out. And the Ghûls must be slain, to keep them from opening it up again, as they did before at Spindle Ford, and the bridge, and perhaps at the other crossings, too. There is this, too: I think Modru uses the Ghûls to reave us, to keep our minds on them and not on the Barrier. Till now he has succeeded, and if the 'Wall is left open, then his Swarm will march in and raze the Boskydells, as Hanlo so aptly foresaw. Hence, we must close the Thornring ere they come."

"You are right, Merrilee," said Patrel. "Even though by closing the Thornwall, we shut the Ghûls in with us, it must be done . . . and that means we will have to slay the reavers rather than drive them out. For to leave the Thornring open invites Modru's Horde to enter, though why they have not already come, I cannot say."

"Perhaps they still loot Challerain Keep," said Danner.

"Nay," spoke up Vidron, "for Modru would not allow petty spoils to disturb his careful plans. Nay, it is something else that delays his hand. Perhaps the Warlord of the Horde was slain in that last battle, and they await a new tyrant to drive them on."

"Hey! The emissary!" exclaimed Patrel. "The one Danner slew at the north gate. Perhaps he was the Warlord you speak of. Mayhap your arrow, Danner, has stayed their hand thus far."

"Be that as it may, it won't stop 'em: If they don't already have a Warlord, Modru will just send another," responded Danner. "Merrilee's right: We've got to plug up the Thornwall now. And then we'll set about killing the Ghûls."

"Ah, but your tactics must change," Vidron said. "The Guula will be wary, now, and no longer fall easy prey to ambuscades. That's why I will leave half of the Wellenan horsemen here in the Boskydells to aid you. The rest I take to Gûnarring Gap to try to break the enemy's hold there."

"The Gap?" said Patrel. "You go to the Gap?"

"Aye," answered Vidron. "When Jarek brought me the news of the enemy at that pass, I knew then that my mission would be to break their hold. I took my Men from Stonehill and we headed for Wellen, but Jarek I sent on to the Weiunwood to bear the news unto the Alliance and to Lord Gildor."

"Lord Gildor?" asked Patrel. "Wasn't he with you?"

"Nay, lad," answered Vidron. "Gildor had turned aside earlier as we went north of the 'Wood. I went on to the Battle Downs and then south to Stonehill to keep the rendezvous, while he went to seek tidings from his kin, Inarion, and to bear to the Weiunwooders the sad news of the fall of Challerain Keep and of the death of King Aurion."

"We saw Aurion slain," said Danner, his voice low. "He fought well and bravely, but there were just too many Ghûls."

"He was a great King and a valiant warrior," responded Vidron, "and his keen sword and royal hand will be sorely missed in the days ahead. If Galen survived, he is King now, and if not him, then young Igon."

"But wait!" cried Patrel. "Do you not know?" Then the buccan smote his forehead. "Ach, how could you? Laurelin's waggon train was Ghûl-slaughtered. All were slain but for Igon and the Princess, and they either escaped or were captured and borne east; at least that's the way it looked to Danner and me when we came upon the wrack, six or seven days after the Ghûls fell upon that ill-fated train."

Vidron's face blenched at this dire news. "When was this, and where?" he gritted.

"It was on the Post Road where it swings west above the Battle Downs," answered Patrel. "And, as to when, I would guess the Ghûls attacked the train on Fifth Yule, perhaps—nearly two fortnights past."

"*Rach!*" Vidron struck a clenched fist into open palm and sprang to his feet in agitation. "That explains the mystery, then, as to why Jarek saw no waggon train bearing south along either Ralo Road or the Post Road as he came north with the news of the Gûnarring Gap. Ai, but he saw no riders either, and so the Ghûls may indeed have Laurelin and Igon, though it is by no means certain."

Like a caged beast, Vidron paced in silence; but then he abruptly sat down once more. "Ah, but my heart cries out to do something—to go after the Prince and Princess . . . but where? They could be nearly anywhere! And their trail has grown cold beyond following. *Garn!*" He fell silent again, then at last said, "When we get to Gûnarring Gap, the foe will pay for this foul deed." And there was a fell look in the warrior's eyes.

At that moment a horse-borne warrior wearing

one of the blue-and-white helms of Wellen clattered up. "Sire, the Men begin to return, and Wee
Folk come at their side," said the warrior. "The
Ghûls are slain or scattered and at the moment
are no threat."

"Hai!" exclaimed Vidron. "Now if these *Waldfolc*
can but get the Thornwall plugged, then with the
help of the Wellenan warriors who remain behind,
this Land will be made safe again."

And as the herald wheeled his steed and can-
tered off, Danner and Patrel and Merrilee looked
at one another in astonishment and then fierce
joy. For, less than two hours past, they were plunged
into despair fleeing a dreadful foe—knowing that
the fate of the Bosky was perhaps teetering on the
brink of doom—but now, with the arrival of the
Men of Wellen, their fortunes had entirely reversed.

Vidron beamed down upon them, and his hearty
voice said, "I think my promise to your Thornwalker
Captain Alver has been kept."

"Captain Alver?" burst out Patrel. "Do you know
Captain Alver? And what promise?"

"Aye, lad," answered Vidron. "Alver and I met
when I rode through the Boskydells on my way
from Stonehill to Wellen."

"You rode through the Bosky? Why, of course,
you *had* to. Down the Crossland Road?" At Vidron's
nod, Patrel exclaimed, "Then *that's* who it was! It
was you and your sixty-odd Men who thundered
past in the Shadowlight while Danner and I bed-
ded down in the loft of the stable of the Happy
Otter Inn at Greenfields. *Again* we just missed
you!"

"The fortunes of War turn on small moments,"
replied Vidron. "That we missed each other in
Stonehill and then again in your Greenfields may
have had little to do with this War, but on the

other hand may have altered its course beyond measure. And we will never know what would have been had we met in either place."

"If you'd met in Stonehill," said Merrilee, "I think all of you would have ridden in pursuit of the Ghûls who perhaps stole Princess Laurelin and Prince Igon, and the Warrows of the Bosky would not have dealt with the Ghûls as we did. How else we might have faced them—in what other fashion —is beyond our knowing. But that did not happen, you did not meet, and so it was Danner and Patrel who rallied us in our time of need, and you, General Vidron, who rescued us when all hope seemed lost."

"Lass, you and I, we are right about one thing: we will never know," answered Vidron. "And if Captain Alver had not given me and my Men food and shelter as we rode toward Wellen, then I would not have heard of the Guulen strongholt here in the ruins of Brackenboro, hence I would not have brought the Wellenen to fall upon them. But, my chance meeting with Alver near your village of Rood changed all that, and I *did* hear of the strongholt, and we *did* fall upon it just as soon as I returned with the Men of the eastern garrison of Wellen. And it was only the happenstance of keeping my promise to your Captain Alver to purge this place of the Guula that we were here at all to hear the Horn of Elgo blowing in distress, calling us to the attack. A long string of slim chance led us here, and a longer string may lie before us. In any case, on the morrow I will take half the Wellenen and make for the Gûnarring Gap. And thus will I see what my improbable string of chance will lead me to henceforward."

"Improbable or not," said Patrel, "I am glad your path led you here . . . and in the nick of time at that, else we three would be the deaders and not the Ghûls."

"Hoy, look!" exclaimed Danner. "Here comes Luth and some others."

"There's your dad, Danner," said Merrilee, pointing. "I am so happy for you."

And as Danner ran down the street to meet his sire, tens and twenties of Warrows came into the village of Brackenboro, some on foot, some on ponies, and here and there amidst them rode the warriors of Wellen. And some of the Warrows wept, for they were from Brackenboro, and it was Rollo who said it best for them all: "The 'Boro may lie in charred ruins, its buildings burnt and sundered, but, by Adon, it is our home, and now it is free again."

Men began to drag the corpses of the Ghûls to a nearby ravine to burn in a great fire made there, and billowing smoke rose into the Shadowlight where it was lost in the blot above. The bodies of the slain Men and Warrows were recovered, and there began the raising of a great common burial mound on the bracken-covered hillside. And warriors large and small alike wept to see their comrades laid in the earth.

Men and Warrows continued to straggle in, and camp was made outside the ruins. And a council of Captains and Lieutenants was held and tallies taken to judge the losses: Of the nearly one thousand Ghûls, four hundred twenty-one dead were counted, two hundred seventeen of which had been felled by Warrow bolts. Of the three thousand Men, ninety-two were known to be slain, though another one hundred twenty-three were missing; some were known to be yet on Ghûlen track, while others could be lying dead or wounded. Of the one thousand eighty-six Warrows, one hundred fourteen were known to be dead, and nearly three hundred were missing, though Hanlo and others believed that most of these were alive and cautiously making their way back to the Eastwood rendezvous points.

Parties were sent out to scour the hills, and to sound the trumpets to assemble. Warrows were dispatched to the Eastwood rendezvous locations and to the camps to spread the word of the victory.

And in the council, plans were made to leave half the Wellenen in the Boskydells under the command of Captain Stohl. Warrows would join forces with Men to run the surviving Ghûls to earth, for the reavers would yet be a formidable force in the Boskydells should they reassemble. Plans also were made to plug the Thornwall at Wenden, Spindle, and Tine fords, and to stopper the way across the bridge over the Spindle River, and to close off the old abandoned Northwood tunnel, for there was still the Horde to keep out of the Bosky should the Spawn march from Challerain Keep.

Then the council turned its thoughts to the freeing of Gûnarring Gap. And it soon became obvious that Vidron could use the sight of the Wee Folk to see for him in the Dimmendark. Danner and Patrel looked at one another, and Danner nodded to Patrel's unvoiced question, but ere he could say aught, Merrilee spoke up:

"Kingsgeneral Vidron, you will need Warrow eyes to see for you in the Shadowlight. Were my Tuck here, he would go with you; but he is not, and I will go in his stead. Yet you must take more than my eyes alone, for should I be slain, still you will need the Warrow sight. I deem ten of us will be enough, and I see that Danner and Patrel would go with you also. That leaves us but seven more to choose, and so I ask my kindred: Would any of you come with us?"

There was a great uproar among the Warrows, as some cried *No! You are needed here!* while others leapt up to join the quest south. Luth Chuker smiled to himself, for he alone seemed to appreciate Merrilee's canny maneuver: By speaking first as she had done, it was she who had set forth the terms of Vidron's need, and she had gauged it well, for ten Warrows spaced the length of a two-mile-long horse column would more than fill Vidron's requirements; and by speaking first, Merrilee had established her *right* to go with Vidron, though some might have said it was no place for a damman had she merely volunteered to go after another had set forth the identical plan; but as it was, none questioned her *right* to go, they only questioned whether or not she—as well as Danner and Patrel—would be more valuable in the Bosky-dells than in Vidron's strike force. And so, while Luth sat back and smiled, some Warrows argued over the merits of losing these three to Vidron, while others argued over their own right to fill the last seven open slots.

Finally, it was Hanlo who "set them all straight," for, when he at last held the floor, in an uncharacteristically quiet voice he turned to his bucco and asked, "Would you go on this mission, son?" At Danner's nod, Hanlo said, "Captain Rushlock, who would you appoint in your stead?"

"Luth," answered Patrel, "Luth Chuker."

"Damman Thornwalker Merrilee Holt," asked Hanlo, and by this very statement he established for all time the recognition that Merrilee was indeed a full-fledged Thornwalker, damman or no, "who would you take with you?"

"Two more from the Company of Whitby's barn,

and five from the Eastwood Company," answered
Merrilee. "That's five from each, even-handed."

"Then make your choices," said Hanlo, "for in
this entire matter we would not gainsay you. General
Vidron deserves the best, and you *are* the
best."

Hanlo sat down again, and none raised his voice
in protest. Now it could be seen where Danner got
his air of command: Like sire like bucco, they
always say, and in this case the saying was true.

And so it was that Merrilee, Danner, Patrel, Teddy
Proudhand, and Arch Hockley—all from Whitby's
barn—and Rollo Breed, Dink Weller, Harven Culp,
Dill Thorven, and Burt Arboran—from Eastwood—
were selected to go with Vidron's force to free
Gûnarring Gap, or if not to free it, then to harass
the enemy until reinforcements came from Wellen.
For even now the muster went forth in that Land,
and a portion of the levy was to come south if
needed.

At last Fieldmarshal Vidron stood. "We can plan
no more here this 'Darkday, for we have come to
the limits of speculation. Let us now take to our
beds, for on the morrow we must set forth on our
missions. But ere we adjourn, this I say: Long
shall the bards and tale-tellers speak of the alliance
of *Waldfolc* and Men, and their words will be
glorious, and their sagas full of valor, for we do
battle with the forces of darkness and evil, and we
shall prevail!"

A great cheer broke forth from the assembled
council, and spirits were aflame. Though none knew
what the morrow would bring, still they were filled
with confidence and faith, and they were *proud*,
for on this day they indeed had met the evil foe,
and they *had* prevailed.

*   *   *

Early the next 'Darkday, Vidron set forth with fifteen hundred Men and ten Warrows, the Warrows mounted upon lightly loaded packhorses, for ponies would not be able to match the pace of a Valanreach long-ride.

As they rode forth from the ruins of Brackenboro, those remaining behind—Men and Warrows both—stood along the streets and gave them a rousing cheer to send them on. And, in turn, those departing cheered the ones who remained behind to sweep the Bosky clean of Spawn and to plug shut the Thornwall. And so, shouting goodbyes and good fortune, Vidron's force wended eastward through the downs to turn southerly along the margins of the Eastwood as they followed the South Trace, making for the Tineway, which they would then follow southeastward and out of the Boskydells at Tine Ford.

All 'Darkday they travelled thus at the varying pace of a Valanreach long-ride. And they saw no sign of friend or foe, for the land seemed deserted. At last they came to the Tineway, some twenty miles east of Thimble.

Now they swung along the tradeway, heading east and south for Tine Ford. But they rode no more than ten miles down the Tineway, for they had come some fifty-two miles that 'Darkday alone.

The Warrows were weary, and, soon after their meal, all but the one on watch quickly fell asleep; for they were not used to the rigors of a Valanreach long-ride, and they welcomed the comfort of their bedrolls spread upon the hard, frozen ground.

The next 'Darkday was much the same as the previous one, the unremitting miles of cold 'scape passing by as hooves hammered at a canter and fast trot, and clipped at a slow trot, and clopped at a walk, as Vidron varied the pace to save the steeds, stopping now and again to feed and water the horses and to stretch legs and take care of other needs. But even while the mounts were eating grain from nosebags, at times the Men would walk forward leading the steeds, bearing ever toward their goal.

It was late when they made camp at the road junction where the Wendenway met the Tineway. They had come to Downdell. The next 'Darkday would see them leave the Bosky.

Mid of the third 'Darkday, the two-mile-long column came to the Thornwall at Tine Ford. But *lo!* this crossing was guarded by Thornwalkers. As their Captain Willinby said, "Yar, they came lots, but we just hid out in the Thornring itself, and when the Ghûls were gone, back we went on guard, putting the thorn plugs back in place. Finally I guess they got tired of unplugging the tunnel, 'cause they've not come in a while."

Danner and Patrel shook their heads in admiration at the pragmatic persistence of this dogged Downdell company, and they thought that if the other Thornwalker companies had only used this tactic, then the other ways into the Boskydells would now be Thornguarded, too.

Little did they know that even as they rode out through the thorn tunnel and across the frozen Spindle River at Tine Ford and beyond the thorn barrier and into Harth, far to the north the vanguard of the Horde from Challerain Keep was at that very moment marching down the abandoned Northwood tunnel and into the Northdell of the Bosky. And some ten leagues behind, swarming across the southern plains of Rian, came the seeth-

ing Horde, marching to the beat of a great Rūcken
drum: *Boom! Doom! Boom! Doom!*

Late that same 'Darkday the Wellenan column
made camp where the Tineway met the Post Road,
some one hundred twenty miles south of Stonehill
and the Battle Downs.

The next 'Darkday Vidron's force turned southeastward along the Post Road, riding through the
bleak Winternight. Down through the southern
reaches of Harth they rode, and the ground-eating
pace of the Valanreach long-ride hammered away
at the iron-hard, snow-covered 'scape, and miles of
frozen land faded behind them.

Seventeen or so leagues a day they rode—fifty or
more miles a leg—and the Warrows were glad
each time camp was made, for they were weary of
riding. In the beginning their muscles had protested mightily each 'Darkday, especially when they
arose to break their fast. Yet each 'Day they had
become more inured to the rigors of the long-ride,
and the Warrows now suffered only an occasional
twinge.

The horses, too, settled in to the long hours of
travel, the varying pace conserving their strength.
And all the riders, including the Warrows, saw to
it that the steeds were frequently fed grain and
given enough to drink and rubbed down each 'Night
ere the warriors saw to their own comfort.

Late on the second 'Darkday upon the Post Road,
the column made camp deep within the western
margins of the Riverwood, a great forest stretch-
ing out many miles to either side of the Isleborne
River and growing along its length for fifty leagues

or more. And some miles ahead, at the heart of the
Riverwood and upon the banks of the Isleborne,
stood the ruins of Luren, once a great trade city,
but destroyed in elden times: first devastated by
the terrible Dark Plague that swept all of Mithgar
and slew nearly one out of three; then, years later,
ruined by a great fire—and this time Luren was
abandoned. Both the plague and the fire were said
to be sendings of Modru.

The next 'Darkday the column rode through the
ruins; but the wind had begun to howl, and flying
snow obscured their vision, and so they saw nought
of the remains. But even had the wind not been
blowing and the snow not flying and their cloak
hoods not drawn tightly over their heads, still Luren
had fallen into such utter decay that little would
have been seen of the former great city in any
event.

They crossed the frozen Isleborne at Luren Ford,
and Vidron's force turned southward along Ralo
Road; this was the road that would bear them
across the Grimwall through Ralo Pass and then
down through Gûnar to the Gûnarring Gap.

But the Warrows were not thinking of their route,
for the shrieking wind doubled its fury and the
fling of snow lashed at them; and they ducked
their heads and were glad that the packhorses
they rode were being led on tethers behind riders
who seemed to know where they were bound.

And the howl tore at them, and white snow flew
and spun, raging past. Yet the column pressed on
into the blast . . . and suddenly they were come
out of the Dimmendark and out of the flying snow
and into overcast daylight.

*   *   *

And glad yells sounded above the howl of the wind along the Black Wall.

When Merrilee was led forth upon her packhorse out of the Dimmendark, waiting for her were Danner and Patrel, joyous smiles upon their beaming faces, eyes brimming; and the damman looked at the blear light of a dismal day and, overwhelmed, she burst into tears.

The rest of the day they rode southward through the winter Riverwood, and there was much singing along the horse-borne column, even though the overcast skies darkened as a brewing storm drew nigh. For Man and Warrow alike were filled near to bursting with the joy of the *day*, and they reveled in Adon's light; even the horses seemed glad to see the daytide.

That evening they made camp still in the Riverwood, and a miserable driving sleet lashed at them. Even so, the joy of day persisted. Folk would glance up from the ground and look through the frigid ice-rain at one another, and great smiles would burst forth upon their faces as they shuddered and shivered in the blast.

When dawn came it fell through grey skies onto a frozen, ice-laden land, and a chill wind blew from the west along the great arch of the Grimwall and over the Riverwood. But even though the coming day promised to be bleak and of little comfort, still all the column broke their fast in high spirits, for it was *dawn* they witnessed, the first they'd seen in more than a month, the first since the Shadowlight of the Dimmendark had swept down from the icy Wastes of Gron to grasp the northlands in the frigid clutch of Winternight.

That day they rode down through the southern reaches of the Riverwood, and as they rode the leaden cast of the sky began to lighten. By midday great swatches of blue sky slashed overhead, riving the clouds to the wonder and delight of the south-bearing soldiers. And just as they rode from the last of the Riverwood, the Sun broke through, and a great jubilant cry rose up to greet it.

Up through the foothills of the Grimwall they rode, up toward the mountains standing before them; warrior songs of the road spontaneously burst forth from their lips as the cavalcade pounded over the crystalline 'scape toward the Ralo Pass ahead.

In early afternoon they came to the rise of the gap, and Vidron called a halt, for the pass was fully fifty miles through. And although here the Grimwall could be crossed at this time of year, night would fall ere they had gone halfway, and he did not want to camp upon the icy heights.

But on the morrow they would make the crossing in a single day, to come down into the abandoned Land of Gûnar and thenceforward across its open plains to come to their goal: the enemy-held Gûnarring Gap.

The Sun of the next day found the column deep in the icy channel of Ralo Pass, southbound over the Grimwall, and the breaths of horses and Men and Warrows alike gushed forth in white plumes and rose into the bitter-cold mountain air. To either side of the wide col sheer rock buttresses glared icily down upon the passing warriors, and the ringing echoes of driven hooves shocked and shattered among the frozen crags.

And the Sun had set and darkness had fallen when they came at last down out of the pass and into the southern foothills. At last they were come into Gûnar.

Over the next four days, Vidron dropped back the pace but sent horseborne scouts ranging to the flanks and fore, and across the plains the fifteen hundred riders went.

At night they camped, but burned no fires, for they did not want to be revealed to unfriendly eyes.

On the fourth day into Gûnar, the scouts went forth with special caution, alert for sight of the enemy, for late on this day they would come nearly to the mouth of the Gûnarring Gap.

At midday the Ralo Road came to the sparse forest northwest of the Gap, and onward pressed the column. Southeast they rode, and the Sun fell towards dusk. And the closer to the Gap the cavalcade drew, the more dense became the woods to the west of the road. In midafternoon they passed the junction where the Gap Road came south from Gûnar Slot and joined the Ralo Road, and on pressed the warriors. Just ere sunset, the column turned aside to ride in among the trees; here they would make camp concealed from any who might pass along Ralo Road.

Scouts now were sent forth to ride the last few miles to the Gap, there to spy out the strength of those warding it.

And it was late in the night when they returned, and their news was dismal. "Marshal Vidron," reported the chief among the scouts, a Wellenan named Brûd, "there are many warriors guarding the Gap—five or six thousand, I ween. Hundreds of campfires we saw, and here and there were huge fires—special fires—but what they were for, we could not get near enough to tell. Yet we did

creep close enough to make certain that it was no
ruse of the enemy, that warriors surely were at
each pyre—and indeed they were there, for we saw
them from afar. But pickets rode Moon-lit perimeters, and had we come closer, they would have
discovered us. Yet we counted the fires—more than
five hundred in all—and we judged from that count
the number of warriors. Too, they have horses—
many, many horses. Perhaps it is a cavalry we
looked upon, though we cannot be certain, for the
bulk of the herd was beyond the Gap, moving like
a great black shadow out upon the winter grass of
Valon. Nought else have I to report, Hrosmarshal
Vidron." Brūd fell silent and looked to the scouts
that had gone with him, but they said nought.

Vidron turned to his advisors, Wellenan and
Warrow alike, seated in council. "Our course is
clear then: we must use tactics that will allow our
force of fifteen hundred to defeat an army of five
or six thousand."

Vidron paused, and before any could say aught,
Patrel spoke: "Strike and flee."

"Hai!" exclaimed Vidron, the light of the quarter Moon shining pale upon his silver beard and
white teeth. "My thoughts exactly. Harass them as
the Horde was harried by Galen, now King if he
yet lives. But, lad, you spoke first. Say on."

"Kingsgeneral," said Patrel in a clear voice, looking to Vidron, "I deem that the Wellenen can strike
hard and unexpectedly and withdraw in haste ere
the enemy can group to give chase. Even if the foe
sends pursuit, most of them will be left behind to
hold the Gap. Hence, only a token will give chase,
if any. We can regroup in these woods to assail the
pursuers, should they come. If I am wrong and a
great number follows, then we will fade away without engaging them.

"But it will take more than one assault to vanquish the foemen, and it is to the second strike and the third and all thereafter that we must give extra caution, for the enemy will be on guard and wary. Here the quarrels of the Warrow bows will be most valuable, for we are the Wee Folk and can move as quietly as the falling leaf. And our arrows will be used to strike down their sentinels in silence, to breach their warding ring and let the Wellenen through to lash forth without warning.

"That is the gist of my thought, Fieldmarshal Vidron. It is the only way that I think fifteen hundred can prevail over six thousand." Patrel fell silent. And Merrilee, seated next to Vidron, nodded to herself in agreement with the buccan's strategy.

Vidron rocked back, a look of admiration upon his face. "Ho, Waldan, but I am glad you are not my enemy, for your battle plans are most formidable."

"Perhaps, Fieldmarshal," responded Patrel. "Yet I am not the tactician of this group of Warrows. Merrilee Holt holds that place."

"Hai, lass!" cried Vidron, slapping a hand to his leg in pleasure and hugging the damman over to him with one arm. And the air whooshed from Merrilee's lungs and her tilted blue eyes flew wide in his fierce embrace. Then Vidron released her, and as she struggled back to an upright sitting position, he spoke on: "Tactician or not, Captain Patrel, your plan is sound, and your thoughts match mine. We will follow that course, at least until more Men muster in Wellen and join us.

"Yet there is much we must speak on to flesh out the tactics of this stroke, for all must go smoothly. We must set forth the order of the companies, the direction of the strike and withdrawal, the horn signals to be used, and much else. Yet, I would fall upon the enemy at the morrow's dawning, for then we will come out of the shadows of the pass as a catamount striking from dark crags." Vidron turned to his Captains. "What say you? How shall we carry forth with this plan?"

Thus it was that the detailed plans were made to strike the foe in the Gûnarring Gap and then to withdraw unto the woods. In this first strike the Warrows would play no role, for the enemy expected no attack and their guard would be sparse and lax. Hence, along with a few herdsmen to watch over the packhorses, the ten Wee Ones would take shelter in the forest to the west of Ralo Road. But in subsequent strikes, Warrows would lead the way.

The council met until after mid of night, but at last the plans were set and the orders relayed. In the dawn the Wellenen would foray against the force in Gûnarring Gap.

It was yet dark when the column set forth from the woods and went upon the Ralo Road to the southeast: dark shapes in the waning starlit night, moving out of the trees and toward the Gap ahead. And the Warrows stood at the fringe of the woods and watched the raiders bear off. When the last one had ridden by, the Wee Folk turned to go in among the trees, and behind them the sound of hooves faded southerly as the skies greyed in the east.

Vidron rode at the head of the force, and after him came the full of his strength, save those few left in the woods. And the Hrosmarshal's eyes strove to pierce the gloom of the foredawn and see through the enshadowed Gap to the warders at the far side.

Into the slot rode the fifteen hundred, lances and sabers at the ready. And the skies lightened to the east as they rode onward in the cloaking dark of the Gap.

When the Sun lipped the rim of the world, a mile or so ahead the warriors could see where the Gap came to an end. And there the Ralo Road split in twain: Bearing leftward and to the east ran the Reach Road, passing hundreds of miles across the plains of Valon to come at last to Vanar, the city in the center of that Land where King Aranor had his throne; rightward went Pendwyr Road, reaching southeastward all the way to Caer Pendwyr, nearly three hundred leagues away, where dwelt the High Kings of Mithgar.

But Vidron's eyes were not upon the junction of the roads nor beyond to the Land of his home. Instead he looked where stood a great cavalry, warriors mounted upon horses as if for some ceremony. And although their flags were unfurled, no wind blew, and so he could not see their sigil to say if they were from Hyree, Kistan, or some other Realm. And their numbers were very great, and Vidron knew that his strike would have to be lightning quick and swiftly withdrawn, for to stay and fight would mean defeat.

Even as the outriding scouts fell back to join the oncoming ranks, the Hrosmarshal gave a silent hand signal that passed back along the column, and the Wellenen spread wide in attack formation. At another signal they lowered their lances and began a trot forward. And the long line of warriors moved as one great military unit.

Onward they went, and now Vidron signalled once more, and the horses broke into a canter. The Fieldmarshal's eyes swept left and right along the formation and then to the force ahead, and those warders had not yet seen the oncoming Wellenen, for they stood in ranks with their backs to the Gap.

Vidron raised his black-oxen horn to his lips, and when the long file burst forth from the shadows of Gûnarring Gap, he blew a mighty blast that echoed up and down the line as the horns of Wellen took up the call. And they raced forth at a headlong run, deadly spears leveled to strike: Death flying upon thundering hooves.

Now Vidron couched his spear and urged his racing steed to greater speed. Yet even as he flew over the ground, his eyes were locked upon the horsemen in the closing distance. And Vidron gasped in dismay, for with great precision they wheeled about and swiftly spread wide to meet the oncoming Wellenen, *and began a charge of their own!*

And Vidron knew that his force would not survive the shock of their clash.

CHAPTER 2

ENCOUNTER AT GÛNARRING GAP

Tuck, Galen, Gildor, Brega and Aranor looked to see the unknown force charging out of the shadows of the Gûnarring Gap. Ubrik barked a command in Valur, the ancient War-tongue of Valon, and horns sounded, and the files of the Vanadurin wheeled and swiftly formed to face into Gûnar, lances and sabers at the ready.

Galen flashed Steel-heart from its scabbard, and Gildor drew Bale, and as Ubrik cried another command, the High King and the Elf Lord spurred forth with the Harlingar and to the fore of the answering charge.

King Aranor cursed his wounded arm but caught up a spear in his off hand and thundered after.

Tuck and Brega standing upon the ground, looked at one another, and then the Dwarf took Drakkalan in hand and growled, "Come on, Tuck."

And the Dwarf and Warrow ran on foot after the horse-borne warriors, Brega bearing his black-hafted axe, Tuck his arrows and bow.

And now the buccan could hear the horns of Valon blowing wildly as the riders raced toward one another, spears lowered for the death-dealing clash.

But *lo!* bugles sounded in the oncoming force, and the file veered left! *They were sheering off the attack!* And now the horns of Valon sounded, too! *And the charge of the Vanadurin turned aside, also!*

Spears were raised and sabers lowered as the two forces swerved oppositely. Trumpets blew and were answered by black-oxen horns, and then the armies rode together to mingle.

Tuck and Brega ran toward the now-milling warriors, and the Warrow could see the standard borne by the others: white falcon upon blue field—*the flag of Wellen!*

And as Tuck dodged among the seething tide of shifting horses and stamping hooves and worked his way toward the center of the mass, he heard the familiar hearty laughter of a silver-bearded Hrosmarshal and looked up to see Vidron clasping Galen's hand.

CHAPTER 3

THE VALANREACH LONG-RIDE

Now the mighty cavalcade thundered northwest through the Gûnarring Gap, six thousand five hundred strong, for Vidron's fifteen hundred Wellenen had joined the five thousand Harlingar; and among the column and near its head rode a Warrow and a Dwarf upon stirrup-shortened saddles, each of their steeds led on a long tether by a warrior riding before them, and the strength of the Dwarf's grip upon the fore cantle made his knuckles white. Wellenen, Vanadurin, Warrow, and Dwarf: they all rode in the Legion of King Galen, and their goal was the cruel Iron Tower in the Wastes of Gron.

They rode into Gûnar. First they would gather Vidron's packhorses from the woods west of the Ralo Road, and then they would swing north to begin the long-ride to Claw Moor. The Hrosmarshal had smiled mysteriously at Tuck but had said nought other than he had a "special gift" awaiting the buccan back in the forest by the road, though what this surprise might be, Tuck could not imagine.

And they rode along the margin of the woods, the Wellen horns pealing the calls of assembly, the sounds ringing among the trees.

At last the calls were answered, and Tuck could see the shapes of horses and Men moving through the forest to come to the verge of the road. And then his sapphirine eyes saw smaller shapes: *Warrows!*

Now the column halted, and, his heart pounding, Tuck leapt down and trotted toward his kith. And *lo!* he saw among them one taller than the rest: *Danner!*

"Danner!" he yelled, running now, nearly stumbling in his haste, "Danner!"

Warrows turned at Tuck's call. *There was Patrel, too!*

But another figure broke forth from the Warrow ranks and ran toward the oncoming buccan. "Tuck! Oh, Tuck!" she called his name, and he saw that it was *Merrilee!* And then she was hugging him and kissing him, and Danner and Patrel were pounding him on the back in jubilation, and unabashed tears streamed down all of their faces, while smiling Vidron sat upon his steed and looked down at them as he wiped the tears from his own eyes, too.

What are you doing here? How did you escape the Ghûls at Challerain Keep? Did you know that Aurion is slain and Galen is now King? Are these others from the Bosky? Questions flew back and forth, but no answers.

At last Tuck threw up his hands. "Wait!" he cried. "We've a long trip ahead of us and plenty of time to tell our tales and hear the stories of the others. Just let me ask this: Dammia I know not why you are here, nor how you came unto this place, but you must have come lately from the

Bosky. What news is there of Woody Hollow? And how fare my sire and dam?"

At his question Merrilee's face fell, and new tears brimmed her eyes. She took Tuck by the hand and led him away from the others. And Danner and Patrel watched from afar as she stood and spoke softly to her buccaran, telling him of the last hours of Tulip and Burt, and of the burial in the glade in the Dinglewood. When she was finished, she wept and stroked his hair and clasped him to her as he held on tightly and cried.

Horns and bugles blew the calls to mount up, and though he wept still, Tuck went to his horse and was lifted to the saddle, for the press of War yields no time to grieve. And once more the column started forth while horse-borne scouts scattered to the fore, flank, and rear.

Lord Gildor glanced up at the Sun standing near the zenith and spurred forward to ride alongside Galen. "Galen King, the Iron Tower lies nearly three hundred leagues to the north as the horse runs. And exactly twenty days from this very hour will come the Darkest Day: The Moon will eat the Sun, and Gron will stand in the utter blackness of the 'Darkday. We cannot delay, for though I do not know how we may upset the Evil One's plans, we must do so ere that darkest moment comes." Gildor fell silent.

"I do not plan to tarry, Lord Gildor," responded Galen. "Yet our horses must last long enough to get us there, and the Wellenen have already come some eight hundred miles at the pace of a Valanreach long-ride. Their steeds may not endure unto Gron and the Iron Tower." Galen held up a hand to forestall the protests coming to Lord Gildor's lips. "Aye, Goldbranch, I know. And if need be, we will ride on without the army Vidron brought from afar. Yet I would rather have their strength with me when we assail the Kinstealer's holt than leave them behind in our wake."

Gildor inclined his head and then dropped back to ride alongside Brega, but what they spoke about is not told.

North the cavalcade turned, north along the Gap Road, heading toward Gûnar Slot, that great cleft through the Grimwall where the mountains changed course, running away westerly on one side of the Slot, curving to the north on the other.

It was after sunset when they made camp in the margins of sparse woods to either side of the Gap Road. The Warrows gathered about their own campfire, and Tuck held hands with Merrilee as he exchanged his story with Danner and Patrel and the damman, while the other buccen listened and commented and added to the story of the Struggles. And occasionally Tuck would glance in his diary to recall a point or date. And all the Warrows *oohed* and *ahhed* when Tuck told of the harrowing pursuit of the Ghûls that led to the Dusk-Door, and their flight from the Krakenward, and the slaying of the Gargon.

But as he listened to the tale of the Struggles—of the reaving of the Bosky, and of Merrilee's rescue of Danner and Patrel, and of the battles of Budgens and Brackenboro—Tuck's face would now and then cloud over. Tears would well from his eyes, and he would walk away to stand weeping in the darkness with Merrilee at his side. And when he returned to the fire, the tale would go on, taking up where it had left off as if it had not stopped at all.

And even while they talked and hoped fervently that the Thornwall had been closed up tight, the

Horde raged across the Boskydells—ravaging, pillaging, slaughtering—while Warrows fled before them.

Three more days the cavalcade hammered to the north, and at last they reached the Gûnar Slot, camping near the woods at its mouth. And during these same three days, Tuck slowly recovered his good spirits, though a look of sadness would sometimes haunt his eyes. But then, whether he was staring into a campfire or the night, or whether he was riding during the day, Tuck would look up to see Merrilee gazing at him, and he would lose himself in her warm smile and grin foolishly back at her.

The next day they rode into the vast cleft, ranging in breadth from seven miles at its narrowest to seventeen at its widest. And the walls of the mountains to either side rose sheer, as if cloven by a great axe. Trees lined the floor for many miles, though long stretches of barren stone frowned at the riders from one side or the other. The Gap Road ran for nearly seventy-five miles through the Gûnar Slot, and so the Legion camped in the great notch that night.

The following day they pressed onward, coming out the north end of the Slot near the noontide and swinging slightly west for the ford on the River Hâth. And Brega grumbled that it seemed he was getting nowhere, for this was the very same route he had followed some five weeks past.

That night they camped just south of Hâth Ford, where the Gap Road came to the Old Rell Way. Before them stood the hideous Black Wall, the wind and snow rumbling along the great ebon flank of the Dimmendark. On the morrow they would enter once more into the cruel Winternight, and the hearts of all the warriors of the Legion fell because of it. And many sat up late into the night and watched the silvery full Moon and the glittering stars wheel overhead, for they knew it would be a long time ere any saw them again.

And Tuck and Merrilee sat with ams about each other and gazed at the Moon and whispered gentle things, and the argent orb sailed through the spangled night and shone its silver rays down upon them.

But Lord Gildor looked at the Moon with another thought—a dire thought—in mind; for he knew that just under fifteen days hence, the gentle Moon would consume the fiery Sun, and the Darkest Day would come unto Gron, to the woe of all Mithgar.

In the morning they passed through the howling wind and driving snow to enter the spectral Shadowlight, and Warrow eyes took over the chore of scouting. And all that 'Darkday they fared northerly along the Old Rell Way.

At mid of 'Darkday the Legion passed by the mouth of the Valley of the Door, and Tuck pointed out to Merrilee the vale where stood the Dusk-Door carven in the Grimspire, unseen in the Dimmendark. And Merrilee shuddered, for she knew that in the distant Shadowlight in a black mere dwelled the monstrous Krakenward.

On the second 'Darkday the cavalcade continued north and passed by the road leading up to Quadran Pass, and onward up the Old Rell Way they went. Soon they came to the place where Brega's Dwarven company had battled the vanguard of the Horde.

And as they rode by, Tuck gasped in shock, and
Merrilee turned her eyes down and away and did
not look up again through her tears of distress; but
Brega looked upon the Warground and his frame
shook with rage, for the Horde that had come later
had mutilated the slain Dwarves: Hands and arms
and feet and legs had been sundered from the
bodies, and heads stood on poles driven into crevices in the frozen ground, and dead eyes stared
from maimed faces at the passing Legion; and the
Spawn had committed other unspeakably foul acts
of butchery that turned the stomachs of many a
staunch warrior. And as the column rode past,
Brega raised his face to the Dimmendark and cried
out in anguish, *"Châkka djalk aggar theck!"* and
cast his hood over his head and said no more. And
what his words meant—what oath of vengeance or
cry of sorrow he had uttered—none could say.

In the following 'Darkdays the horses of the
Wellenen began to weaken, for they had come an
enormous distance these past twenty-five days:
more than one thousand miles in all, from Wellen
across the Boskydells and down to Gûnarring Gap;
then north through the Gûnar Slot and past the
Quadran; and all of it at the pace of a Valanreach
long-ride, which, although it got the most distance
from a steed at the least cost to the horse, never-
theless took its toll in the long run. Each 'Darkday
the Legion rode north was one more 'Day of nearly
fifty miles of travel, and the Wellenan horses began to flag as the cavalcade rode through the spur
of the Grimwall that stood across the Old Rell
Way and turned aside to make for Rhone Ford
across the frozen Tumble River. Galen King had
chosen to leave the ancient Rell tradeway, for, as
Gildor reminded him, it was the route used by

Spaunen to travel to and from the region of the Crestan Pass along the western side of the Grimwall. And although the Legion had seen no signs of the foe, still it would not do to meet up with a south-bound Horde. And so the column rode for the ford leading into the Rhone and crossed into that Land ere making camp.

The following 'Darkday they swung wide around a dense winter-bared forest growing along the western side of the River Tumble and then pressed back northward and east to come at last to the southern margins of Drearwood, where once more the Legion made camp. And now the talk around the campfires was whether or not the Wellenen would continue on, for their steeds were clearly showing the fatigue of the long journey they had made.

But on the 'Darkday next, once again the entire cavalcade bore onward. Up the narrow plain between the Drearwood and the River Tumble they went, at last to camp just north of the Crossland Road where it crossed the Tumble at Arden Ford. Galen spent a lengthy time inspecting the horses of Wellen, and there was a brooding look upon his face when he took to his bed for sleep.

And Tuck sat by the campfire and scribed in his diary, his sapphire gaze often straying to his dammia who was sleeping nearby. And out on the perimeter—alongside Men—stood two Warrows at watch, their tilted Utruni eyes scanning the spectral Dimmendark.

The following 'Darkday saw the Legion ride alongside the high Arden Bluff. Beyond the stone massif lay the hidden Arden Vale, and Tuck wondered what the Lian were doing. And he told Merrilee about the food and baths and clean cloth-

ing he and Galen had enjoyed in the Hidden Refuge. Merrilee Holt thought back and realized that
she had not had a bath in nearly four weeks, since
three days after the Battle of Budgens—and that
one had been but a quick laving from a basin,
hastily done in a stall in Whitby's barn, and not a
proper bath at all. And Merrilee longed to be in a
real tub full of warm soapy water, and her eyes
stung with tears.

That 'Night they camped at the northern reaches
of the Drearwood. They had come only thirty-two
miles that 'Darkday, for the horses of Wellen could
no longer hold the pace.

"They are nearly played out," said Vidron. "Oh,
some can go onward—in fact they all can—but no
longer at the pace of a Valanreach long-ride. King
Galen, I am troubled, for the Wellenen are nearly
a quarter of your Legion. I would not have you
face the Enemy in Gron at less than full strength.
This I advise: drop the pace back to eight leagues
a day—say at most twenty-five miles, no more—
then we will ride with you all the way to the Iron
Tower, and thence you will arrive at full strength."

"At full strength, yea," spoke up Lord Gildor,
"but far too late. For the Darkest Day will arrive
less than nine days hence. Let the Wellenen come,
Galen King, but at their own pace, for they may be
needed in the times ahead. Yet we must fly onward, and leave them behind, for the Moon is a
clock that none of us can stay. We have no other
choice."

Galen looked up from the flames of the campfire, but what he would have said is lost forever,
for at that moment a horseman rode up. "Sire!"
called the rider. "The Waldan at the north watch
reports a small party on horses riding towards us!
He says they are Elves!"

*   *   *

It was Lord Talarin! And he came with an escort of six Lian. And at his side, astride Rust, came Igon! And when the Prince saw Galen's fire, he spurred the great roan forward and came at a gallop before the others, the steed's strides devouring the distance. With a glad shout—"Hai, Igon!"—Galen leapt to his feet as Rust pounded forward, at last to thunder to a halt, and the Prince sprang down; and the two brothers embraced. And the youth of fifteen summers looked hale once more, for under the Elves' ministrations he had recovered his strength.

Galen spoke: "My brother, your eye is clear and your grip firm, and for that I am most grateful. No doubt you have been hacking some training manikin to shreds with your sword, or puncturing it with spear."

Igon laughed. "You are right, elder brother. I *have* tattered Lord Talarin's devices to a fare-thee-well. Yet those times are at an end now that you are here, for I propose to join you and go against the *Spaunen*."

A troubled look crossed Galen's face. "Igon, I ride into grave danger. I would not have both of Aurion's heirs fall to the Enemy in Gron in a single battle should the tide turn against us. Together, we can both be felled at one and the same time; apart, Modru has to come at us twice and win both times ere we are foredone. I would that you stay somewhere safe."

"Brother of mine," replied Igon, "you seek the same solution as did our sire." A fleeting look of pain crossed both their faces at mention of slain Aurion, yet Igon continued: "But heed! He sought to send me away south to safe haven, yet I was nearly killed by Ghol sword stroke; it was only the smiling face of Fortune that spared me.

"My meaning is this, Galen, King: Nowhere in Mithgar is safe today, for the enemy is everywhere. You would have me seek refuge in Arden instead of face the foe at your side, yet Arden itself is on the brink. And so, I ask this boon: to go at your side. But ere you say yea or nay, listen first to the words of Lord Talarin, for he bears tidings of import, and perhaps they will influence your decision."

The King nodded his acceptance of Prince Igon's terms and turned to watch Lord Talarin and the escort ride up. "Hál, Warder of the Northern Reaches of Rell!" called Galen.

"Hál, Galen King!" cried Talarin as he reached the fire and leapt down from his steed and bowed. At the High King's nod, acknowledging the Elf Lord's courtesy, Talarin's eyes sought his son, Gildor, and the two Lian smiled each upon the other. And Talarin clapped a hand to Tuck's shoulder. "Hai, but we meet again, Waerling."

And among the Elves now moving into the light of the Kingsfire came a Lian whom Tuck recognized: Inarion! It was Lord Inarion from the Weiunwood!

But then came an even greater shock to Tuck, for now there stepped from among the Elves ... *Flandrena!* Flandrena, who had ridden into Gron with Vanidor and Duorn and Varion! And now he was here! And both Gildor and Galen were shaken, too, on seeing the Lian warrior. But neither said aught, for Inarion was speaking, and he held on a long tether a grey horse; and tears sprang to the Warrow's eyes, for it was Wildwind, slain King Aurion's steed.

"Galen King, I have brought you the horse of your sire, though that was not my purpose when I took him from the Weiunwood, for I did not expect to find you on the bounds of Arden. Yet he is a swift steed, and my urgency was great, for I rode in haste to the Hidden Refuge to bear dire news, and I had vital need for a fleet remount to aid my own Wingfoot. But now I give Wildwind over from my keep into yours: from Sire to Son, from King to King, goes this noble steed. Care for him well, for he is a horse befitting the High King of all Mithgar." Inarion handed the reins of Wildwind to Galen and bowed.

Galen took the horse and stroked Wildwind's muzzle, and the glitter of the fire shone brightly in the King's eyes. And Wildwind looked upon Galen and then lowered his head as if in obeisance, but then quickly raised it and whickered.

"We shall get along well, old fellow, you and I," said Galen, his voice husky with emotion. "But now you are wanting some grain, no doubt, and perhaps the company of other steeds. But most of all, I suspect, you would like to gambol in a sunny meadow, or graze quietly under the Moon and stars. Perhaps one day. Perhaps . . ."

At a gesture from the King an attendant came and took the steed, and Galen led all of Talarin's party to council around the Kingsfire. As soon as all were seated in a great circle, Talarin turned to Galen. "Word came to me by swift riders of your yester camp at Arden Ford, and the sentinels atop the long Arden Bluff have signalled of your progress along your course. Yet why you come this way, I cannot say, and I would ask that you quench my curiosity."

"We ride for the Iron Tower in Gron," responded Galen, and Talarin's eyes flew wide at this news.

Talarin turned to Inarion. "Ai! This may explain your tidings, Alor Inarion."

Then Talarin turned once more to Galen. "There is much we have to speak upon, Galen King, fell news from the west. But I am troubled by your course, for you have less than seven thousand in your Legion, or so my scouts say. Yet to attack Gron—the Iron Tower—seven *times* seven thousand seems hardly enough to breach those walls."

"We have no choice, Father," said Gildor. "Vanidor . . ."

Talarin's face clouded with grief.

"Vanidor called my name at his dying," Gildor continued. "And he thrust this rede upon me:

> *'The Darkest Day,*
> *The Greatest Evil. . .'*

And though we know not for certain what it means, these are our thoughts: The Darkest Day . . . will be when the Moon eats the Sun over Gron less than nine days hence; the Greatest Evil . . . is Gyphon." Talarin gasped, and grim looks fell upon his Elven escort. Gildor spoke on: "We think Vanidor warned that Modru plans something most vile on the Darkest Day."

"So *this* is the rede Rael felt pass her by!" declared Talarin. "And dire it is if you have guessed its meaning. Yet, how can it be? Gyphon is beyond the Spheres!"

"Yet the Hyrania and Kistania believe that the Great Evil shall return," responded Gildor. "And we must attack the Iron Tower and turn Modru's energies aside ere he can, somehow, *release* Gyphon."

"Then why have you not brought more warriors?" asked Talarin.

"Even as we speak, Lord Talarin," answered Galen, "the Lakh of Hyree and the Rovers of Kistan

stagger the Realm in the south. They have cast
down Hoven and Pellar, and now the struggle to
whelm Jugo and Valon goes on. All the Hosts are
needed in those battles, and even then their numbers may not be sufficient. This Legion, made up
of Vanadurin and Wellenen, is all that I could
bring and still hope to reach the Iron Tower ere
the Darkest Day."

"But I do not think seven thousand enough to
cast it down," responded Talarin. "What say you,
Flandrena?"

"Can seven thousand cast down the Iron Tower?
That I do not know, Alor Talarin," answered the
slim Elf after some thought. "For even were there
not swarms of *Rûpt* upon its walls, still it is a
deadly fortress, and to breach it is a task perhaps
beyond doing."

"How know you this?" growled Brega.

"I was there, Drimm," replied Flandrena, his
eyes glittering in the firelight, his voice sinking
low. "With Vanidor, Duorn, and Varion, I was
there."

None said aught for long moments, then Gildor
spoke: "Say on, Flandrena for I would hear of my
brother."

Tuck put his arm about Merrilee and drew her
to him as Flandrena told his tale:

"Six 'Darkdays and some, we rode north from
Arden—swift across the Wastes of Gron—and at
times we had to turn aside from the path to avoid
the patrols of the Evil One. Yet at last we came
unto Claw Moor, and thence to Modru's dark
bastion.

"Long we lay and watched the ones within, counting the *Spaunen* numbers, gauging their considerable strength. Modru has held back perhaps eight
thousand *Rûpt* to ward his Iron Tower. Too, we

watched the wall patrols, and crept around the perimeters of the chasm that berings the holt while looking for a way to enter, for it was in all our minds to clamber o'er those palisades and rescue Princess Laurelin.

"But the crevasse is deep with sheer walls, and the iron drawbridge is Troll-guarded. Yet we continued our search. At last Duorn saw a thin crevice on the far side of the chasm, running from floor to rim. And Varion deemed we could climb it ... as well as one corner of the fortress wall.

"Yet Vanidor said that one of us would have to bear word of the count of Modru's strength back to Arden, for then if the mission to rescue the Princess failed, all would not be lost.

"As Captain, Vanidor chose to try the walls, and Varion he asked to go with him, for Varion was the most skilled at climbing. That left Duorn and me to decide between us who would get to go with them and who would ride south. But we both argued to try the bastion, and so Vanidor plucked two dry blades of grass and held them out for us to choose. I pulled the short blade and lost—hence, I would bear the word back to Arden, while those three would breach the walls.

"We said our farewells, and when last I saw them, they started down a rope toward rift's bottom. I went back to where the horses were concealed and mounted my steed and rode southward for Arden.

"Many miles I had ridden, yet still I was on Claw Moor when I felt Vanidor's cry: *'Ride, Flandrena, ride!'* was his desperate last command ... *'Ride, Flandrena, ride ...'* " Flandrena's voice sank to a whisper, and his eyes stared deeply into the fire. Tears welled in Tuck's eyes, and Merrilee gripped his hand tightly, her own eyes misting over. And Brega sat with his hood cast over his head.

At last Flandrena continued. "Vanidor had given me his last command, yet I nearly turned back. But his call echoed and rang in my mind, and I could not refuse it. And so, weeping in rage and anguish, I spurred forth, for I knew then that the mission to rescue Princess Laurelin had failed and that I alone would carry to Arden word of Modru's strength.

"Swiftmane ran as he had never run before, and the leagues fell away beneath his hooves. He would have run until his heart burst, if I had asked it— but I did not. Still it was not four full 'Darkdays ere we came into the Hidden Vale.

"That is my tale, Alor Gildor; that is my tale, Galen King. But it is a story as yet unfinished, for I would return to Gron with you and avenge my lost comrades. How? I cannot say, for the fortress is formidable, and even though it is defended by less than a full Horde, still it will be hard to break ... perhaps impossible. Yet I would go with you to try." Flandrena's Elven eyes held a steely glint.

"If your Lord will give you leave, I welcome your sword in my Legion," said Galen, and Talarin inclined his head in assent.

"My King," Vidron spoke, "you have gained one warrior, but you are about to lose fifteen hundred: The horses of Wellen cannot hold the pace. Perhaps the Lian of Arden Vale can provide us with mounts."

Galen turned to Talarin, and the Elf spoke: "Galen King, ere I answer your unvoiced request, first you must hear the news Alor Inarion carries, for I think it will bear heavily upon what we decide in this council."

All eyes turned to Inarion, and the Elf Lord

spoke: "Six 'Darkdays past, the Horde sent by
Modru to whelm the Weiunwood broke off their
attack against the Alliance and began force-march-
ing eastward along the Crossland Road. Forty miles
a 'Day they raced—"

"Forty miles a day!" burst out Vidron. "But they
are on foot! At least the Drōkha and Rutcha go
afoot. Do the Guula ride with them, or do they
come ahead?"

"The Ghûlka ride with the *Spaunen* and drive
them unmercifully eastward," answered Inarion,
"yet none knows why, though we had guessed that
they strike for Arden Vale to cast down the Hidden
Refuge. But now another reason has come to mind:
perhaps they thought to intercept your Legion,
Galen King."

"Six 'Darkdays past, you say, they began their
march . . . ai, I deem it was then that we had just
come into the Dimmendark at Hâth Ford," re-
flected Galen. "Yet how Modru could have known
of this—"

"Spies!" spat Brega. "His spies must watch the
roads inward."

"But then how did the Horde in Stonehill know
of this?" asked Patrel.

"His emissaries," answered Tuck, and Lord Gildor
nodded. Patrel shuddered, for Tuck had told him
and Danner and Merrilee of Modru's hideous power
to *possess* another. "But why the Horde in Stonehill?" asked Tuck. "I mean, why not the one in
Drimmen-deeve? All they would have had to do
was march over Quadran Pass and stand athwart
the Old Rell Way. Surely Modru would have chosen them to intercept us."

"Mayhap they are still trapped in Kraggen-cor,"
proposed Brega. "Mayhap they cannot cross the
Great Dēop, for the bridge is felled."

Talarin looked curiously at the Drimm, for here was a tale the Lian of Arden had not heard. But before the Elf could ask aught, Galen said, "I deem it was the Evil One's agent we slew in the Black Hole, yet whether this severed Modru's command of that Horde, I cannot say."

"What about the Horde in Challerain Keep?" asked Danner. "Do they march this way, too?"

A look of pain crossed Inarion's features. "I am sorry, Wee Ones, to bear you evil tidings, but the Horde of Challerain Keep has gone into your Land of the Thorns."

What! Danner and Patrel and Tuck all leapt to their feet, and Merrilee buried her face in her hands.

"In the Bosky? The Horde is in the Bosky?" demanded Danner, his fists clenched, his entire body quivering in rage, his words guttural and but barely understandable.

"I am afraid it is so." Inarion's eyes were filled with deep sadness. "Three weeks past."

"Three weeks?" Tuck's legs gave way under him, and he slumped down by Merrilee. Then he saw for the first time that she wept. Tuck reached out and put his arms around her and drew her close.

Patrel smacked a clenched fist into open palm. "Danner, we've got to go back. We never should have left. They need us more than ever now."

Danner's lips were white, and he gave a short jerky nod, but then Merrilee looked up through her tears and cried, "No! That's not the way! West to the Bosky is not the way!" Her sharp cry split through the shell of rage engulfing Danner, and, blinking, he looked down at her. Patrel, too, turned toward her. "North!" she spat. "Our way lies north!" Then her voice became deadly calm. "In Gron dwells the source of the evil. Brega has the right of it: the best way to kill a snake is to cut off its head.

And that's where we are going, to snare the viper in its nest.

"Why do you think he sends his Horde to intercept us? He is frightened! That's why! We give him good cause to fear us, though we know not why. Perhaps he simply fears that we will upset his careful plans, as Lord Gildor has suggested is our mission's purpose. But whatever the reasons— whatever are Modru's fears—we should act to make the most of them. And so I for one say we strike north unto the very Iron Tower itself. Let us go forth and slay this serpent." Merrilee fell silent, and Lord Talarin, as well as King Galen and many others, looked upon the damman in wonder, for, unlike Patrel and Danner, they had never before heard a female speak as would a warrior. And first Patrel and then Danner reluctantly bowed to the wisdom of her words, and the two buccen grudgingly sat back down.

But Vidron voiced a doubt he held: "Perhaps you are right, lass. Perhaps Modru *does* fear us and sends a Horde to intercept us ere we can gain Gron. Yet there are other explanations, too: The Spawn may be marching upon Arden Vale, as Inarion first guessed; they may have some other target in mind, perhaps even beyond the Grimwall; *or they may be seeking to trap us in Gron, to fall upon us from behind as we attack the Iron Tower.*"

"But then, Hrosmarshal Vidron," said Galen, "Modru would need to know that we head for Gron. How could he have knowledge of our goal?"

"He is evil and suspicious, Galen King," answered Gildor. "I think the bringing of the Legion into the north surprised him, for he did not expect his grasp on the Gûnarring Gap to be broken, nor any of the southern defenders to come north in any event . . . at least not as long as the Hyrania and Kistania assail the Realm. There is this, too: Where else would we be bound if not for Gron? Modru asks himself that question, and the answer he finds is not to his liking, I deem, and so he acts in haste to prevent the upset of his plans."

Gildor fell silent, and Talarin, whose eyes had widened at mention of the hold on the Gûnarring Gap, seemed about to speak. Yet he held his silence, and it was Galen who spoke: "Lord Inarion, where is the Horde now? And what is their strength?"

"Five 'Darkdays past, I took Wildwind and Wingfoot from the Weiunwood and rode to intercept the Horde," responded Inarion. "I came upon the *Rûpt* at Beacontor, where they rested, and I stayed beyond the range of their vision and watched them and counted them. I deem their ranks to be ten thousand strong. And I waited to see if this march of theirs was a feint or not . . . waiting to see if they would bear onward, or would turn upon Weiunwood once more.

"The next 'Darkday they pressed forth again, tramping east along the Crossland Road. At the end of that 'Day, I knew it was no ruse. They were truly bound eastward, and sought not to attack the Weiunwood by surprise maneuver.

"I left them encamped in the land north of the Wilder River, and I hied up through the Wilderness Hills to Drear Ford and across Rhone to Arden, riding apace to warn the Hidden Refuge. And so I saw the *Rûpt* not again, but if they have kept up their quickstep along the Crossland Road, they are now camped along that pike midway through the Drearwood."

Vidron gasped. "That is but two 'Darkdays' march behind us at the hard stride they set!"

"Aye," said Ubrik, "but at the pace of a Valanreach long-ride, we shall slowly draw away from them."

"But the Wellenan horses!" exclaimed Vidron. "they cannot keep the pace! They have at best but one or two more hard rides left in them, and then they will need long rest. Now more than ever, Lord Talarin, we need fresh steeds. Can you supply them?"

"Not enough to mount fifteen hundred warriors," answered Talarin, "nor even a third of that count. The Lian of Arden are far flung on forays against the *Spaunen:* along the Old Rell Way, and in the approaches to the Crestan Pass. Even now the recall order goes swiftly forth, and Lian will come at speed back unto the vale to defend it if the Horde seeks to attack the Refuge. But were they all here now, their steeds would not number enough to give you relief."

Vidron turned to Galen in anguish. "Sire, the Wellenen then cannot keep the pace. They will come, but late . . . perhaps too late to aid you in your time of need."

"Hrosmarshal Vidron, my time of need is now," said Galen, "and my needs are changed by this Horde at our backs. I would not have them fall upon us from behind as we assault the Iron Tower." Galen paused and looked the Kingsgeneral straight in the eye. "I have a most fearful duty to thrust upon you, for only you have the Valonian battle skills to be able to lead the Men of Wellen and do what I need done: I would have you take the Wellenen and stop this Horde for as many 'Dark-days as you can hold them."

Tuck's eyes flew wide. "But, Galen King," he protested, "there are ten thousand of the maggot-folk and but fifteen hundred Wellenen!"

"That I know full well, Wee One," acknowledged

Galen. "But the Horde is two 'Darkdays behind us now, and when our Valanreach longride comes to the Iron Tower, they will be a full four 'Days' march in arrears. And each 'Darkday of additional delay that Vidron can win for us will be one more 'Day we can assault the Tower ere we must turn our energies aside to meet a foe falling upon us from behind."

Galen turned to Vidron. "Hrosmarshal, this is the plan I propose: Set the Wellenen athwart Grūwen Pass; it is strait and the Yrm will have great difficulty bringing their numbers to bear upon you. You will be a barrier of iron that they will find hard to sunder."

"Aye, Sire," responded the Kingsgeneral, "your plan is sound, yet the horses are all but spent." Vidron clenched a fist and smote his palm. "But by the very bones of Sleeth, we *will* bar the way of the Horde!"

At mention of the Dragon's name, Brega growled low in his throat, but he held his tongue.

Talarin spoke: "Galen King, not long past I pledged to you in the name of the Lian of Arden Vale that when you need us we will be at your side. This then *is* the hour of your need, and we *are* at your side. My Guardians and I shall aid Kingsgeneral Vidron in holding Kregyn—Grūwen Pass —to buy you time at the Iron Tower. Our horses will be fresh and our arms stout."

Galen's eyes glittered in the firelight, and his heart was filled with emotion, and he could not speak; but Vidron leapt to his feet and flashed his sword to the darkling sky and cried in the ancient War-tongue of Valon: *"Hál, Deva Talarin! Vanada al tro da halka!"* (Hail, Elf Talarin! Together we shall be mighty!)

Talarin raised his hand in salute and smiled,

and then he turned to one of the Lian. "Feron, hie
to the hidden entrance and down into the Refuge.
Gather the returning Guardians and have them
prepare to come forth and join in the blockade of
Kregyn. The scouts along Arden Bluff will track
the *Rûpt*. Come forth with all my strength when
this Horde is a 'Darkday's march south of the
pass."

Feron leapt up to go, but Talarin held up a hand
and called, "Wait!" And when Feron turned once
more to him, Talarin said, "This, too, I think should
be done, Feron: Seek out the Lady Rael. Tell her of
Vanidor's rede:

> *'The Darkest Day,*
> *The Greatest Evil . . .'*

Perhaps she will divine the meaning of his warning, for she is versed in such things."

Of course! Tuck thought. *The Lady Rael should be
told the rede and her counsel sought. Perhaps she
can shed some light upon this darkness.*

Talarin nodded to Feron, and then the Lian herald was gone.

And as the drum of the hooves of Feron's horse
faded to the north, Prince Igon turned to Galen
and spoke: "Galen King, now I ask that you grant
my boon: I would fight at your side. And as you
have known, and heard again in this council tonight, no place is safe from the Evil in Gron: not
Arden, not Rian, not Pellar; neither Harth, nor
Rell, nor Rhone; not Hoven, Jugo, Valon, Gûnar,
or Riamon; not even the Land of the Wee Folk.
Aye, it is to Gron you go, yet Gron is no more
dangerous than elsewhere, for the foe is everywhere—if not now, then he soon will be.

"You have said it would be better if we were

apart, for then Modru will have to strike twice and succeed both times to end the House of Aurion, and that is true. But heed me! If you have guessed aright, then the Darkest Day will bring the Greatest Evil less than nine 'Darkdays hence. And if that Evil is Gyphon, then the House of Aurion is ended then and there, for no mortal can withstand Gyphon—nor can the Elves.

"And so this I say: if we are to be defeated, my brother, let it be as we stand shoulder to shoulder; but if, on the other hand, we are to win, then let that victory come as we stand shoulder to shoulder, too." Igon fell silent.

Galen thought long, staring at the fire, and at last he looked up and nodded his assent. Igon let out a sharp cry—*"Hai!"*—and leapt to his feet in joy, as all the council smiled at this youth-warrior verging into manhood. Abruptly Igon sat back down again, his face drawn into solemnity, but it was a solemnity often broken by an inward smile.

And Talarin turned to Galen. "Now, Galen King, you must tell me your tale, for I have many times wondered this 'Night at the path that has brought your footsteps nearly full circle to my door."

Galen looked to Gildor and nodded, and Gildor turned to Talarin and said, "First, Father, this I must say: *Va Draedan sa nond . . .*"

After the council ended, Tuck lay wearily down to sleep. But his mind churned with chaotic thoughts: *The Horde is in the Bosky. Ai! What foul news! And Danner and Patrel feel as I do: They would run the hundreds of miles on foot, if necessary, to go back and help, whether or not it would do any good. Yet, I did not like the look that came over Danner—his rage was awful to behold; it may be his undoing one day.*

But what if we have guessed right about the Darkest Day, the Greatest Evil? Then Gyphon will somehow come and it will be the end of the world as we know it. And if that is true, then whether or not Vidron delays the Horde behind us will not matter, for Modru and Gyphon will cloak Mithgar in an evil wrap that will smother all that was once good. Does that mean that Vidron's stand in Grūwen Pass is all for nought? Perhaps. But what if we have guessed wrong, and the Darkest Day does not come? Then Vidron's stand will buy us more time to assault the Iron Tower. Yet, if we cannot throw it down, or if Modru's power is too great . . .

Tuck fell into a restless dream-filled sleep: dreams of years of no summer, no crops, starvation, famine—the babies, oh the babies, swollen bellies—plague, cruel slavery, death. And he would start awake to escape the nightmares, and then fall back asleep exhausted. And nearby, Merrilee moaned in her own dark dreams.

At the breaking of camp the next 'Darkday, Danner, Patrel, Merrilee, and the other Warrows that had been mounted upon the packhorses from Wellen were placed instead upon steeds from Valon—packhorses whose loads of food and grain had become light with the long-ride. And once more Galen's cavalcade set forth, the five thousand Harlingar leaving Vidron and the Wellenen to come after. And Tuck felt as if they were somehow abandoning or being abandoned by the silver-bearded Hrosmarshal and his warriors. Yet north rode the Vanadurin, the Thornwalkers in their company—as well as two Elves and a Dwarf.

Three hours later the column came upon the Lady Rael and her escort of Lian Guardians as they stood beside the Legion's route where it swung close to the concealed entrance into the Hidden Stand of Arden Vale. Galen and much of his War-council turned to the side to speak to Raél, as the long line of horse-borne soldiers passed.

And Rael's eyes widened at the sight of Merrilee in this company of warriors. As for Merrilee, she had never seen anyone or anything quite as beautiful as golden Rael, and the damman felt awkward in the presence of Rael's Elven grace. Yet Rael took her by the hand, and all reserves between them melted.

"Galen King," said Rael, inclining her head in courtesy as Galen stepped down from Wildwind and bowed.

"My Lady Rael," Galen spoke with regard. "Though I would stir up no painful memories, still I must ask: Know you what Vanidor's rede means?"

"Nay, Galen King," answered Rael, her eyes filled with ache and sorrow. "Had Vanidor Silverbranch called my name at the last, then his final message would have been thrust upon me and not Gildor Goldbranch. Yet, although I would have spared my eldest that blow, still I think I would know no more than I do now. I can add nought to your interpretations. The Darkest Day comes on the eighth 'Darkday hence—if that is its meaning. And the Greatest Evil is indeed Gyphon, the High Vûlk."

As they rode away, Tuck looked back and waved at Talarin and Rael as the sad-eyed Elves stood and watched the Legion press onward. And somewhere behind—beyond Tuck's vision—riding at a slower pace came Hrosmarshal Vidron of Valon and the Wellenen, while even farther away marched the pursuing Horde.

* * *

All that 'Darkday the Legion rode, passing swiftly over the frozen stony ground at the pace of a Valanreach long-ride. And slowly the slopes around them rose as they came into the approaches of Grūwen Pass where the land veered upward to meet the Rigga Mountains.

Up through the rising canyon they rode, toward the rift through the mountains, and the ice-clad walls glinted darkly in the Shadowlight.

Into the notch they went, cloaked in the frigid Winternight. And as the air grew thinner, the steeds labored, yet the pace did not slacken, for they could not camp at these heights.

Onward they pressed, up through the frozen stone of Grūwen Pass cracking in the hoarfrost and rime. Now the floor of the col became more or less level, and they rode steadily northeastward through the blacklimned crags. Hours passed, and the notch swung northerly and began sloping downward. On they went, the ring of hooves knelling back at them from the sheer walls.

At last they came down through the Dimmendark and into the Land of Gron. And the horses and riders were weary, for they had ridden nearly sixty miles that 'Darkday alone—a long 'Day, even for a Valanreach longride.

And after he had tended to his steed and taken a meal, Tuck spoke briefly with Merrilee and others, and recorded a bit in his journal, ere falling into exhausted slumber.

Over the next three 'Darkdays the Legion rode north across the barren Wastes of Gron. King Galen had slackened the pace a bit to allow the horses to recover from the long trek through Grūwen Col, and at the end of the third 'Darkday they camped near the southern edge of the frozen Gwasp. A raw wind blew down upon them from the Gronfangs off to the east as they sat around cheerless peat fires and shivered in the blast.

"Hey!" exclaimed Danner. "I just thought of something. If Modru is the Master of the Cold, why hasn't . . . why *doesn't* he just summon up a blizzard and stop us here and now? He could freeze us solid, us being out in the open—no shelter, no firewood. Is it that he cannot control the cold? Is that just an old dammen's tale?"

Merrilee shot Danner a squint-eyed look and responded. "Perhaps, Danner, it is instead just an old *buccen's* tale, generated by an overdose of ale down at the One-Eyed Crow."

"Ar, Merrilee, you know what I mean," squirmed Danner.

"And you know what I mean, too, loud buccan," shot back Merrilee.

"Hold on now," soothed Tuck. "We are all tired and cold and cross. Let us not to argue amongst ourselves out of sheer weariness."

"Danner's got a good point, though," spoke up wee Patrel. "I mean about Modru being the Master of the Cold, and all. Why *doesn't* he just bury us with a blizzard? Or *is* his reputation false?"

"Modru has the power, alright," spoke up slim Flandrena. "He *is* Master of the Cold. And he *could* bring a blizzard down upon us, for that is his most terrible weapon. Yet why he does not use it now, I cannot say. Perhaps it requires all of his power to do so, and he is saving his energy for some other reason . . . mayhap saving it for the Darkest Day."

At Flandrena's words, Tuck felt a deep foreboding race through his veins, and he shivered with its dire portent; and he glanced up to see a dark look in Merrilee's eyes, too.

"Well," yawned Danner, "I don't know either, but I am just too tired to stay awake and dwell upon it any longer." And the buccan spread out his bedroll and prepared to sleep. And as if that were a signal to the others, they too crawled into their blankets.

But ere Tuck fell into slumber, long ululating howls shuddered through the Winternight as Modru's curs wailed in the Wastes of Gron, and a cold chill ran up the buccan's spine.

And far away to the south, at the mouth of Grūwen Pass, Vidron, Talarin, the Wellenen, and the Lian Guardians all watched as the Swarm of *Spaunen* marched northward toward them, northward up the approach to the col: ten thousand Wrg marching upon two thousand defenders.

The next 'Darkday saw the Legion ride across the wastes to the north end of the Gwasp, where they made camp.

And once again the juddering howls of Vulgs called through the Shadowlight, other cries sounding to the northward and beyond, as if yawling messages were being relayed to the north, to the dark fortress of Modru.

And to the south at Grūwen Pass, that same 'Darkday had seen the Horde launch four attacks upon the Men and Elves, and four times Vidron's Host had hurled the *Spaunen* back. But each time, like a great battering ram, the Horde had smashed into the defenders, and each time the Alliance of Wellen and Arden had been driven reeling backwards, deeper into the pass.

Another 'Darkday passed, and the wayworn Legion rode through Claw Gap and onto Claw Moor, driving northward toward Modru's strongholt. No enemy barred their way or sought to strike at them, though Modru's curs—Modru's spies—hounded their flanks and yawled shuddering messages across the moor. The Legion at last made camp and rested in the mid of the high frozen land. On the morrow they would reach their goal.

And at Grūwen Pass, thrice more on this 'Darkday the Spawn sought to break through Vidron's Host. And thrice more the spent horses and exhausted Men and worn Elves rallied to hold the gap shut to the *Rûpt*. And the count of the slain mounted as the hammer of the Wrg smashed into the anvil of the Allies, driving them another eight miles deeper into the pass.

It was noon, the only time of 'Day that the faint disk of the Sun could be seen through the Dimmendark, and then but barely and only by knowing exactly where to look in the Winternight. And now the dim orb stood shadowy vague at its brumal zenith. High King Galen, son of Aurion, sat astride Wildwind and looked high in the southern sky at the dimly seen circle, while behind him sat unmoving the five thousand warriors of his Legion. And as he looked at the shadow-faint disk, Galen knew that in just two more 'Darkdays, at this very hour, the unseen Moon would eat the Sun, and the Darkest Day would come, and the Greatest Evil.

And Galen dropped his gaze to the east and looked at the dark fortress standing before him. Massive it was, and formidable, and beringed by a deep crevasse plummeting into ebon depths below. The great iron bridge was drawn up 'gainst sheer walls of black stone blocks rising up to towering battlements. And in the center, from atop the highest tower, flew the Sun-Death standard, a scarlet ring of fire upon a field of black. And now more than ever the Sun-Death sigil seemed to hold dire portent. Galen took a deep breath, and his eyes swept the ramparts for some sign of weakness, some place of entrance, some chink by which this bastion could be cast down. For the Legion stood now before their goal: They had come at last to Modru Kinstealer's holt. They had come at last to the dreaded Iron Tower.

CHAPTER 4

THE IRON TOWER

The 'Darkdays following Vanidor's torture-murder had been 'Days of anguish for Princess Laurelin. Yet whenever her mind stumbled into the black memories of those endless moments in Modru's chamber high in the tower—moments filled with hissing questions, and the *Clack!* of a Troll-driven rack wheel, and raw screams of agony—whenever Laurelin's mind returned to that hideous time, visions of a golden Elfess guided the Princess past the pain and horror and into a quiet domain of mourning. Laurelin grieved, but no longer did her wits fall stunned, nor did her heart plunge into an icy pall, and no longer did her soul flee through an unending labyrinth of despair. Instead she wept for the lost promise of Vanidor, and through her tears, her spirit began to heal. And even though she remained in the clutch of the Enemy, his will had not broken hers. And slowly she returned from that place of no hope to come back into the realm of reality, and she began to take note of her surroundings.

The chamber in which Laurelin was held was along a main corridor of the Iron Tower, and through the massive door she could at times hear fragments of snarling conversations of Yrm passing in the hallway as they went to and fro on their vile errands. Often they would be speaking in the Slûk tongue, and the Princess could not understand this foul, slobbering, guttural speech; at other times, though, a debased form of the Common Tongue would be used, and then she could piece together some of what was said. Yet she learned little from their talk, for most of it consisted of cursing and threats and insults aimed at one another.

The foul Rukh that grudgingly brought her food and drink and tended her fire was no source of information either, for he had no tongue and did not speak except to snarl at her. And when he came to do his chores, he was ever leering and prowling about, and his eyes followed her every movement. And whenever his small figure scuttled in through the door, Laurelin was repelled by the loathsome creature and took pains to ignore him.

Even so, the Princess did learn something of the course of the War—from the Evil One himself.

Not forty-eight hours following Vanidor's death, Modru's enraged shrieks echoed throughout the tower, and slapping footfalls of fleeing lackeys could be heard scrambling along the hallway past Laurelin's room. And the small filthy Rukh that served the Princess came scuttling in through the door, slamming it shut behind.

Hissing a tongueless snarl at Laurelin, the Rukh pressed his ear to the portal and listened intently. Modru's shrill cries of wrath rang in the corridor; yet abruptly the Evil One's stridor fell silent.

Now the Rukh listened even more intently to the ominous hush beyond the heavy panel, but he could hear nought.

Suddenly the door burst open, sending the mute asprawl, and Modru stalked into the chamber, his eyes glaring in rage through his hideous iron mask.

To the Princess he strode, and she stood defiant before him. The mute Rukh fled the room, limping and gibbering in fear.

"They will pay! They will pay!" Modru's wrath lashed out at her. Then his voice fell to the hiss of a poison-laden viper. "I will find them out—these four—when I am Master of all Mithgar, and they will suffer endless days at my hands. I will make them eternally regret that they strode through the *Dubh* caverns. They will forever rue the day that they slew my Negus of Terror."

Laurelin knew not of what event Modru spoke, nor what were the *Dubh* caverns, nor who or what a Negus of Terror was; but it was plain that four unknown heroes had thwarted some vile plan of the Evil One. And the Princess smiled in triumph at Modru.

The Evil One snarled and loomed above her and raised a black-gauntleted fist to strike, yet Laurelin did not flinch or cower before him. And just as it seemed his clench would crash down upon her, Modru hissed unto himself, "Unblemished," and he spun in rage upon his heel and strode from the room, his black cloak billowing behind.

In the long 'Darkdays that followed, Modru came often to gloat—his viperous mouthings, his sibilant whisperings, filling the room with malignancy as he boasted of his victories in Pellar, in Hoven, in Aven, and especially in the Realm of Riamon, where Laurelin's father, King Dorn, ruled: "Your dotard of a sire falls back before my power in the Rimmen Mountains. Dael soon will be mine. I think I shall make of it a great bonfire, and I will let King Shallowpate Dorn witness the burning . . . from a seat in the midst of the pyre!''

Though Laurelin knew he told her these things to break her spirit, still she listened carefully, for amid his sibilant puff-adder hissings was news of the War: news of the *Dubh*—the Dwarves—trapped in Mineholt North, "where they think to defy *me!* —*sstha!*—the foul-beards will be grovelling at my feet ere long, begging for mercy, but I will chain them to their forges, where they will eat and sleep and toil, and their hammers and anvils and sweat will serve Gron ever after"; news of the Baeron— the woodsmen of the Great Greenhall—fighting in the fastness of the Grimwall Mountains above Delon, struggling to close the secret Rukken doors upon the mountain slopes, "drooling imbeciles who will forever regret that they strove against *me—sss* —when they are in fetters, I think I shall have them carve new doors and new chambers in the flanks of the Grimwall, for I hear that they walk tall beneath the open skies and through the forests, and so stooping grinding labor in the dark laby- rinths under the mountains seems a most . . . fit- ting task, *tsss, sss''*; and news of the *Dolh*—the Elves—with their bright swords and swift steeds, "stinking lordlings—*sssth*—who shall not escape *my* wrath, for even Adonar will not be a haven when I am victorious. And I will drag them kick- ing and screaming back into Mithgar, and I will sit and watch while they hew down to lie in rot each and every one of those obscene trees of theirs. And then I shall bring the *Dolh* north and see if they can . . . *sss* . . . dig through the muck and find the bottom of the Gwasp.''

Hissing and gurgling, Modru's vile gloating seemed endless. Yet it was not among his boastings that Laurelin gleamed tidings that kept alive the spark of hope within her heart; it was instead in his moments of rage as some fortune went 'gainst him that the Princess found faint glimmers of promise.

Two 'Darkdays after he had last burst into her chamber prison—raving that his Negus of Terror had been slain—again Modru's wrath rang throughout the tower, this 'Day twice. And when next he came with his sibilant whisperings, Laurelin found among his mutterings and threats indications that the four heroes had somehow escaped his grasp. Modru also hissed a vile pledge to torture and starve the "runtish scum" that had twice ambushed his reavers.

Inwardly the Princess smiled, for here were two more things that buoyed her spirit. Yet whether the four heroes were in any way associated with the "scum" and the ambushing of Modru's Reavers, she could not say.

Four 'Darkdays later Laurelin found out who the "runtish scum" were, for Modru came to gloat and hiss, saying that the Horde that had destroyed Challerain Keep was "even now marching through the ring of thorns and into the Land of the Runts."

And Laurelin's heart wrenched, and in her mind rose the faces of Tuck and Danner and Patrel, and her soul cried out to these gentle Folk of the Boskydells.

And when Modru left the chamber, Laurelin sat by the fire and wept.

It was in this time that Laurelin began to think upon escape, and she carefully examined her plight:

There were but two possible ways to leave the chamber: There was the door, but it opened out into a hallway heavily trafficked by the Spawn; further, the door was kept shut by a great brass bolt on the outside. And there was a single narrow window overlooking a courtyard, but the window was barred and was some twenty-five feet above the rough cobbles.

Neither way seemed to hold much promise of her escaping. And too, if she *could* get out, what then? How to avoid the teeming Yrm to slip across the courtyard? How to get beyond the walls and drawbridge? How to cross the Wastes of Gron? Horses? Nay, for the *Spaunen* rode Hèlsteeds. And although she had ridden one of these vile beasts to the Iron Tower, it had been led by a Ghol, and Laurelin was not certain that a Hèlsteed would permit a human to guide it. And what about food? And clothing, too, must be considered, for the garments provided by the mute Rukh were not suitable for travel o'er the Wastes in the bitter Winternight cold.

Laurelin did not know the resolutions to these considerations or to the others that came to her mind; yet, in spite of her broken arm, she began working to loosen a bar from the sill of the window, chipping with a fireplace tool at the mortar, praying that the heavy drapes would muffle the sound of her work ... praying, too, that neither Modru nor the Rukh would come upon her unawares. And grain by grain, chip by chip, the mortar slowly, infinitesimally, began to yield.

Five more 'Darkdays passed, and Laurelin continued to chip at the mortar in which the bar was embedded, stopping whenever she heard the doorbolt *thunk!* back as the Rukh or Modru came. And they would find her prodding the fire with the iron.

Such was the case when Modru came to gloat on the fifth 'Day, and she stirred the blaze and then set the iron aside as Modru's hissings began. Among his reptilian mouthings, Laurelin gleaned that a battle between the Vanadurin and the Hyrania had begun.

The next 'Darkday, Laurelin managed to free the lower end of the bar, and she started chipping away at the upper end. And while she worked, she began to think upon how to twist or braid a rope out of cloth so that she could lower herself to the courtyard below.

Again Modru came and boasted. And Laurelin came to know that the fighting still raged between the Vanadurin and the Hyrania, and that it was at Gûnarring Gap. And the Evil One crowed at how clever he had been to seize the Gap at the War's outset.

Still his malignant hissings went on, and he spoke of many things. Laurelin was repelled to hear of the future he planned for Mithgar, but she gave no outward sign of her revulsion.

And as Modru prepared to leave her chamber— his malevolent gloating done—the Princess spoke to him for only the second time since arriving at the Iron Tower:

"Vile One, Yrm may thrive on fire-smoke and confinement, yet I would walk in the fresh air." Laurelin stood and spoke with the air of command of a royal Princess, yet inside she was wound tense as a spring, for she *needed* Modru to grant this request. Her only knowledge of the fortress was made up of chaotic memories from that time twenty-one 'Darkdays past when she had been led captive into the hold. Yet if she were ever to escape, she would need to know more of the arrangement of the strongholt ere attempting flight.

Modru's maleficent eyes glared at her through his iron-beaked mask. "*Ssstha!* Perhaps instead I will fling you back into my dungeons." And as Laurelin's heart plummeted to hear those words . . . "But then, *sss*, your health *is* a consideration." Modru spun on his heel and left.

An hour or so later the bolt slid back, and the filthy Rukh hobbled in bearing quilted Rukken garments, and boots, and a cloak. He flung them all in a pile in the center of the room and limped out.

The garb was crawling with vermin, yet Laurelin clasped it to her breast. Her heart pounded with glad excitement, for here was the clothing necessary for her survival in the Winternight cold while she crossed the Wastes of Gron.

And she washed the garments with the harsh soap provided for her bath and hung them before the fire to dry.

The next 'Darkday two iron-helmed Lōkha came and snarled at her to get dressed for her outdoor stroll. And as they walked the Lōkha spoke in a debased form of the Common Tongue, but their talk was of a revenge they planned upon one of their own kind and so Laurelin paid them little heed; instead her eyes sought ways she might escape.

The escort took the Princess across the rough cobbles toward the soaring battlements, and everywhere she looked was filth. Yammering Yrm snarled at one another and quarreled. Dark squatty Rukha, swart Lōkha and dead-white Ghola swarmed within the walls. A great iron portcullis barred the way to the drawbridge, and it was Troll-guarded.

As she mounted up the ramps to the bastion parapets, the Princess saw the stables where the Hèlsteeds were kept, just inside the gate. And there, too, stood a Troll guard—a leering Ogru dressed in nought but black leather breeks in spite of the cold—and Laurelin's heart leapt with shock upon seeing the foul hulking creature, for it was the same Troll that had slain Vanidor on the rack. Her heart pounded with rage and loathing as the Lōkha led her up to the ramparts.

They walked along the battlements, and Laurelin deliberately shoved the vile image of the Elf-slaying Ogru from her mind and looked down through the Shadowlight at the great fissure that split the stone to encircle the fortress with a deep chasm.

She thought upon all that she had seen, and her heart plummeted, for she knew that she could not get out unless she could somehow pass undetected across teeming courtyards to take a Troll-guarded Hèlsteed and ride through a barred portcullis past its hulking warder and across an iron drawbridge above a black chasm.

When she returned to her chamber, the Princess took up the fire iron and chipped at the mortar holding the upper end of the bar, and tears ran down her face as she toiled in what she now believed to be a hopeless cause.

Again Modru's enraged screams resounded throughout the tower, and once more the bolt shot back and the small filthy form of the mute Rukh scuttled through the door, slamming it behind.

But this time the Evil One did not come, and after a long while the Rukh hobbled out.

*   *   *

The next 'Darkday Modru ranted, now promis-
ing to lay waste to the Land of Valon: "No horse,
no rider, no filth of a Harlingar, nothing—not even
the smallest blade of grass—shall escape my wrath!"
And Laurelin then knew that at the Gûnarring
Gap the Hyrania had suffered defeat at the hands
of the Riders of Valon, and her heart sang.

Six more 'Darkdays passed, and Modru's maleficent boastings hissed unremittingly, and there was
nought to buoy Laurelin's spirit. But on the seventh 'Day:
"Fools! They enter *my* darkness now," spat the
Evil One. "And though my minions in the *Dubh*
caverns are not yet able to come at them, I have
broken off my attack against the Weiunwood and
sent my Horde marching east along the Crossland
Road to intercept this paltry Legion. These riders
will rue the 'Day that they set forth to come against
me."
Laurelin knew not where this Legion was from
nor where it was headed, yet she hoped with all
her being that Modru's plans would be foiled.

On the next 'Darkday the window bar came loose.
Laurelin took it from the casement and saw with
relief that she could now squeeze her slight form
through the resulting gap. Carefully she set the
bar back into the sill so that all would appear
normal to the casual eye.
Now she turned her mind and hands to the man-
ufacture of a cloth-strip rope, and she set about
acquiring more food for her journey across Gron:
"Yrm, your evil lord wants me in perfect health,"
she couched her voice in hauteur and imperiously
demanded of the mute Rukh, "yet how can I become hale when you bring me not enough proven-

der to feed a sparrow? Shall I speak to your master
of your neglect?"

The foul Rukh snarled at her, but each meal he
brought thereafter held extra bread and more
vegetables—turnips, potatoes, and the like.

And Laurelin began concealing food in a pillow-
case she planned to use as a knapsack.

Each 'Darkday she plaited more of her escape
rope, carefully tearing strips of her bedding sheets
and twisting and tying and braiding the cloth,
praying that it would hold her weight.

And each 'Darkday her Lōkken escort would take
her to the battlements for her "fresh air." And still
her eyes did not see and her mind could not imagine how she might escape.

But still she toiled onward.

And a week of 'Darkdays passed.

And on the seventh 'Darkday they came to remove the wrap from Laurelin's arm. It had been
eight weeks and three 'Days since the time of her
capture, when her arm had been broken, and a
month since it had been lapped in the stiff bind-
ing. And while the nervous Rukha worked, peeling
away the layers of plastered cloth, Modru looked
on and seethed in rage at events miles from the
Tower:

"*Tsssth!* I would set a blizzard down upon this
ragtag Legion that has come through Grūwen Pass
and into Gron," sissed the Evil One, "a blizzard
they would not survive. But I am forced to con-
serve my energies for the coming Darkest Day . . .
Careful, fools! I would not have her arm broken
again!"

A Legion in Gron? Laurelin's heart leapt with hope, but she gave no outward sign and instead watched the plastered cloth come loose. Laurelin was as anxious to see her arm as Modru seemed, for she knew she would need it to be strong and healthy for her climb down the rope when the time of her escape came.

At last the wrapping was off. Her right arm was thin, and the skin was scaly and sloughed off in large flakes. She could not straighten her elbow. And her muscles felt . . . stiff . . . fibrous.

"Sssath!" spat Modru, his vile eyes glaring malignantly through the hideous iron mask. "One week till the Sun-Death. That's all the time you have. You will carry a weight to straighten the limb. And you will flex the arm to strengthen it. And you will clean the skin, and treat it with oils. You will do this for hours each 'Day. And if you lag in your progress, *ssss,* I will have it done for you. For in one week will come that Darkest Day I have waited four thousand years to see. And you, my Princess, at that time must be . . . presentable. *Sssth, sss, sss, tsss!"*

Long grueling 'Days of pain and effort followed as Laurelin stressed and flexed and worked her arm, striving to straighten her elbow and bend it full, and to stretch the muscles and strengthen them. Slowly the arm began to respond as the tissues lost their fibrous feel and started to take on the tone and flexure of healthy sinews. She worked hard at restoring her arm not because Modru had so bade her; instead she did this so as to be able to climb down a rope and escape.

She did not know what Modru's long-awaited Darkest Day would bring, nor her role in it; yet she feared it, for she knew that it had something to do with Gyphon's return, and she planned to fly ere then. But her arm was terribly weak, and whether she would be able to manage the climb in but a few more days was questionable. Yet she worked with a single-minded determination.

And Modru came each 'Darkday to check her progress and sissed at her to work harder; yet he did not set his lackeys upon her to force her arm beyond its limits.

And each 'Darkday he hissed news of the War: "My Vulpen scouts slink upon their four legs and stay hidden in the scrub and track the ragtag Legion as they ride across Gron. *Ssss.* It seems as if these *fools* come to assault the Iron Tower itself! And the howls of my Vulpen report that this paltry Legion is but five thousand strong. *Sss, ssth, sss, tsss!* Five thousand, where *fifty* thousand would fail! *Imbeciles!* Little do they know that my Horde marches upon their trail."

"Fools!" spat Modru the following 'Darkday. "Do they hope to stop me? Ten thousand of *my* minions against but two thousand or so of them? I shall batter through Grūwen Pass in less than a 'Day! Then once again will my Horde come after the ragtags."

The next 'Darkday, Modru did not come, and so the Princess learned nought of the conduct of the War. But the following 'Day she listened to the guttural slobberings of her Lōkken escort as she walked upon the battlements, for they spoke first of Modru, then of fighting in the south:

"He's in a foul mood, they say," said one guard.

"Har! When ain't he?" barked the other.

"Ar, you stupid gob," snarled the first, "I mean

worse than a foul mood. I won't cross his path if I see him comin'.''

"They say somethin's wrong at Grūwen. The Horde's been stopped by Men . . . and, *sss*, Elves," said the second Lōkh. "And more Men camp on Claw Moor . . . a Legion, they say . . . comin' here!"

On Claw Moor! Laurelin's spirit leapt with hope, yet plummeted again when she thought of the impossibility of throwing down this mighty fortress.

The Lōkha said little else of interest as they led her back to her chamber, but Modru was there to inspect her arm. And what he said caused her heart to cry out to the Men coming toward the Iron Tower.

"*Ssss*, I will show these fools who come to my dark citadel. From Aven and from your Riamon, through the Jallor Pass to Jord, and thence by secret ways through the Gronfangs, my reavers come. And this puling ragtag Legion that now camps upon the moor . . . *tssah!* My Hèlsteed cavalry will soon slam the Gap shut behind them and fall upon them from the rear. *Sssth, tsssth, ssth!*"

That 'Night, Laurelin sat in deep thought. Through all of Modru's hissings and rantings she had striven to strengthen her arm. And slowly it had improved. Soon, she felt, she could attempt her escape. But still she did not see how to accomplish it. And her daily walks out to the walls and around the battlements and then back to her chamber did nought to shed light on how she should set about fleeing.

And though she did not know who made up this "ragtag" Legion, her heart leapt with hope to hear that they came toward the Iron Tower and plunged in despair to hear that a great force of Ghola was now gathering to fall upon them from behind.

Yet she thought that if the Legion *did* come,

then perhaps they would provide the diversion needed for her own escape. And it seemed as if indeed they were coming to the Iron Tower, and soon, for now they camped upon Claw Moor itself, and the moor led to the very gates of Modru's fortress.

The next 'Darkday the Princess was taken for her walk, and great turmoil filled the courtyards as Rukken horns blatted and Yrm rushed thither and yon, bearing weapons up to the battlements.

And when Laurelin strode up the ramparts and looked out through the crenellations, out through the Shadowlight, out upon the moor, there before her she saw arrayed a great force of horsemen, a forest of spears stirring to and fro.

And she gasped, and her heart hammered wildly, and her spirit soared up to the sky, and joy flooded her being.

For there flew the white and green of Valon . . .

And the scarlet and gold of Pellar . . .

And in the fore stood proudly the grey steed Wildwind, yet upon his back sat not High King Aurion, but instead a Man clad in scarlet armor—*the scarlet armor of. . . Lord Galen!*

Her beloved had come at last!

Laurelin caught her breath and tears filled her eyes, and she would have called out, but the Princess knew that the Legion was too far away to understand her words. Yet her heart cried out for her somehow to warn her Lord Galen that Ghola in force were even now riding from Jord into Gron to come to the Tower and fall upon the Legion from the rear. But she must not let the Lökken escort know what she would shout, else when the

warriors *did* come nigh enough to hear, she would
not be permitted upon the walls.

Since she saw no way to give the warning, she
held her tongue and brushed aside her tears as the
Lōkha marched her along the ramparts. And all
about her Yrm rushed to their stations and made
ready their weapons: cauldrons of hot oil; sinuous
bows and black-shafted arrows; scimitars, tulwars,
dirks; hammers, cudgels, bludgeons, iron bars.
Above the gate, with a harsh clatter of gears, Lōkha
wound taut a great crank-bow, and they laid a
spear-length iron-pointed shaft in the launch groove
and pivoted the weapon upon its pedestal and aimed
it at the Legion.

But Laurelin did not see this writhing turmoil
atop the ramparts; her eyes were locked upon the
figure of her beloved. She could not seem to see
enough of him, and her gaze drank in his distant
form, and her heart sang, for he had come at last.
And as she was marched along the walls, she looked
long at him. But at last she tore her eyes from the
scarlet-clad figure upon the grey horse and turned
her gaze to scan among the warriors of the Legion,
searching for others she knew. And with a rush her
heart leapt to her throat, for there was a horse she
knew could be not any but Rust, and upon his
back sat ... Prince Igon! *Yet, how could this be?*
With her very own eyes she had seen him slain at
the waggon train! And she herself had given the
command for Rust to flee. Yet here they were—
and Igon was *Alive!*—and they stood before the
gates of the Iron Tower.

She shook her head as if to clear it of phantoms,
yet the Prince remained solid and real. And then
she knew that, somehow, Igon had survived the
cut of the Ghol tulwar that had cloven through the
youth's steel helm and smashed him down.

Again her eyes scanned the fore of the Legion, and there was one she took to be Lord Gildor, yet she was not certain, for the Elf was not astride Fleetfoot.

There, too, were the small forms of—*Waerlinga!* But whether Sir Tuck, or Sir Danner, or Captain Patrel was among them, she did not see, for at that moment she was marched down from the walls and back to her chamber.

When the door was slammed shut and bolted, the Princess sat and tried to assemble her chaotic thoughts. At last much of Modru's disjoint hiss-imgs became clear in her mind: *This* was the Legion that had ridden north through the Dimmendark—a Legion from Valon, a Legion led by her beloved Lord Galen. Perhaps this was the same Legion that had defeated the Hyrania at the Gûnarring Gap. If so, then they had come north through Grūwen Pass and had left a rear guard behind to stave off a pursuing Horde. Yet, how came Lord Galen to be at the head of this force? And upon Wildwind? Where was Aurion King?

Fa! The answers to none of these questions mattered now. Instead, all that mattered was that she must warn Galen of the force of Ghola gathering to attack him.

And she had to warn Galen that Modru planned some great vileness in but two days, for that was when the Evil One's Darkest Day would arrive.

Laurelin began to pace the floor in agitation, for now more than ever she knew that she had to escape . . . Yet how? Although she could climb through the window and down, and perhaps win her way across the courtyard, still, how could she pass the walls? And how could she cross the ravine? Until she had an answer, did she dare attempt aught? For if she were caught in an unsuccessful try, Modru would lock her in other quarters—quarters with no windows, no bars, no hope of escape.

Moaning in distress, Laurelin jerked bolt upright in her bed, her eyes flying wide as she shocked awake from a hideous dream of terror and bondage. Her heart pounded frantically, and her entangled bedding was knotted and twisted about her and was wet with perspiration. Fragments of her nightmare clung to her mind like wisps of chill mist. Yet all she could remember of the dream was a great sucking maw of blackness coming to swallow her whole, and she could not flee, and behind her *Spaunen* had jeered and thrummed some monstrous instrument of torture.

As the Princess struggled free of the bedclothes, *Thuunn!* she heard the deep twanging sound of her nightmare, and it was followed by the raucous japing of Spawn.

For a moment Laurelin's dream terror struck at her heart; but she knew that what she heard now was real and not some phantom of sleep. She padded from her bed to the window, stepping behind the heavy drapes and peering out through the Shadowlight.

Thruum! There it was again! And amid the howling jeers of the *Spaunen*, the Princess could hear a harsh clatter of gears. Although she could not see it from her window, Laurelin knew that the great crank-bow on the battlements above the gate was being wound taut by Lōkha, soon to hurl another iron-pointed spear at the Legion.

Laurelin's eyes drifted to the courtyard below, and she gasped in dismay, for there, directly under her window, a pair of Lōkha stood watching as Rukken lackeys parcelled out gobbets of stringy meat and bowls of cold gruel to squads of Yrm coming from the walls. And to one side stood one of the corpse-foe—a Ghol watching o'er all. And even as she looked, he turned his dead black soulless eyes to her window, and his red gash of a mouth split in an evil grin, his rows of pointed teeth gleaming yellow in the Shadowlight.

Thuunn!

Tears welled in Laurelin's eyes, and she turned from the window and made her way back to the bed. And her heart despaired, for even though she did not know how she could have gotten past the ramparts and beyond the ravine, still she had thought that escape somehow might have been possible. Yet now she could not even climb down from her window, for that way led directly into the clutch of the *Spaunen* below.

That 'Darkday no Lōkken escort came to march her around the walls. Neither did Modru come. And the Princess knew that they prepared for War.

And all 'Day long Laurelin frequently checked the window, but the Yrm feeding station remained below. Her mind raced, yet no plan came to light as to how she could even escape her room, much less reach the ranks of the Legion.

And throughout the 'Day the deep-pitched *Thuunn!* of the spear-hurling crank-bow thrummed upon the wall.

The next 'Darkday, Laurelin paced her chamber as would a caged animal. Her mind screamed at her to *do something!* Yet just as loudly her thoughts cried, *What? What can I do?* She was dressed in her quilted Rukken garb, and she was ready to fly . . . but Yrm stood below her window, and the door to her chamber was bolted.

And this was the 'Day Modru had raved about: this was the Darkest Day.

Time lagged as moments turned into long spans of minutes, and the minutes dragged into hours, and the 'Day slowly seeped toward the time of the Sun-Death.

Laurelin frequently trod to her window, and yet nothing changed; and her heart despaired, and she felt as if something foul—something evil—was drawing nigh. But what it was, she did not know.

Now it was nearly mid of 'Darkday, and once more she strode to the window. And as she stood looking, a great hubbub broke out atop the walls. She could hear the harsh blats of Rukken horns. And there came the clash and clangor of weapons, and hoarse snarls and shouts, and she could see Yrm running upon the ramparts in the direction of the unseen gate.

And in the courtyard below, with harsh cries the Spawn beneath her window snatched up their weapons and rushed toward the uproar.

Now was her chance!

Quickly Laurelin donned her cloak and removed the window bar, setting the thick iron rod aside. She tied the cloth rope to a remaining bar and cast the braided line out the window, her knapsack tied to the distant end of the braid, where it dropped to within a few feet of the stone cobbles below.

As she tugged on the rope, testing the strength of her knot, she heard the enraged screams of Modru ringing throughout the tower, and there sounded the slap of feet running past her door.

There was a moment of silence, and then *Thunk!* the bolt on her door shot back, and although she could not see, she heard scrabbling footsteps hobble in and the door slam shut behind. There were the hash gasps of labored breathing, *and then the limping steps and blowing breath came straight toward the window!*

Behind the heavy drapes, her heart hammering, Laurelin silently took up the loose iron bar and raised it on high, girding herself to bring it crashing down upon the intruder's head in a killing blow, and then make good her escape.

CHAPTER 5

THE DARKEST DAY

Astride Wildwind, King Galen turned his steel-grey eyes from the faint disk standing at its zenith in the southerly sky and looked eastward toward the Iron Tower. The dark battlements rose upward in the Shadowlight, the black fortress looming balefully in the Dimmendark. And in the forescape and curving beyond seeing 'round the stark walls, a black chasm gaped.

To Galen's left, Brega stood upon the frozen ground, his dark gaze surveying the bastion; the Dwarf stroked his forked beard and muttered under his breath. Upon Galen's right Lord Gildor sat ahorse, his own sight still locked upon the pale circle, wan in the darkling sky. And behind the King, drawn up in long files, sabers unsheathed and spears stirring to and fro, was mounted the High King's Legion.

"In but two 'Days comes the Sun-Death, Galen King," said the Elf, turning his eyes away from the faint glow and to the ramparts.

Galen merely grunted, his sight searching the stone of the dark citadel, seeking a weak chink through which the Legion could strike. And somewhere in the Kinstealer's holt his beloved Princess Laurelin was captive—if she still lived.

And in a rank immediately behind the King, the Warrows talked among themselves:

"Hoy, Tuck," exclaimed Danner, his voice low, "look at the central tower—the tall one."

"I see it, Danner. I see it." Tuck's voice was grim, for he too saw that all about the top of the spire a dark nimbus streamed. "Lord Gildor," called the buccan, "see you that black halo around the tallest tower?"

The Lian warrior shifted his gaze to the pinnacle. "Nay, Tuck, I do not. Your Waerling sight alone descries it."

"Perhaps in that tower lies some hideous device of the Evil One," speculated Patrel, his viridian eyes watching the fluxing blackness enshrouding the spire.

"Mayhap the heart of the Dimmendark lies in that pinnacle," suggested Merrilee after a moment. At her ominous words Tuck's heart hammered within his breast, for with his sapphirine gaze he saw the awful darkness pulsating forth. And in that moment Tuck knew that from this tower emanated not only the Shadowlight of the Dimmendark, but all of the evil that now beset Mithgar. The buccan shuddered at this thought, but said nought as all stared at the looming fortress.

Long moments they sat upon their steeds in silence and peered at the dark citadel, and then at last King Galen spoke: "Sound the call to make camp, and summon the scouts to me. Set the wards and pass the word to be ever vigilant, for we know not what Modru plans."

Ubrik raised his black-oxen horn to his lips and split the air with resonant calls, and the mounted ranks of the Legion broke for camp. And Galen once more donned his quilted jacket, for the High King had shown his colors and his armor to the enemy in challenge, but the foe had not deigned to answer.

Camp was made out upon the moor to the north and west of the drawbridge road; scouts were dispatched to encircle the dark citadel, to seek ways the Legion might enter into the fortress, and to spy out the paths by which the foe might issue forth to fall upon the Host.

Hours passed, and one by one the riders returned with the word that the ravine ringed all, that Wrg patrols paced the far side, and that atop the battlements Spawn warders jeered from afar. And the riders reported that there seemed to be no means of ingress or egress to or from the strongholt other than over the drawbridge and through the gate.

Now the Warrows set forth with the scouts, for it was suggested that in the Dimmendark their jewel-hued eyes might see fine detail of the fortress that Men's eyes saw not. Gildor and Flandrena went also, their Elvensight to probe the bastion. So, too, went Brega mounted behind Flandrena upon Swiftmane, for, as the Dwarf said, "Châkka eyes will gaze upon these defences as well."

Long they searched while the weary Legion slept within a ring of warders, and the hours fell away. Yet these scouts, too—Men, Warrows, two Elves and a Dwarf—came at last to King Galen to report no success in their quest.

Thus did the 'Darkday pass.

*   *   *

Thuun! Tuck was awakened by a deep thrumming sound. He sat up in his blankets and rubbed sleep from his eyes and looked up to see Merrilee standing and gazing toward the dark fortress. Tuck, too, got to his feet; he stepped to her side and put an arm about her, and she leaned her head upon his shoulder without taking her eyes from the distant battlements.

"What is it, my dammia?" asked Tuck, peering toward the walls.

"I know not, Tuck," she answered. "I was awakened by . . . a sound."

Thuunn!

"There! There it is again!" exclaimed the damman. "And look!" She pointed.

Both Warrows saw a great shaft soar upward through the Shadowlight to arc down toward the Legion.

"Wha—what can hurl a spear like that?" breathed Tuck as he watched the flight of the shaft.

From behind them came the answer to Tuck's question: "The Wrg have a great crank-bow mounted above the gate." Marshal Ubrik stepped beside the Warrows, his eyes, too, following the flight of the spear.

The shaft lanced into the earth amid warriors scrambling to get out of the way, and the far-off gibes of Spawn jeered out from the walls and onto the moor.

Thrumm! The ballista hurled forth another spear to arc through the Shadowlight and strike among the Legion, and once more the hoots of the maggot-folk fleered from the battlements.

Feartoken, thought Tuck. *This is another feartoken of the Evil One.*

Yet Ubrik said, "Worry not here about this weapon, for where we now stand the shafts are easily avoided. The Spawn but use the crank-bow to harass us. It amuses them to see us jump. Only if we have to cross the drawbridge will it make a difference, and then it will fell warrior and steed alike. That is its purpose—to ward the bridge—and then it becomes a mighty weapon; then it is a most dread device."

Thuumm!

All that early 'Darkday the strum of the crank-bow sounded, but none of the warriors had yet been struck by the spears, for, as Ubrik had said, here the shafts were easily avoided. Yet as the 'Day crept forward, tempers began to fray, for the enemy hurled insults as well as spears, and the Legion did not strike back.

And as the noontide came, the faint glow of the pale disk began to show dimly—a glow that would last for but a quarter hour or less as the enfeebled darkling Sun rode past zenith in the Winternight sky.

Thumn!

Lord Gildor turned his eyes from the dimly seen disk. "Galen King, we must do something soon, for at this time on the morrow the Darkest Day will come."

Galen nodded and spoke: "Lord Gildor, it is in my mind that we must strike at the right time, a time that will upset Modru's plan. If we try too soon and fail, then our effort will have gone for nought. And if we wait too long, then no endeavor will succeed. Aye, we must strike at a time that will give us the best chance to distract the Evil One. Then, whether or no we succeed or fail to overthrow the fortress, still we may cause his plan to fall into ruin.

"Yet, you are right: We must do something soon.

I deem now is the time to gather the War-council together to discuss Flandrena's plan." Galen turned and spoke to Fieldmarshal Ubrik: "Call the council unto me. Let us begin this War."

Tuck and Merrilee came last to the War-council, joining the circle already seated, taking their places between Danner and Patrel. Tuck's eyes swept 'round the ring—a ring of Men, Elves, Warrows, and a Dwarf. High King Galen sat before all, his visage stern. To his right was Prince Igon and then Marshal Ubrik and four more grim warriors of Valon. To Galen's left came two Elves and then the four Warrows. And opposite Galen and completing the circle sat Brega his Dwarven axe, Drakkalan, held across his lap in a two-handed grip.

Galen spoke: "You have all seen the quandary of Modru Kinstealer's holt: High are the ramparts and well warded by *Spaunen*. These walls *alone* would be difficult to o'ertop even had we the siege towers to do so; yet we do not, and no forest lies nearby to yield the timber for their construction. But e'en were a woodland nigh, still we could not surmount the walls by normal dint, for a mighty chasm rings the fortress entire—a chasm that has never yet been crossed by siege engine. Over this ravine is but one road into the holt, and that way passes across a drawbridge, a span now held tight 'gainst the bulwarks.

"This, then, is our problem: How do we bring the Legion to bear upon the Yrm within? How can we cross the chasm and top the walls and throw this dark citadel down?"

Galen let his questions hang upon the still air for a moment. Then he nodded to Flandrena, and the slim Elf's soft voice broke the silence: "Galen

King, as you have said, there is no means at hand to build the mighty siege engines needed to span the gulf and top the walls. Yet even if there were the means, still we have not the time to construct them ere the Darkest Day arrives. Hence I deem we have no choice but to try this plan: While the Legion provides a diversion, a small force must go in secret to scale first the ravine and then the walls of Modru's fortress, as Vanidor, Duorn, and Varion did. And then this squad must gain the drawbridge winch and lower the bascule while raising the portcullis. And when this is done, elements of the Legion can charge across the span and into the courtyards within and engage the Horde until the Host entire arrives.

"Aye, it is a simple plan, but it is the only one I deem can succeed in the allotted time. Yet the plan is fraught with danger, for much has changed since Vanidor, Duorn, and Varion scaled the walls: Now *Rûpt* patrols walk the ravine at the base of the ramparts. Now *Spaunen* teem upon the bulwarks. And the route taken by my brethren up the chasm side no longer can be used, for now there is a station along the lip of the ravine near the crevice they climbed—a station used by the *Rûpt* as a reporting place for their chasm patrols.

"Still the crevasse can be climbed; yester 'Darkday Drimm Brega and I searched for another way up that far chasm side, and his eyes found one."

Flandrena held out his hand toward Brega, and the Dwarf stood to speak, still holding Drakkalan in a two-handed grip.

"King Galen, like all the Châkka well do I know stone." Brega's rough voice held a note of pride. "And among my Folk I am accounted a good climber. Yet this I say unto you: that ravine has been worked by Grg pick to thwart easy access up the sides, for it is mattock-smoothed for most of its length. The place where Vanidor and his comrades climbed was one of the few places where the rift wall can be scaled, and that is only because the cleft fissures most deeply, and for the Grg to have smoothed it would have undermined the battlements.

"Yet, given time, any section of the ravine could be scaled, using rocknails and jams and rings and rope. But we have not the time for a slow climb, and even if we did, the sounds of our hammers would bring the Squam running. Nay, what we must do is mount up swift and silent, and there is but one place to do so: 'round on the eastern side of the fortress, where an outjut clambers from bottom to rim.

"But the stone at that place is layered, and subject to crumbling under stress. And so the climb will be dangerous—not only because of the Grg patrols and Squam upon the battlements, but also because the stone may give way and carry the climbers to their deaths.

"This then is what I propose: I will take a small squad up that ravine side, for I have the skills to lead that climb. But those who come with me must be, first of all, good climbers and, second, light of weight, so as not to stress the stone. Lastly, they must be of a stature to pass for Úkh, Hrōk, or Khōl, for we must still climb the battlements and then march as a Grg squad along the ramparts and to the distant gate."

Amid a murmur among the War-council, Brega sat back down crosslegged and laid Drakkalan across his lap.

"Drimm Brega," Lord Gildor spoke up, "what weight can a warrior be and still not break the stone?"

"Elf Flandrena is slim enough, Elf Gildor," answered Brega, "but you are taller, heavier, and I would advise King Galen to send only those of Elf Flandrena's weight or less."

Again a murmur ran 'round the War-council, and Ubrik protested: "But Dwarf Brega that would rule out most if not all of the Vanadurin. Aye, it is true that we Harlingar have little or no experience climbing stone, for we ride the flat grassy plains and come not often into the mountains. Still, your words would rule out all Men from this mission."

"Not all Men, Marshal Ubrik." The speaker was young Prince Igon. "I deem I fall under Flandrena's weight. And I have scaled many a wall."

At Igon's words a look of distress crossed Galen's face, but he said nought.

"But that is only three." The words came from one of the Vanadurin, Raiklen by name. "Who else can undertake this mission?"

Patrel stood. "We can go."

Ubrik groaned. "King Galen, I deem we send but lads on a Man's mission."

Brega growled and leapt to his feet, his dark eyes blazing in ire. "*I* am no lad, Man Ubrik! And Flandrena holds a hundred times your years. Prince Igon is young, it is true, yet I know of his feats and I would have him with me. And as to the Waerans, I have walked through darkness with one at my side, and no finer comrade, no better warrior, could I ask for." Brega stepped to Tuck and placed a gnarled hand on the buccan's shoulder. "This Waeran helped slay the Ghath—the Gargon. Have you warriors in your company who can say the same?"

Tuck felt embarrassed to be the center of all attention, and he was surprised at Brega's fervent outburst, yet at the same time a quiet pride filled his being, for Brega's words meant much to the buccan.

Tuck stood and spoke: "I would not debate that there are better warriors in this company than I am. Yet, as I understand it, this mission calls for those who can climb and are of slight weight. Among the Warrows are some who fill this need: Danner for one, and I, for many a time we have clambered up the stone face of the High Hill near Woody Hollow. And we are skilled with bow and arrow . . . and in a pinch I have been known to use this." Tuck flashed Bane from scabbard and held it on high, and the blade-jewel streamed blue flames down the sharp edges, shouting of the nearby fortress filled with evil Spawn from the Untargarda from Neddra.

The Men of Valon gasped to see such a potent token of power in the hands of a Waldan, and they looked upon the Wee One with a new respect.

Tuck sheathed the blade. "There is this, too, Marshal Ubrik, said by one of your own riders upon the banks of the Argon. We are squatty, the likes of Rutcha . . . given the slightest disguise. Only we can hope to march upon yon ramparts—cloaks soiled, hoods up, snarling among ourselves—and stand a chance of reaching the gate unchallenged. For we will have the look of a squad of Rūcks—the Warrows and Dwarf Brega—and Prince Igon and Flandrena will be our Hlōk masters."

Tuck sat down, his words done, and none said aught for a time. Then King Galen spoke: "So be it, then. We shall try this plan. Captain Patrel, how many of the Waerlinga can ascend stone? And Marshal Ubrik, what diversion can we provide to distract the Spawn and give Brega's climb a chance? And lastly, Warrior Brega, how long will you take, and when should we strike? Tomorrow is the Darkest Day."

And so the planning went forth, and none but Tuck noted the quiet tears sliding down Merrilee's face, for she knew full well she had not the skills to make the climb, just as she knew that her buccaran did: Tuck would go without her.

In the end, along with Brega, Flandrena, and Igon, six Warrows were selected to go: Tuck, Danner, Patrel, Rollo Breed, Harven Culp, and Dink Weller. Of all that company Flandrena had the least experience climbing stone, though he *had* clambered among the crags of Arden Vale; yet his skill was deemed enough for him to join the raiders. Too, his green eyes burned with an inner flame that cried out for the revenge of his lost comrades— Vanidor, Duorn, and Varion—and none would deny him the right to go.

And when all the planning was done, King Galen gave over the Atalar Blade to Patrel, the long-knife a sword in the Warrow's hand. "Take this edge, Captain Patrel, for it cleaves Evil. This was the blade that hacked into the Krakenward to spare Lord Gildor. I deem you might need such a weapon upon those walls; it will serve you well."

Patrel took the silvery blade from its scabbard and gazed at the golden runes. "I will bear this sword in honor, King Galen," said the Warrow. And then he sheathed the weapon and girted it to his waist.

Ubrik barked an order in Valur to the Vanadurin in the War-council, and swiftly, long-knives were given over to all the Warrows, Ubrik's own blade going to Danner. And though the Wee Folk knew little of sword play, they graciously accepted the gifts, for they knew well that these edges would be needed ere their dangerous emprise came to an end.

That 'Night, Tuck held Merrilee in his arms as she wept softly, for on the morrow he would depart with the raiders on their desperate mission to open the way. They would set out six hours ere the Sun-Death—a scant six hours ere the blackest depth of the Darkest Day. And no one, perhaps not even Adon, knew their destiny.

The time drew nigh, and before the High King stood the nine climbers: Brega, Flandrena, Prince Igon, Tuck, Danner, Patrel, Rollo, Harven, and Dink. Grime had been smeared on the faces of the raiders and filth splashed upon their clothes to give them a Rūckish look.

King Galen stepped to their ranks, and one by one he embraced them each, saying a few words to most. But when he clasped Tuck unto him, and then Igon, Galen said nought, for he did not trust his voice. Lastly, he gruffly hugged Brega and gripped the Dwarf's gnarled hand, saying, "Lead them well, Warrior Brega, for on this climb depends the fate of all Mithgar."

Tuck's heart hammered to hear such words—*the fate of all Mithgar*— but Brega merely grunted and nodded.

Now King Galen stepped back from the raiders and spoke to them all: "Once again the world is faced by the forces of darkness, and once again an alliance of Men, Elves, Dwarves, and Wee Folk is called upon to cast Evil down, and, yea, once again the fortune of the world pivots on the valor of but a few.

"The Evil One squats in his dark tower like a

bloated spider and spins his vile webs of doom to the woe of the world, for he would snare the hearts of all free things and bind them in despair.

"Yet Modru is but a shadow servant of the Great Evil, and perhaps it is Gyphon's will we see at work here.

"We know not what the darkest hour of the Darkest Day will bring, yet it will be utterly evil, of that we can be certain. And we must do all that is within our power to deflect Modru's vile plan, and in doing so, perhaps we can save Mithgar from a hideous doom.

"I cannot promise you that we will be victorious; yet hearken: If we are to suffer defeat, to perish, then let us rain havoc upon our foe as we ourselves fall. And if we can cause the ruin of Modru's evil scheme, even in defeat we will have won.

"I have but one more thing to say, and it is this: May your eyes be keen, your shafts fly true, and your blades be sharp. And may Adon go with you."

Galen fell silent, and no one spoke for a moment. Tuck looked to see Merrilee weeping, and unshed tears stung his own eyes. Yet there echoed through his mind High King Galen's words: *. . . the fate of all Mithgar . . . the fortune of the world pivots on the valor of but a few . . .* And Tuck thought, *Oh, Adon, this crushing burden, I have not the strength to bear it . . .*

Yet ere Tuck's thoughts could run on, Brega cleared his throat and growled, "We'll not ope' the gate if we stand here all day. Come, let us clamber through a black ravine and up a dark wall. The fortress awaits, but the Sun and Moon do not."

And as the raiders turned to go, Merrilee flung herself forward and fiercely embraced Tuck, and attempted to smile through her tears. And she tried to speak, yet all she could utter was "Tuck, oh Tuck, my buccaran . . ." before she burst into tears.

And Tuck tenderly kissed her and said, "Don't cry, my dammia," as tears slid down his own cheeks, "for I shall return. After all, I wear your favor, a silver locket, and it has borne me through much."

Lord Gildor stepped forward and knelt beside the damman and put an arm around her as Tuck gently disengaged. Merrilee buried her face in the Elf's chest and sobbed uncontrollably as Tuck turned and ran to catch up to the others on their way to save the world.

"See, there it is," said Brega softly, pointing at the far wall of the ravine. "There's where we'll make the climb up."

The raiders lay upon the backslant of an upjut of rock and stared across the wide abyss yawning just ahead.

Along with Ubrik and a scout named Aric and the buccan Burt Arboran, the nine climbers had ridden from Galen's camp west, away from the black fortress and out into the Shadowlight until they had gotten beyond the pry of the evil gaze of the warders upon the walls. Yet it was not only eyes upon the walls that they had sought to elude: Vulg spies, too, had concerned them, and a small force of Men had ridden out before the raiders to draw Modru's curs away. Hoping that no Vulgs watched them, the raiders then had circled to the eastern side of the stronghold, the steeds of the Warrows and Brega in tow behind Ubrik, Igon, Flandrena and Aric. They had come 'round to the point facing where they would climb, then had turned and ridden straight toward the distant ramparts until once again the eyes of the Men could just make out the distant bulk of the dark bastion; and all the raiders had dismounted and taken down their weapons and the long coils of rope, and had handed Ubrik the tethers of their steeds.

Ubrik had saluted each of the nine and then had spoken an ancient Vanadurin benediction: "May the smiling countenance of Fortune's three faces be turned your way." And so saying, he had spurred back out into the Dimmendark, the string of horses running after.

Leaving the scout and Burt behind—Burt's Warrow eyes to keep track of the mission from afar—the raiders had turned and begun making their way toward the strongholt, flitting silently and one at a time from rock outcropping to brush to mound to ground crevice, using whatever cover they could find. And they slowly had made their way to the crevasse bearing the fortress walls.

And now the raiders lay upon the upjut of rock and peered through the Shadowlight at the gulf and, beyond, at the ramparts of Modru Kinstealer's holt.

"*Ssst!*" hissed Dink. "Up on the wall above: a sentry."

Tuck peered across and upward, and his head plummeted, for high upon the rampart opposite he could see the distant form of a Rūck warder slowly pacing along the parapet, the sentry passing in and out of view as he trod along the castellated walls with its merlons and crenels.

"*Rach!*" muttered Igon, "we can't make the climb under his very nose. Can we not clamber through the ravine elsewhere?"

Slowly the Rūck paced to a corner, then turned and trudged back.

"Nay," growled Brega, his voice bitter. "It is

here or not at all." A questioning look upon his face, the Dwarf turned to Flandrena.

"Your memory does not deceive you, Drimm Brega," Flandrena's soft voice answered the Dwarf's unspoken question. "The guard was not here when we surveyed the crevasse."

"Well, we're going to have to get rid of him or let him watch us climb," hissed Igon. Then the Prince turned to Patrel. "Captain Patrel, can your arrows reach him?"

Once more the Rūck turned and paced back the way he had come.

Patrel shook his head. "Mayhap if I had Grayling's fabled bow I could bring the Rūck down, but without that magic weapon, I have not the skill to make such a shot."

"Danner," said Tuck. "Only Danner might be able to do it."

"Wha—what?" hissed Danner. "Tuck, your mouth speaks what your mind knows is not true. No one can make that shot. Oh, aye, perhaps I can cast an arrow that far, but so can we all. Yet to loose it with accuracy . . . well, it cannot be done. Remember Old Barlo's words: 'The arrow as strays might well'er been throwed away.' Only in this case the straying arrow will clatter upon the wall or against a turret or into a courtyard. And *then* the maggot-folk *will* be warned of our coming."

"You have no choice, Waeran Danner," growled Brega. "We must make the climb, else all is lost. We cannot climb with the Grg there. You have the greatest skill with the bow."

Brega fell silent, his argument done, yet Danner's amber eyes followed the distant guard and still the buccan did not take up his bow.

Flandrena's soft voice spoke: "Though you would not choose to do this thing, believing it will bring ruin, circumstance dictates no other course. It is ever so in War that choice oft is taken from us. Yet think on this: if you do not try, then our mission is ended here and now; if you try, and miss, and alert the *Rūpt*, then again our mission will have failed; but if you try, and succeed . . ."

Muttering under his breath, Danner slid over the slant of the rock to the level ground below. Tuck and Patrel jumped down to join him while the others remained above, watching the guard. Danner took all of his arrows from his quiver and sighted down the shaft of each, choosing this one, discarding that one, taking up another and comparing it to the one just selected. He winnowed and culled until at last he held but three arrows, and these he carefully scrutinized—point, shaft, fletching, nock, weight, balance—and in the end he made his choice.

Now Danner stepped to the edge of the upjut, and his eyes swept o'er the nearby 'scape and up to the patrolling Rūck. "I'll try it from that outcropping over there. It will give me a slightly better angle for this impossible shot."

"Do you want someone to go with you?" asked Patrel.

"No!" Danner's voice was sharp, then softened: "Ar, Paddy, no. It'll be hard enough keeping my concentration without someone breathing down my neck. Thanks but no thanks, Paddy, this one I'll do alone."

Danner turned to go. "Good luck," whispered Harven, and so said they all, and then Danner scuttled away while the Rūck's back was to them as he paced atop the wall.

. Tuck and Patrel clambered back upon the stone and watched as Danner flitted through the Shadowlight across the snow to the nearby outcropping, where he slid into the darkness at the base of the stone. And then Danner paused long, seeming to do nought; but the Woody Hollow buccan was watching the Rūck sentry trod to and fro on his station, his form now shielded by a merlon, now exposed through a crenel, only to be shielded then exposed again as he slowly marched on. And Tuck knew that Danner was counting to himself, timing the Rūck's measured step, gauging the distance and reckoning the length of time the arrow would be in flight.

Now Danner took up his bow and set the selected arrow to string, and then the buccan stood beside the stone and drew the bolt to the full and aimed across the ravine and up toward the pacing guard.

But then Danner relaxed the pull and set the bow and shaft aside and removed his Elven-made cloak. Then he took up the weapon once more and again drew the quarrel to the full.

But again Danner relaxed his aim, for a thin chill wind had sprung up. Slight it was, yet it would deflect the arrow in flight, and the buccan had to take it into account.

Once more an eternity passed as Danner estimated the needed windage, but at last he again drew and aimed.

"Hsst!" Flandrena sharply drew a breath through clenched teeth and pointed northward along the base of the wall; and Tuck looked and saw one of the ravine patrols marching southward on the far flank of the chasm.

Danner, don't shoot! Tuck's thoughts silently cried, for he knew that if the warder atop the wall were felled, then the mission would be detected by the oncoming Rūcks.

"Patrel, Rollo, Harven, Dink," whispered Tuck

urgently, "ready your bows. We may have to slay them all . . . if we can."

"If this patrol is slain," breathed Patrel, as all the buccen nocked arrows, "then others will come looking when this bunch doesn't report in. Let us pray that Danner does not shoot."

Yet Danner, too, had seen the ravine patrol, and he once more lowered his bow and slipped deeper into the darkness of his outcropping.

And at that very same moment, upon the wall a second figure, a Hlōk, stepped into view and watched as the Rūcken squad tramped nigh. "Har, yar!" the Hlōk called from the rampart to those below, his grating voice sounding down the wall and pitching outward to echo from the crevasse "Has yer spotted anythin'?"

"Nar!" shouted up the Hlōk leader of the marching Rūcks. "Nothin's in this stupid hole in the ground!"

"Keep your gummy eyes open, then," yawped down the other. "They say somethin's astir on the far side, north of the gate." After receiving an affirmative grunt from below, the Hlōk above snarled at the sentry and spun on his heel and left the rampart, disappearing from view.

Grumbling and jostling and cursing one another, the ravine patrol marched below the sentry and to the south, passing opposite the raiders and going onward. And on the wall the Rūck warder glared over his shoulder in the direction his Hlōk master had gone, then leaned upon his hands in a crenel and watched the squad tramp away. And so, too, did the Elf, Man, Dwarf, and Warrows watch as the Rūcks marched on.

And time passed.

But at last the patrol tramped out of sight beyond

a buttress, and once more the sentry took up his pacing.

And once more Danner took up his bow . . .

And arrow . . .

And counted time . . .

And gauged the distance . . .

And estimated the windage . . .

And drew . . .

And aimed . . .

And Tuck's eyes flicked from Danner to sentry and back again.

And the Rūck paced toward the corner.

And with his heart in his throat and his inner core wound tight as a spring, Tuck's mind screamed, *Shoot, Danner, shoot! For Adon's sake, shoot!*

Thuun! Danner shot. And the arrow was in flight, arcing upward through the Dimmendark. And the sentry passed from open crenel to shielding merlon. Now the arrow hurtled through its zenith and began hissing downward, and the eyes of all the raiders were locked upon the crenel where the Rūck would next appear, but had not. Now the bolt gathered speed as it sissed down, hurling toward the vacant slot . . . and it struck the Rūck in the throat as he stepped forth into the open! With a clatter, the sentry dropped the pike he had borne and clutched at his neck and staggered forward, toppling from the corner in the wall to fall silently down the rampart face to land with a sodden thud on the edge of the ravine. And then the corpse slid over the rim and down into the blackness below.

Danner had done it! He had made the impossible shot! Behind the rock outcropping, Tuck and Patrel grabbed one another in rib-creaking hugs and clamped their jaws shut to keep from shouting for joy. Igon pounded Brega's back, and Flandrena's eyes sparkled, while Rollo and Dink and Harven held hands and danced around in soundless circles.

Then Tuck and Patrel flitted through the Shadowlight and across the snow to the outcropping where Danner stood. And there they found the buccan with his face buried in his hands.

"It couldn't be done, Tuck. It couldn't be done, Paddy." Danner's voice broke as the tears slid down his cheeks, the buccan weeping with the sudden release of unbearable tension.

"But you did it, Danner, you did it," whispered Tuck, embracing the Warrow.

Patrel took Danner's cloak up off the ground and gently draped it around the crying buccan and fastened it at the throat; and Patrel, too, embraced Danner, then softly said, "Let's go, buccoes, we've a ravine to cross, a wall to climb, and a gate to open."

And so, taking up their bows, the three buccen made their way back to the other outcropping, where they found Brega, Igon, and Rollo anchoring soft pliable Elven-made ropes to the rock—ropes brought from Arden Vale upon Flandrena's packhorse and borne hence into Gron. For ere he had set out to venture again unto the Iron Tower, the Elf had suspected that another attempt to scale the wall of the crevasse might become necessary.

Three long lines were cast over the edge of the ravine to drop all the way to the bottom. Then, because only Brega knew the art of rappelling, he showed each of them how to wrap the line under one thigh, across the body, and over a shoulder so as to slip over the edge and walk backwards down the wall of the crevasse.

And while a fourth line was used to lower weapons and extra ropes into the blackness below, the raiders began their descent, three at a time, Tuck, Igon, and Flandrena going first. With his heart pounding and one hand high and one hand low and using his legs and feet to fend, Tuck stepped backwards over the lip of the yawning darkness.

It seemed to take Tuck forever, the rope slowly slipping through his gloved hands and sawing around his body, his feet at times scrabbling upon the icy rock. And three times he lost contact with the stone and freely twisted and turned like a trapped insect on a spider's strand—or a victim on the gallows. But at last Tuck came to the bottom as Igon reached up in the darkness to brace him, while Flandrena untied the weapons and gear from the fourth line and shook it to signal Brega that all were down and safe.

The fourth line was hauled up through the ebon shadows, only to return with three more sets of weaponry as another trio of raiders rappelled down: Patrel, Dink, and Harven. And when they came to the bottom, once more Flandrena signalled Brega.

The last of the weapons were lowered and the final three raiders came down: Brega plummeting down the rope almost as if he were falling, while Danner and Rollo descended more slowly.

Armed once more and bearing Elven ropes, all followed Brega through the jagged boulders and stone rubble and scree bestrewn across the crevasse bottom; and slowly they made their way through the darkness to the opposite side to come to the layered outjut rising up to the distant rim.

Brega reached forth with a gnarled hand and grasped the stone, and it flaked and crumbled under his grip. "Bad rock," growled the Dwarf. "Worse than I thought. Yet still we must climb it. Use hands and feet to spread your weight, and move only one limb at a time while supporting yourself with the other three. And if we come to places where it is possible, lay your whole body against the stone to spread the load even more.

"We will rope ourselves together so that if one of us slips the others can support him; and let us hope that no single fall will carry all of us to our deaths.

"I will go first and test every step of the way. My instructions are to be passed back down the line as each of you in turn comes to the same place; and my words are to be followed to the letter.

"And this shall be our climbing order: I go first, followed by Elf Flandrena, then Prince Igon, Danner, Harven, Tuck, Rollo, Dink, and lastly Patrel.

"Roll your cloaks and sling your weapons across your backs and shoulders; they must be out of the way and not entangle you nor hamper your ability to climb.

"Now let us tie ourselves together and begin this journey up the rotten stone."

Soon the cloaks and weapons—bows, arrows, swords, long-knives, and axe—were secured across the climbers' shoulders, and the nine were roped together. Brega turned to the outjut and began the slow ascent, Flandrena and the others creeping up after.

When Tuck started up, sixth in line, he could feel the stone flake and crumble under his grip, and pebbles and grains of rock slithered down from those above. And the buccan felt as if at any moment the entire face of the ravine could come crashing down. He wondered how those ahead of him felt, for they were heavier than he. Then it was that Tuck realized how Brega had selected the climbing order—by weight, the heaviest first, the lightest last, for the stone grew weaker with each passing climber. Yet at the same time, Tuck knew that in any event Brega would have gone first, for only he could lead this climb.

And slowly they crept up the crumbling outjut, now all nine climbers upon the face of the ravine. And Brega cursed, for the stone was much worse than it had seemed from afar. At times the climb came to a complete standstill while the Dwarf searched for a route onward. And these were the worst moments for Tuck, for he could feel the rock slowly disintegrating under his grasp, and he strained to maintain his hand- and footholds, while at the same time striving to stress not the stone. And as the nine inched up through the rain of flakes and sand, whispered instructions from Brega were passed back down the line as each came to those same places: *Grasp the crevice to the left . . . Put no burden on the round outcrop . . . 'Ware the slab, it is loose . . . This ledge is solid and will bear all your heft . . .*

Time eroded past like the sand slithering down the face of the ravine, moments gradually edging into minutes, and minutes into hours. And still the raiders struggled on.

As he toiled upward, salty sweat ran down Tuck's forehead and stung his eyes, and his entire body was covered with perspiration. His harsh gasping breath came through jaw-clenched teeth, and his arms and legs trembled from the agonizing strain. His stomach felt as if it were tied in knots, for the stone crumbled and shifted under him, and the bottom of the ravine was lost in blackness some ninety or one hundred feet below. And his heart hammered in his breast, partly from the labor, partly from the strain, partly from the fear. All he wanted to do was simply rest; but even when he stopped there was no relief, for even then the wall eroded in his grasp. And the raiders continued the long upward struggle o'er the disintegrating rock, the lip of the crevasse now but yards above Brega's head.

Stop! The command relayed down the chain of climbers. Brega had come to an impasse: the stone just below the rim was the weakest of all. Long did the Dwarf search, carefully sidling both left and right, and the scree slithered down. Flandrena just below the Dwarf, clung to the face of the sheer, while Igon, next, stood on a narrow ledge. And those below the Prince clung to knob and crevice and slab while standing in cracks and upon outjuts.

At last Brega said, *"Kruk!* It is all of it more rotten than ever and may not bear my weight, yet here will I try it, for this place is least weak. May the spirit of First Durek guide my way."

And Brega started up the unsound stone, testing, probing, then slowly shifting his weight upon the crumbling rock. Pebbles rattled down upon those below as the Dwarf inched his way toward the top, now but a few feet above his reach.

Up he crept, and a rock gave way 'neath his right foot and crashed down. Brega threw himself flat against the wall and clung with two hands and his left foot while he sought purchase with the right. At last his boot found a crack, and he rested but a moment, then went on.

And the rim was nearly in his grasp.

Slowly his trembling fingers stretched for the lip—just inches away—and then his hand fumbled o'er the rim, and gripped it, and he began to haul upwards.

But at that moment, with a sharp *Crack!* the slab he stood upon gave completely away and hurtled downward, and the Dwarf was left dangling by the fingertips of his left hand. Yet whether or not

Brega could have held on will never be known, for the slab tumbled down and knocked Flandrena from the wall; and the Elf fell, his rope jerking the Dwarf's grip loose, and they both plunged downward amid crashing stone and falling rock.

Prince Igon was next in line, and he braced himself as rocks and Flandrena and Brega tumbled past. The line between the Elf and the Man snapped taut as Flandrena plummeted to the limit, and the shock wrenched Igon's grip loose and jerked him down upon the ledge; then Brega hit the end of his line, and Igon was dragged over the jagged edge. But the youth's grip clutched a narrow crevice, and he held on with all the strength he could muster, for he knew that if he fell then all nine would be carried to their doom.

Now Igon got his other hand in the notch, and his left foot found purchase, and then his right. Grinding his teeth, he held on, concentrating all of his strength into clinging to the ravine wall. And below him—dazed—an Elf and a Dwarf swung pendulously, while Warrows watched as their lives and the fate of their mission hung in the balance, depending upon the strength and grit of a highborn youth.

And Igon not only held on, but slowly, *against the full weight of Brega and Flandrena*, pulled himself back upon the ledge! And he struggled to a standing position and, gasping, turned and took hold of the rope and braced his back against the ravine wall!

Danner and Harven, closest to Flandrena—one above, one below—began to sidle across the face of the ravine wall toward the stunned Elf, stone crumbling and showering down. But Brega—quickly recovering and finding a fingerhold here and a toehold there, hence taking much of the strain off

Prince Igon—barked at the two Warrows, "Nay, move not on this rotten stone. Return to the path I climbed. I will aid Flandrena."

Testing each foot of the way, the Dwarf clambered up toward the dangling Elf; but ere Brega arrived, the Lian warrior came to his senses and grasped the layered stone, taking the last of the strain off the now-trembling youth above.

"Elf Flandrena," Brega's voice was low yet filled with anxiety, "how fare you? Are you injured?"

"Nay, Drimm Brega," answered the Lian, "I am not injured. Mayhap bruised, but nothing is broken."

"How fare the rest of you?" Brega asked the others.

"I feel as if I've lifted a horse," softly answered Igon, "yet I'm hale."

"Nought but pebbles rattled down on me," whispered Danner, now back upon the climbing path.

"Yar, me too," came Harven's quiet reply.

"I think my foot may be broken," gritted Tuck in pain. "One of the larger rocks smashed down on it."

"I'm alright," softly called Rollo, "and Dink and Patrel say they're fit, too."

"Tuck, you will just have to put up with it till we reach the top," hissed Brega, "then we will take a look."

Once more the Dwarf slowly inched up the ravine wall—Flandrena creeping behind—while all the other raiders held their positions on the crumbling face. After a long while, once more Brega came to the stone of the rim.

"Hmph," grunted the Dwarf, "the rock uncovered by the fall seems sturdier."

Now Brega began climbing the last critical few feet. Cautiously he went, again testing every grip, every foothold. And all eyes watched up through the falling sand and rattling pebbles; and suddenly the Dwarf was gone from sight as he crawled over the lip of the ravine and onto the rim beyond.

Now Flandrena began, and his climb went more quickly, for Brega, on firm ground above, hauled upon the line.

And as the Elf went up, Prince Igon advanced, too, and so did they all, Tuck climbing in spite of the excruciating pain in his left foot; and the Warrow could feel something *grind* each time the foot bore weight.

Now Flandrena and then Igon disappeared over the edge, and with the three—Dwarf, Elf, and Man— all pulling on the line, the Warrows swiftly went up the face of the ravine and over the top: Danner first, Patrel last.

Flandrena looked up at the raiders gathered 'round Tuck. "Indeed, it does seem broken," said the Elf. "Yet I cannot say for certain unless we remove the boot; but if we do, the foot will swell, so I deem it best to leave it shod. In any case, Tuck cannot go on. Our climb has taken overlong, for less than an hour remains until the Sun-Death— and we have much yet to do. I think ... nay, I *know*, we must leave Tuck behind."

"What?" hissed Danner. "You cannot be serious. We can't leave him behind. The ravine patrols—"

"We have no choice, Danner," interrupted Brega. "We *must* go on. Up that wall." The Dwarf pointed at the nearby rampart. "True, it will be easier to climb than the ravine, for the wall has projections, and it is sturdy. Even so, it is beyond a broken-footed Waeran's power to mount it."

"No—" Danner started to object, but again he was interrupted:

"He's right Danner," said Tuck, smiling in spite

of the fact that his heart was sinking. "They're both right. And though none has said it, for me to try to come with you would endanger the raid beyond measure. You've *got* to leave me behind. You *must* continue the mission. And none can stay with me, for all are needed to drop the bridge and raise the gate." Tuck raised his hand to forestall Danner's objections. "I know: the ravine patrols will come by, and soon. Well, help me to that jumble of rocks yon, and I will hide out as they draw nigh. But me no buts, Danner, for there is *no* other choice. Hurry now! For you all must be on your way."

And so the raiders carried Tuck to a pile of boulders next to the base of the wall. And with tears in his eyes, Danner fastened Tuck's cloak about the broken-footed buccan's shoulders. And Tuck hoarsely whispered, "Thanks, bucco . . . now go! I'll be alright."

At that moment there came to their ears the juddering howls of roving Vulgs. "*Hsst!*" breathed Flandrena sharply. "Modru's curs. We must hasten, for they may have spied us." With quick farewells to their injured comrade, the raiders swiftly returned to the corner and began to climb upward. And, blinking back tears, Tuck watched them go.

Upward the eight began to climb, the outjutting stones on the angle of the wall giving them easy purchase—for when the fortress had been constructed, Modru had not dreamed that any could gain these walls to scale. But suddenly the raiders froze, dark blots on a dark wall.

Wha—Tuck wondered why they stopped. Then he saw: a ravine patrol! Coming this way!

Pain lancing through his foot, Tuck scuttled backwards into the boulders. And the patrol came on:

snarling, jostling Spawn. Tuck's eyes followed the Rūcks' progress. *Don't look up!* he willed the maggot-folk. *Keep your eyes down!*

And the dark shapes of the eight climbers moved not.

Onward came the squabbling patrol, now even with, now striding past the rampart corner, passing below the silent raiders frozen but a few feet above.

Then the quarreling *Spaunen* were beyond the corner, and they had not glanced up. Tuck breathed a sigh of relief and slithered further back among the jumble of rock, where he no longer could see the patrol.

Yet hark! It sounded as if the Rūcks—or at least some of them—were coming toward the rocks of the Warrow's hiding place!

Desperately, his foot shooting agony up his leg, Tuck scrambled even deeper among the boulders, squirming through small crevices between the huge stones, shoving his bow and quiver ahead of him. He crawled over a rusted iron gate lying between two huge rocks and squeezed forward into a black hole but barely large enough for him to enter.

Behind he could hear the muffled sounds of maggot-folk speaking the harsh Slûk tongue. Trying not to grunt, Tuck wriggled onward in the blackness, the hole so tight that he could not raise his head.

Ten feet he went, then twenty, the stone scraping along his chest and back; and he prayed that he would not get stuck as he pressed on; and there were places where he had to exhale just to go forward, but forward he went, for he knew that if he tried to back up, his own cloak and jacket would roll up along his body and jam him tight.

And so, not really wanting to go ahead but afraid to back up, Tuck wriggled on.

Tuck did not know exactly how far forward he struggled to get through that long constricted hole—twenty, thirty, forty feet, or more—yet at last he hauled and pressed and wormed his way to its end. And when he emerged he found that he had been crawling through a channel, a drain channel, one that ran under the fortress walls, for when he emerged to painfully stand in a shallow recess along the bulwark, Tuck discovered that he was in Modru Kinstealer's holt. He had crawled under the cold stone walls of the dread fortress of the cruel Iron Tower!

The eight raiders held absolutely still upon the wall as the ravine patrol marched beneath them. Only the eyes of the climbers moved, following the track of the Rūcks below. Patrel, climbing last, did not even breathe as the maggot-folk tramped past not fifteen feet under, so close that the small buccan felt as if he could almost reach out and touch them. All that the Rūcks would have to do would be to glance up, and the raiders would be discovered. Yet the maggot-folk snarled at one another and cursed and jostled, so intent upon elbowing and shoving and squabbling that they saw not the eight Free Folk on the wall above.

Past the corner the Spawn marched and on toward the south. Yet wait! Two of the Rūcks swung wide of the squad, *and they strode toward Tuck's hiding place!*

Upon the wall the raiders watched in anguish, and Danner made as if to descend. But Prince Igon reached out and grasped the buccan's arm and whispered, *"No!"* and Danner froze once more.

Now the two Rūcks came to the rocks, and

snarled in the foul Slûk tongue as they stood and relieved themselves. And then they turned and rejoined the squad, marching on southward.

The eight raiders breathed a collective sigh of relief, for injured Tuck had not been discovered. And when the Rûcks disappeared from view beyond the distant buttress, once more the eight began to climb.

Up they mounted the soaring ramparts, their hands and feet finding ready purchase upon the outjutting rock in spite of the hoarfrost and rime. And upward they climbed.

At last Brega came to just below the crenel, where he stopped, and so did all the others—for the Dwarf would signal if the ramparts were clear, and then the eight would o'ertop the walls.

But Brega gave not the sign to proceed, for there came to the Dwarf's ear the sound of scuffling Rûck feet as one of the Foul Folk came at the change of the watch; yet the guard he came to relieve was gone, lying slain at the bottom of the ravine. And below the slot at the lip of the rampart, Brega clung with only one hand to the stone while with his free hand he unslung the axe Drakkalan, for he heard the unseen Rûck mutter and pick up the dead guard's fallen pike and then step straight toward the opening.

As Ubrik came riding back into the King's camp, leading the long string of horses used to bear the nine raiders to the eastern side of the dark fortress, he found Galen and Gildor discussing the strategy of the Legion.

"Ho, Ubrik!" called Galen, seeing the Marshal return. "Fared they well?"

Ubrik dismounted and handed the tethers over to an attendant. "Aye, King Galen, as far as we went. Yet grave danger will face them not until they come to the ravine. The Waldan, Burt, and my scout, Aric, now watch the progress of the raiders and will report to us when the nine scale the fortress wall."

Galen grunted and handed over a warm cup of tea to the Reachmarshal. "Let us then review one last time the tactics of our ruse."

Their plan was simple: the Legion would ride to the north of the gate, where the ravine was narrowest. There they would send forth a force of Men in plain view with ropes and shields and escorts of archers, and this force would make as if to scale the ravine under the cover of arrows. In this, the remaining Warrows—led by Merrilee—would join the archers from Valon.

Meantime a second force, proceeding in apparent secrecy, would move even more northerly and act as if to cross over the crevasse and mount the walls. It was expected that here too the Men would be seen, and it was hoped that the Rūcks would think that *this* was the true mission to breach the fortress, and thus would not look elsewhere for raiders.

And while these things were going forth, Lord Gildor would hold a strike force on the southern flank of the main body of the Legion. This group would mill about as if part of the whole, yet its purpose was to drive across the bridge—if and when it was felled by the raiders—and through the gate where they would hold the way until the whole of the Legion arrived.

Lastly, during the entire ruse King Galen in his scarlet armor would ride Wildwind along the fore of the Host and draw *Spaunen* eyes to him and away from Lord Gildor upon the flank.

"Argh!" growled Ubrik. "I like not this plan of

mine, for it accomplishes nought if the nine do not succeed. I think we have put too many, nay, *all* of our horses in but one byre, and if it should burn ... My meaning is this: if the raiders fail, then there is nought can be done to halt the Evil One."

"Aye, Ubrik," responded Lord Gildor, "yet what else would you have us do? Were there siege engines, scaling ladders, and assault bridges, then would we act in a different manner. But there are none of these things at hand. This plan, as plain as it is, should draw the *Rûpt* attention to us and away from the eastern wall. Our only hope is that the *Spaunen* will flock to jape at us and taunt us and sneer at our feeble attempts. Pray that their eyes turn toward us and not toward their own ramparts."

"It is the sneering of the Wrg that bothers me most, Deva Gildor," rumbled Ubrik. "I admit it. I realize that drawing Spawn in great numbers to jape at us is at the core of what we do. But I do not have to like it."

"Yet you are right, Reachmarshal Ubrik," said Galen, "if the raiders fall, then so do we all."

Galen turned to the Lian. "Where stands the 'Day, Lord Gildor?"

"In but five hours, Galen King, comes the Sun-Death," replied the Elf.

"Then it is time to begin." Galen stood and girted Steel-heart to his waist. "Like it or no, Reach-marshal Ubrik, now is the moment to draw Spawn jeers. Sound the signal to the Legion, for the hour has come."

Ubrik raised his black-oxen horn to his lips, and an imperative call split the air. It was answered over and again as company after company signalled that it stood ready.

Galen, Gildor, and Ubrik mounted their steeds

and set forth at the head of the Legion, riding
toward the Iron Tower: Ubrik on the left flank,
Gildor on the right, and King Galen in the center.
And just after Galen, rode the Wee Folk: Merrilee,
Dill, Teddy, and Arch, all upon steeds being led by
mounted warriors. Then came the widespread ranks
of the Vanadurin, steel helms glinting darkly in
the Shadowlight, spears couched in stirrup cups,
sabers sheathed in saddle scabbards, and some
warriors bearing bow and arrow. And far to the
north rode fifty Harlingar: the false assault force.

Amid the jingle of armor and the rattle of weaponry and the drum of hooves, the peals of black-
oxen horns rang forth, calling challenges to the
forces of Modru Kinstealer's holt.

Yet from the distant Shadowlight behind and to
the north of the Host there came the chill howls of
Vulg spies, calling unto the Iron Tower. A shudder
ran through Merrilee, for she guessed that Modru's
curs reported that a small band rode to the north—
the false assault force—and the damman wondered
if Vulgs had also seen the raiders. Did Modru know
that Tuck and the others were coming, too? Or
had the Vulgs been fooled, drawn off, missing the
raiders altogether? Merrilee knew not the answer
to her questions, and she could but hope that all
had gone well.

Closer loomed the dark citadel, and Spawn could
be seen rushing thither and yon atop the battlements. And an occasional arrow would be launched
from the rampart as the *Spaunen* tested the range.

Still nearer drew the Legion, until they came to
the limit of blackshafted Rücken arrows. Reachmarshal Ubrik's horn call split the air to signal
along the ranks, and the Legion ground to a halt.

In the fore-center, warriors with shields and ropes
dismounted and marched toward the dark cre-

vasse. Behind them came the bowmen, and in this company went the Warrows; and they took advantage of the great fangs of rock thrusting up through the land, using them for protection.

Closer they came to the black ravine, and closer still. Now the Men with ropes and shields came unto its edge. They tied their lines to jut and boulder and cast the loose ends over the edge and down into the blackness below.

And Rūck and Hlōk and evil Ghûl looked upon these Men in disbelief: Did these *fools* think to scale the ravine and breach the walls under the very eyes of Modru's Horde? Raucous jeering rose up from the *Spaunen* ranks.

Then a clamant blat of Rūcken horn sounded, and a sleet of blackshafted barbs hissed down upon the Men, thudding into shield and earth and flesh alike.

The arrows of the Host hissed up to the battlements in reply, the shafts for the most part to sail o'er the walls or to shatter against the carven stone, though a few bolts found foe.

A great prolonged shout rose up from the Legion, for the High King in a scarlet chain-mail corselet rode along the forefront of his Host, and Steelheart flashed in the Shadowlight as Galen exhorted the ranks.

Still the black-shafted quarrels rained down upon those at the ravine, and arrows flew back in return. But at last, at a signal from their Captain, the Men abandoned their ropes and retreated back to the Legion, the archers firing shafts up toward the walls and backing away, too.

And along the battlements the *Spaunen* jeered in revelment, their strident wrawls, their japing shrieks, wauling out after the fleeing allies.

And along the left flank, Ubrik ground his teeth in rage at the fleering of the Wrg.

Yet all was going as planned.

Brega gripped Drakkalan's black helve, the Dwarf's eyes locked upon the open crenel just above. He could hear the Ükh scuffling toward the opening. Brega grasped the stone of the wall with his left hand and thrust his feet deeper into the crevice supporting the bulk of his weight. Now he could hear the rasp of Ükh breath, the scrape of pike along stone, the slap of hand down upon the sill; and then the Grg leaned out of the opening to look below.

Chok! Drakkalan sheared through the side of the Rück's skull, sending bone and split helm whirling off below; and dark grume splashed upon merlon and wall and warrior. And the corpse slid backwards out of sight to collapse in a grotesque sprawl upon the ramparts.

Brega hoisted himself up and peered cautiously along the banquette. It was empty of guards! Signalling the ones below, the Dwarf quickly slipped over the top and onto the wardway; and the remaining climbers scrambled up after. As the others joined him, Brega raised the slain Rück overhead, and with a heave of his powerful Dwarven shoulders, he flung the corpse out and away from the wall, hurling it into the ravine below, and then cast the two pikes after.

"We must hurry," hissed Flandrena, his voice filled with urgency. "Less than a half hour remains ere the Sun-Death, and we have far to go to reach the gate, and much to do once we get there."

Hastily the raiders donned their soiled cloaks and cast their hoods over their heads. Then, falling into ranks—the Warrows and Brega to the fore,

Flandrena and Igon coming after—they began marching along the wall toward the distant gate, jostling and snarling among themselves as would the *Spaunen* do.

I'm inside! Inside the fortress! Tuck's heart hammered wildly as he peered forth from the recess along the wall. Hundreds upon hundreds of Spawn swarmed across the courtyards before him, some carrying crates or kegs, others bearing weapons and marching up ramps to the battlements above, and still others jostling and snarling as they tramped 'round corners and away or marched toward the buccan. Among the teeming Rūcks, cruel Hlōks plied whips and snarled orders; deadly Ghûls sat upon Hèlsteeds and watched o'er all.

Tuck pulled his hood as far over his head as he could, hiding his face deep in a fold of shadow.

Out of the frying pan, thought Tuck. *Now what? Back into the hole? Nay! I came to get into the fortress, and I did—by an unexpected route, to be sure, yet I am in.*

Once again Tuck peered forth from the recess. The swarming of the maggot-folk had not abated one whit. And the dead black eyes of a nearby Ghûl swept across the courtyard before him. *Alright, bucco, now that you are in, do you think you might get to the gate? The raiders will need you there, you know. Due west, the gate is due west . . . straight across the fortress from here, straight through a hold teeming with the enemy. All you have to do is pass undetected through the entire Horde. But first, you have to get past that watching Ghûl.*

Again Tuck peered out and ducked back quickly, for a snarling Rūcken company marched along the wall toward his hiding place. *Tramp, tramp!* Forward they came, and Tuck pressed deeper into the darkness of the recess and slipped his bow and quiver across his shoulders and back. *Tramp, tramp!* On marched the Rūcks, and Tuck could now hear their quarreling snarls. *Tramp, tramp!* Now the first ranks strode past the buccan, and he moved not in the darkness of the wall. *Tramp, tramp!* Hlōks grated orders, and the jostling Rūcks bore onward. *Tramp, tramp!* Rūcks streamed by, and Tuck prayed that none would peer in to see him. *Tramp, tramp!* Now the last of the ranks hove past.

This is it, bucco! Tuck thought. And when the final Rūck passed, the Warrow stepped forth from the shadows *and joined the marching Spawn.*

With each step he took, lancing agony shot up his left leg, and he could feel something *grinding* within his boot; yet he strode onward, his jaw clenched to keep from crying out in anguish, his heart hammering in fear—a lone Warrow marching at the tail end of a company of squabbling Rūcks. *Like a foolish lamb in Wolf's clothing,* Tuck's mind gasped between strides.

South they tramped, alongside the wall, and then they turned westward, following a stone-cobbled way between squat buildings and stark towers. At the rear of the company Tuck hobbled, refusing to yield to the stabbing torment of his foot, yet afraid that he would scream or collapse at each and every step.

Past the watching Ghûl they marched, his dead black eyes flicking but lightly over this jostling company as west they bore. Tuck kept his face down and hidden and held his hands beneath his cloak as he limped past the Ghûl. And the Hèlsteed snorted and grunted as the Warrow hitched by, and the buccan knew that the beast had scented him. Yet at that very moment the corpse-foe reined the 'Steed and rode away toward three companies of violently squabbling maggot-folk, the Ghûl paying no heed to the squeals and grunts of the creature that bore him.

On Tuck limped, at the rear of the tramping company of Spawn, passing across a courtyard, only to turn north. Tuck could see a way bearing west, and as the *Spaunen* swung 'round a corner, the Warrow stepped aside into a shadowed doorway as the maggot-folk marched on.

Savage pain shooting up his leg, Tuck hobbled back to the courtyard and across it, keeping to the darkened buttresses shoring up the buildings to the north side.

Into the western way he limped and found himself in a narrow twisting labyrinth of alleyways. Yet westward he strove, coming at times to dead ends where he would retrace his path and choose an alternate route. And with each step a sickening *grind* shot agonizing stabs of searing pain jolting through his frame.

Tuck hobbled along the narrow mews between the buildings and came to a great mass of stacked crates and kegs; slowly he worked his way through the wares to come at last to an exit from the twisting maze. Again he faced a courtyard teeming with Rūcks, and across the cobbles stood a great dark tower. Tuck glanced up and saw the black nimbus streaming forth from the top of the spire, wrenching at his Warrow eyes, and his heart hammered, for the buccan knew that he looked upon Modru's Iron Tower. And as he stared upward—

Ssshthack! The thongs of a scourge lashed across Tuck's shoulders and whipped under his hood to cut his lip and welt his face. The Warrow whirled, and there before him stood a snarling Hlōk. And as the buccan's hands under his cloak reached unseen for Bane ... *"Theck dral, guth!"* rasped the

Spawn, raising the cat-o'-nine-tails for another strike, and behind the Hlōk four Rūcks stepped forth from the shadows.

Thrice more the Legion sent warriors forth as if to scale the ravine, archers firing arrows at the *Spaunen* upon the walls. Each time there came a hail of black-shafted bolts raining down from the ramparts; and the great crank-bow above the gate thrummed—*Thuun!*—and hurled the ironpointed spears into the ranks of the Host. And thrice more the assault upon the crevasse was shorn off, the warriors and archers returning to the main body of the Legion while Yrm jeered and hooted in derision and blatted harsh calls upon brazen Rūcken horns. And Ubrik ground his teeth in rage.

Merrilee and the Warrows came back to stand at the fore-center of the Host and watched as King Galen and other riders of the Legion raced along the front and brandished weapons.

Thuumn! A spear arched northward from the gate to hurtle down and shatter 'gainst a stone upjut midst scurrying warriors.

And upon the walls, Spawn jittered about in revelment.

Yet Merrilee's eyes saw a large force of maggotfolk break off and race northward along the top of the rampart. And as Galen came back to the center of the Legion, a horse-borne scout thundered in from the north. "Hai, King Galen!" shouted the warrior, hauling his horse to a stop. "The Wrg have seen the Vanadurin company sent north to scale the ravine, and now the black arrows fall upon those Harlingar, too."

"Then all goes according to plan," responded Galen. Yet his eyes turned south, seeking to see Aric and Burt bearing word of Brega's raiding party, but he saw nought. "Damman Holt, see you aught of scout and Warrow bringing news of the climbers to us?"

Merrilee turned her tilted sapphirine eyes southward and searched the distant Shadowlight, then shook her head no.

"*Rach!*" Galen smashed a gauntleted fist into palm. "We know not whether the raiders have succeeded or failed—or yet strive to scale the walls. But time grows dangerously short." The King tore his gaze away from the south and called, "Mount the fifth assault! Let us hold the *Spaunen* eyes upon us!"

And as a company of Harlingar took up their shields and started toward the ropes, the archers went forward with them; Merrilee strung arrow to bow and advanced, too. Her thoughts were a chaotic whirl as she agonized o'er the fate of Tuck and Danner and Patrel, of Rollo and Dink and Harven, and of Brega and Igon and Flandrena; yet how they fared she knew not as black-shafted arrows began to hiss forth from the walls.

The raiders, their features concealed deep within their hoods, tramped southwesterly along the high banquette atop the dark ramparts of Modru Kinstealer's holt. Below them, inside the walls, they could see swarms of maggot-folk rushing thither and yon upon the cobbles and marching in squads and companies to the harsh commands and lashing whips of Hlōk overseers. And here and there the dead black eyes of Ghûls watched over all.

Yet the gaze of the raiders did not dwell upon the mill within the courtyards nor on the teeming ways below; instead they stared across the hold past the great central tower—the tower that wrenched at Warrow eyes—and to the distant gate in the

west wall. And their hearts plunged, for a great
swarm of maggot-folk clustered atop the ramparts
near the portal.

"They are gathered to repel the Legion," growled
Brega.

"Look, to the north, another swarm," whispered
Dink.

"The false raiders," said Flandrena softly as they
now tramped westerly. "All goes according to plan:
the Legion acts as if to cross near the gate, and
'round to the north the lone company of the
Harlingar draws *Spaunen* eyes away from us."

"But there are too many Rūcks atop the gate
itself," hissed Danner.

"Perhaps—" began Brega, but he broke off what
he was about to say and began jostling and elbowing and snarling, as did they all while Flandrena
lashed at them with a piece of Elven rope, cut to
resemble a whip. And growling and cursing they
marched past a Rūcken sentry, who gave them not
a glance, fearing that if he took his yellow eyes
from the ravine below, the whip would lash him,
too.

Onward marched the raiders, tramping from angle to angle as they swung along the walls in a
great zagging arc, bearing ever toward their goal.
And they were not challenged as they passed warders and marching Rūcks alike along the high stone
way. Now the eight of them marched upon the
western wall, and they could see the Legion out on
the moor beyond the crevasse, King Galen's scarlet armor drawing their eyes as he rode up and
down the fore of the Host. There, too, they saw
Gildor's strike force milling on the southern flank
of the Legion, ready to charge across the bridge if
and when it fell. Lastly they saw a small force of
warriors dashing toward ropes hanging down into

the ravine; some of the Men had already reached the crevasse, and black-shafted arrows rained down upon them while the quarrels of archers flew back in return.

But then the raiders saw no more, for now they were come upon the very rampart holding the gate itself, and they marched the last leg toward their goal. Before them they could see the huge Hlōk-driven crank-bow—*Thuun!*—and hear the clatter of gears as it was rewound and armed with another steel-tipped spear. And amid the raucous jeers of the maggot-folk, the raiders strode toward their prizes: the great winch of the iron drawbridge, and the hoist of the barred portcullis.

Thung! Clk-clk-clack-clk-clk-clk! The rattle of the ratchet on the great crank-bow clattered forth, and the Hlōks laid another spear in the groove. The captain of the gate guard turned to see a hooded squad step toward the drawbridge winch.

"Shugg du!" snarled the Hlōk, moving to block them, and the squad came to a halt. *"Shugg du!"* he barked again, only to be met by silence. *"Arg tha! Shugg du!"* The Hlōk stepped forward, rage upon his features, reaching for the cat-o'-nine-tails at his belt while at the same time shoving back the hood of the figure directly before him. *And the Hlōk's eyes flew wide, for he stared upon the forked-bearded features of one of the hated Dubh!* It was the last thing that the Hlōk ever saw, for Drakkalan clove the Squam's head from his body, and battle exploded upon the wall above the gate.

At sight of the four Rūcks behind the Hlōk, Tuck's mind raced, for he knew that he could not wield a sword well enough to slay them all before one would sound the alarm.

"Theck dral, guth!" snarled the Hlōk again, gesturing toward a group of kegs. Now Tuck saw that

the Rūcks were bearing off toward the Iron Tower, and they had casks hoisted upon their shoulders.

He thinks I am a Rūck! Quickly Tuck limped forward, stooped and lifted a keglet to his own shoulder, and hobbled after the maggot-folk striding toward the spire, leaving the Hlōk behind overseeing other Rūcks coming to carry cargo.

Again excruciating pain jolted up his leg, and Tuck nearly fainted from the agony; yet onward he strove, sucking and spitting blood from his whipcut lip, limping across the courtyard. And he saw that the Rūcks before him bore their burdens toward what appeared to be a feeding station. There two Hlōks oversaw the unloading of the casks, Rūcks breaking the containers open to dispense the food inside. In the background stood one of the dead white corpse-folk, the Ghûl's 'Steed at his side.

If that Hèlsteed catches my scent ... As Tuck desperately looked for a means of escape, directly before the buccan a Rūck stepped forth through a door in the tower, coming down the three steps and past the Warrow and scuttling off across the courtyard.

The door! thought Tuck. *The Rūck left it open!* Without pause the buccan struggled up the treads and through the portal. As he pushed the panel to, a distant clash and clangor of weaponry fell upon his ears. But whence came these faint echoes of battle—from what direction—he could not say, for at that moment with a hollow *boom!* the door of the Iron Tower shut behind him and closed all sound away.

Tuck set the cask down and rested a moment, his eyes searching the gloom. Before him stretched a long hallway with guttering torches casting writhing shadows along its length, closed doorways to left and right. There too, yawning darkly, stood stone arches marking where cross halls bore away. To Tuck's left a staircase mounted upward, and to his right a stairwell led down to a closed door.

Suddenly enraged shrieks rang throughout the tower, and there came the slap of footsteps running toward him; and Tuck scrambled up the stairs to his left, pain crashing through his entire being as he hobbled upward. He came to a landing, and still the raging cries resounded. Rūcks and Hlōks raced down the hall toward him. Once more Tuck hitched up another flight of stairs, and maggot-folk ran past him down the steps, paying little heed to the hooded figure going upward.

As Tuck came to the next landing, the piercing shrieks fell silent. But more Spawn came toward the Warrow, and Tuck knew that if but one of them stopped him, he would be revealed. The buccan turned to the nearest door and shot back the brass bolt and stepped inside, slamming it shut behind.

Pausing but a moment to catch his breath, Tuck surveyed the room: a canopied bed, a fire, a doorway through which he could see the corner of a bathing tub, and heavy drapes covering what had to be a window. From the outside the buccan could hear skirl of battle muffled by the curtain, and, too, there came the sound of a great *Blang!*

The raiders! Have they reached the gate? Still breathing heavily, Tuck limped toward the window and reached to pull the drapery aside.

And as the cloth swung away from the wall, a figure dressed in quilted Rukken garb lunged forward out of the blackness and swung a heavy iron bar down at the buccan, the thick rod glancing painfully down Tuck's arm and back as the Warrow twisted and sprang aside, rolling on the stone floor, arrows spilling from his quiver, the bow across his back clacking against the flag, his cloak twisting around his body as he struggled to draw Bane.

And the hood fell back from his head, and he looked up with his tilted jewel-hued eyes to see the flaxen-haired female leap forward, bar raised for the killing blow.

"Princess!" he shouted.

Clang! Laurelin dropped the bar and threw herself to her knees beside the fallen Warrow. *"Sir Tuck!"* she cried, clasping him to her as he sat up. "Oh, Sir Tuck." Laurelin wept uncontrollably and rocked back and forth and fiercely held on to the buccan, and Tuck put his arms around her and stroked her hair and soothed her and wondered at the workings of Chance that had led his footsteps here.

Through the window came the trumpeting sound of a bugle, and Tuck knew that the silver call came from no other clarion than the Horn of the Reach borne by Patrel. "Come now, Princess," said Tuck, "we must get gone from here."

"Tuck, the Ghûls!" cried Laurelin, rocking back on her heels, then scrambling up. "We *must* get out of here and to my Lord Galen. I must warn him: a great force of Ghûls rides o'er the Wastes of Gron, coming to fall upon the Legion from behind."

"Ghûls? Coming across Claw Moor?" At Laurelin's nod, Tuck's face blenched. "You're right, my Lady, we've got to warn the Legion!"

Thuun! The thrum of the great crank-bow sounded through the window as Tuck painfully got up from the floor: broken-footed, lip whip-split, face wealed, and arm and back bruised by an iron bar. Quickly he inspected his bow—none the worse for having been rolled upon—and then he began gathering the arrows strewn on the stone and putting them in his quiver.

"And Tuck!" added the Princess. "Modru plans something horrible this 'Day. What it is, I know not, yet it is evil and concerns Gyphon . . . Gyphon's return!"

"Aye, Pricess, we suspect as much. Our hope is to disrupt Modru's vile scheme." Tuck snatched up the last arrow and glanced at Laurelin. "Your hair, Princess," Tuck's voice snapped with authority, "hide it under your cloak and hood. We've got to pass through a Horde."

Quickly, Laurelin unfastened her cloak and shook her hair down her back, then donned the cloak over it, pulling the hood up to hide her face. "We can leave by the window," she said. "Down a rope."

"The door is unbolted," responded Tuck, "and we are less likely to get caught walking down steps than climbing down ropes."

Laurelin scooped up her bar and stepped toward the door. "Let us be gone then, Sir Tuck, for I sense the Ghûls come even now."

The sounds of the black-oxen horns of Valon drifted in through the window as Tuck cast his own hood over his head and took his bow in hand and limped to Laurelin's side.

Taking a deep breath, he grasped the latch and looked up at the Princess, and at her nod he opened the door.

And there before them stood a figure dressed in black, with raging eyes glaring through a hideous iron mask.

Ere the Warrow could move, *"Ssstha!"* hissed Modru, and he struck down with a whelming blow of metal gauntlet, the heel of his hand smashing into the Warrow's forehead, the clawlike fingers ripping down the buccan's face and neck and tearing through cloak and jacket to the silveron armor concealed below, one finger striking the catch of the silver locket and springing it open as the hideous hand ripped past. Tuck reeled back, stunned, and fell to the stone, his helm striking hard, his bow lost to his grip.

Laurelin lashed the bar at Modru with all of her strength, yet the Evil One threw up a hand and— *Chang!*—caught the thick rod and wrenched it from her grasp. Then, like a striking viper, his free hand whipped forward and clutched her wrist, and he jerked her toward him.

"So, you sought escape. *Fa!* Did you think the *runt* would save you from your fate?" Modru dragged the Princess toward the form of the fallen Warrow, who lay stunned on his back, face clawed and bleeding, cloak and jacket rent apart, and the silver locket bearing Merrilee's portrait lying open and glittering upon the buccan's armored chest.

Modru raised the bar. "We shall see which is stronger—this iron rod or your *rescuer's* head!"

As Laurelin wrenched and struggled in Modru's iron grip and screamed *"No, no, no!"* over and over again, the Evil One leaned forward above the Warrow to smash the bar down upon the buccan's skull.

And the pure silver mirrored side of the open locket caught a small part of Modru's true reflection and cast it back to the eyes of the Evil One.

With a shrill scream Modru flung the rod *blanging* away, and threw his arm up over his face and reeled hindward, unable to bear what he had seen in the argent speculum of the locket—a locket crafted ages agone in the mystic land of Xian, where it is said that Wizards once dwelled.

Yet even though the polished flat surface had struck Modru a telling blow, the Evil One was not destroyed, for the locket was diminutive and could cast back but a tiny portion of his full image. Hence, as air sissed in through Modru's gritted teeth, he recovered from the heavy brunt. He clenched the gauntleted, taloned fingers of his free hand, curling them into a black iron fist.

Once more he wrenched Laurelin along after him as he stepped toward the felled Warrow, preparing to smash the life from the Wee One. Yet Modru had reckoned not upon the potency of the argent device warding the buccan; for at that very moment Tuck groaned and feebly moved, and the glittering silver of the locket shifted upon his chest, and the sparkling plane of the mirror seemed to turn toward the Evil One, as if seeking him out.

"Sssstha!" Again Modru reeled back, jerking his head aside, away from the token of power lying open upon the breast of the now-stirring Warrow, the Evil One unable to face even this small part of his own true image, unable to come at the helpless buccan.

"Ssss." Air raggedly hissed in and out of Modru's lungs as he paused and gathered strength, and he did not look toward the Warrow, did not look toward the silver bane. And though Laurelin twisted and jerked, she could not pull free, for the Evil One's dinted grip held her fast even as his power swiftly returned unto him.

"Pah!" Modru spat at last, whirling away. "Whether it is now or in but a span, it matters not, for the runt will die . . . yess, die when I fetch my Master, and that moment is at hand. Come, Princess, to the tower above. It is time to meet your fate."

And hauling Laurelin stumbling behind, caught in his grip of iron, Modru stalked from the room, jerking her toward the steps spiralling up to the chamber at the top of the tower, where lay the yawning ebon of the Myrkenstone.

Once again the Legion had been driven back from the ravine, and the Spawn hooted and jeered. And now even King Galen ground his teeth and cursed in frustration at their japing; he had known that the Yrm would fleer at the Host's feeble attempts, for that, too, was part of the plan, yet still their gibes grated upon him.

"Hoy!" cried Teddy Proudhand, one of the Warrows. "Here comes Burt and that Harlingar scout."

Galen upon Wildwind turned his eyes to the south, and hammering forth through the Shadowlight came two steeds bearing riders: Man and Warrow, Aric leading Burt. Along the forefront of the Legion they rode, thundering at last to a halt before the crimson-armored King.

While his steed pranced and curvetted, Aric struck a clenched fist to his heart. "Sire, the raiders are upon the wall at last." Aric gestured to Burt, the buccan having leapt to the ground as Merrilee and the other Warrows gathered 'round.

Burt looked up at Galen. " 'At's right, your Lordship, sir. Long we waited, till I thought as somethin' had gone wrong for certain. But then I saw 'em, climbing up the wall at last, though I counted only eight where there should have been nine . . . One of 'em was missin', and where he's got to, or what's happened, well, it's a mystery right enough. I watched till they topped the wall, then me and Aric hightailed it for here."

Merrilee's heart had plummeted upon hearing that one of the raiders was missing, and a deep foreboding washed over her being, but she did not dwell upon it, for Galen barked, "When did they top the wall? How long ago?"

"Mayhap a quarter hour past, King Galen," replied Aric, "for we rode swiftly and straight away."

Galen wheeled Wildwind. "Vanadurin!" he cried. "Now the moment draws at hand. Pass the word to stand ready, and let us pray that the raiders succeed. But now we must make one last sortie to draw all *Spaunen* eyes to us and away from their own walls." Galen flashed Steel-heart into the air. *"Hál Vanadurin! Hál Harlingar!"*

A great yell rose up from the ranks of the mounted warriors, and Wildwind thundered up and down the fore—from the south flank to the north—rearing and pawing at the air as the High King came to each end. This was the signal to both Gildor and Ubrik to prepare, for it meant the raiders were upon the walls.

Once more a company of Vanadurin took up shields and ran toward the ravine, and with them went the Warrows and other archers. And a great jeering came forth from the Spawn upon the walls, for again these Men, these *fools*, sought to cross the crevasse in spite of the fact that they had failed six times before. And black-shafted arrows hissed downward.

Merrilee's eyes glanced up through the hail of barbed death, and southward—atop the wall above the gate—she thought that she glimpsed combat, struggle; but then she turned her sight once more upon the rampart before her, for her aim was needed here.

When Drakkalan sheared the Hlōk's head from his body, the raiders exploded into frenzied action: knife, sword, and axe, cleaving, stabbing, and hacking. The Hlōks manning the great crank-bow were caught completely unawares, and they fell in their own black gore, with throats cut, breasts split, skulls cloven, bodies gutted.

Nearby Hlōks and Rūcks turned at the sounds of the slaughter as Flandrena and Igon sprang to the great winch to lower the bascule. The two seized the spokes of the winch wheel as cries of alarm burst forth from the Spawn.

The Man and the Elf threw their weight against the radial arms, and maggot-folk charged toward them as Warrows loosed bolts to fell Rūcks and Hlōks in the fore of the oncoming enemy.

And the wheel moved not.

"It's jammed!" cried Igon, straining against the handle, and Dink leapt forward to aid—but still it did not move.

"Release the ratchet!" cried Flandrena but ere any of the three could make a move to do so, Rūcks and Hlōks sprang into the gate cap, and the Prince and Lian warrior took up their swords and began hewing while Dink loosed arrow after arrow.

Now the fighting was too close for bow and arrow, and Danner and Patrel found themselves side by side with long-knife swords in hand, and there came the skirl of steel upon steel as they engaged *Spaunen* scimitars.

Chang! Shang! The Rūck facing Danner fell slain, and the buccan turned to see Patrel in a hand-to-hand struggle with a large Hlōken foe, the tiny Warrow straining to hold the enemy's dirk away from his throat.

Chonk! Danner's blade bit into the Hlōk's neck, and foul dark blood splashed into Patrel's face as the Spawn arched over backwards, dead ere striking the stone. But before either buccan could catch his breath, *Clang! Drang!* once more their swords engaged those of the Rūcks.

Driven by the strength of youth, Igon's sword cut a gory swath, black blood flying wide as the edge clove into the onrushing foe. And Flandrena moved like a wraith—sidestepping, whirling, dodging, swerving—and the Elf's blade licked out time and again, Rūcks and Hlōks falling dead. And Brega bashed scimitar and tulwar aside, Drakkalan chopping through steel, sinew, and bone alike.

Yet still the Spawn came on.

Rollo again managed to use his bow, and he felled a Rūck pressing Danner while Patrel slew another, and they glanced up to see great numbers of the foe rushing toward them, now aware that something was amiss atop the gate. Horns blatting, voices yelling, the enemy mounted a charge; and Harven fell, slain by steel pike.

Danner's eyes rolled white, and spittle foamed on the corners of his lips, and then an amber glare stared out from his distorted face, and dark gutturals snarled forth from his writhing mouth. He ripped off his cloak and jacket and flung his long-knife aside and scooped up one of the long iron bars from the grip of a dead Hlōk.

"Danner!" cried Patrel, but to no avail, for the tall buccan had leapt to the fore and stood in the mouth of the wardway leading into the gate area. And Danner swung the bar with an unmatched fury, for now he was a berserker.

And in the narrow wardway the foe was hurlea back!

Brega sprang to the winch and swung Drakkalan overhead and down with all the strength of his massive shoulders. *Chang!* With a great shower of sparks the black-runed axe *bit completely through the haul chain.* And slowly at first, but with ever-gathering speed, axles squealing in protest, the great iron drawbridge slammed down:

BLANG!

And now Igon and Flandrena leapt to the portcullis hoist and began cranking the barway upward as Brega sprang to Danner's side, for the foe charged once more. Again the Spawn were hurled back.

But suddenly the portcullis stopped moving upward, and strain as they might, Igon and Flandrena could budge it not.

Patrel ran and peered downward.

Below, the great Troll warding the gate clutched the barway, stopping it dead in its track. And the wee Warrow knew that the Man and the Elf could not move the hoist with this monster holding it back. Patrel could see more maggot-folk racing across the courtyards in the direction of the gate.

Swiftly the tiny buccan leapt down the steps toward the gateway below. And when he came to the cobbles, he ran to the Troll and hewed the Atalar Blade into the creature's scaled shank. *Ching!* The golden-runed silver blade glanced downward and did not cut through the Ogru's stonelike hide. Yet the Warrow *had* caught the creature's eye, for with a snarl it swiped a great thick hand at the Wee One, just missing as Patrel sprang backwards.

Ching! Again the blade chopped at the Ogru's calf, and again the scaled hide turned the edge aside. Once more the Troll's evil red eyes glared at the buccan, and its huge hand clutched and missed.

Now Patrel danced out before the Troll, the Warrow slipping under the partially raised barway and shouting at the creature, "Hai! You big stupid oaf! You can't catch me, for I am the golden warrior!" And Patrel threw open his jacket, and the gilded armor shone forth gleaming.

With a snarl, the Ogru-Troll hurled up the portcullis and reached his great clawlike hands for the buccan. And Patrel ran out upon the iron drawbridge, the monster in pursuit—a huge iron club clutched in one thick hand, his great stride over-hauling the Wee One's flying legs.

And up on the wall, Igon and Flandrena spun the hoist to the full and locked it in place, for Patrel's quick wits had loosed the barway from the grip of the Troll, and the portcullis was up and pinned.

Man and Elf turned to the battle, just in time to see Brega felled by Hlōk War-bar and Spawn leap forward to slay the Dwarf. But ere any maggot-folk could reach Brega's side, a black-armored buccan stood above the fallen Dwarf and lashed out with a great iron bar. As the mighty cudgel crunched Rūcken bones, the Warrow warrior cried, *"King of the Rillrock! King of the Rillrock! Danner Bramble-thorn is the King of the Rillroc—"*

A black-shafted arrow hissed through the air to smash through the black chain mail and pierce Danner's side, and a spear burst into his shoulder, hurling the buccan backwards to crash unto the stone. Igon and Flandrena sprang forward, their swords lashing into the oncoming *Rūpt*. And Brega struggled to his feet, his forehead red with gore but Drakkalan in his hand. And Rollo and Dink loosed bolt after bolt, felling Spawn left and right.

Danner lay in a widening pool of blood, and the glazed berserker look faded from his eyes. He tried to struggle upward, but could not, and his cheek lay against the icy stone next to a machicolation. He gazed out through the hole and down upon the iron drawbridge, now spanning the black crevasse. And he saw Patrel out upon the iron, taunting a great Ogru that slowly stalked toward the wee Warrow.

As Patrel darted out through the gate, the Troll coming behind, the buccan's eyes saw Gildor's force flying along the ravine toward the downed bridge.

If the Ogru sees them, he may turn back and slam the portcullis to, thought the wee Warrow. *I've got to keep him from catching sight of the riders.* In the middle of the span Patrel stopped and turned, spreading his arms wide and shouting, "Alright now, you overgrown lummox! See if you can catch me!"

Sensing a trap, the Troll came to a halt. Now he stalked slowly forward, the iron bridge shuddering under his massive tread, his dull wit searching for a snare, his red eyes locked upon this tiny warrior taunting him.

"Hai, jobbernowl!" cried Patrel, darting from side to side. "What's wrong? Am I too big for you?" And the Wee One took the Horn of the Reach—the Horn of Valon—from beneath his jacket, where he had borne it all along, and raised the rune-marked bugle to his lips and blew a lifting call into the air. The silver notes rang and echoed from the crevasse and through the gate and over the walls, and everywhere that Free Folk heard it, hearts were lifted and spirits surged; but everywhere that the notes reached the ears of the maggot-folk, the Spawn quailed back in fright.

The Troll, too, snarled in fear and stared at this small pest on the edge of the bridge. Then the huge Ogru roared and raised the great iron club and strode forward. And Patrel knew that he would not survive the blow.

Thuun! The huge crank-bow atop the gate hurled a steel-pointed shaft with all the might of that great ballista, and the spear flew through the air to crash into the Troll's back and smash through his heart and burst forth from his chest; and black blood flew wide, and where it fell a reeking smoke curled upward from the iron. A look of surprise came over the Ogru's features as he was whelmed to his knees; and—*Clang!*—his club crashed to the bridge, lost to his fingers. The Troll staggered to his feet and clutched at his back, trying to reach the shaft; and, one knee buckling, he stumbled sideways and fell silently into the black depths of the crevasse below.

Stunned, Patrel looked up toward the wall atop the gate, but he could not see who had loosed the great bolt that had slain the Ogru. But a dire feeling of dread washed over him, and he began to run back toward the open portcullis.

And the black-oxen horns of Valon sounded as Gildor's strike force hurtled across the iron bridge and past the running buccan and through the gate of Modru's fortress.

Atop the wall, Man, Warrow, Dwarf, and Elf battled against the Spawn. And a black-armored buccan released his grip from the stock of the great crank-bow and slid down to sit with his back to the pedestal. There was a faint smile upon his face as the blood leaked from his body, for he heard the horns of Valon sounding. And slowly the golden light dimmed in his eyes and then was gone: Danner Bramblethorn had loosed his last arrow.

When Galen King's signal came that the raiders were upon the ramparts, Lord Gildor swept his gaze along the wall above the gate. The Lian warrior's eyes searched for sign of Brega's band, yet he was too far away to tell whether there were any members of that small party among the multitudes that swarmed there. Yet wait! Did his Elven eyes see sign of struggle upon the rampart? Perhaps. He was not certain. Yet he called a warrior unto him. "Stand ready with your horn, Captain Brate, for if we are to succeed or fail, the next few moments will tell."

The next few moments ... Gildor's green eyes leapt to the sky where the faint glow of the Sun could just now be discerned as it swung toward the zenith. And most of the feeble disk was even now occluded, for the time drew nigh. There remained less than a quarter hour till the Sun-Death would come full. Gildor stood in his stirrups and then sat back down, and his knuckles were white, so tightly did he clench the reins, for still nothing seemed to be happening atop the gate.

Then, with a slow majesty that belied its hurtling rush, the iron drawbridge separated from the wall and toppled out and down across the chasm to fall to with a dinning *Blang!*

"*Now!*" cried Lord Gildor. "*Ride! For Adon's sake, ride!*"

Brate raised his black-oxen horn to his lips and blew a sundering blast that echoed across the moor. And, as one great body, Gildor's strike force wheeled and raced for the bridge, flashing hooves now flying along the edge of the chasm.

And behind, King Galen turned his warriors, too, and they hurtled after, with Reachmarshal Ubrik's brigade following.

Lastly, the company at the ropes broke off their ruse and ran for their horses, and with them came the archers—Merrilee and the buccen among the latter.

And as the ravine company fell in with the riders of Ubrik's force, now thundering past, Dill Thorven cried, "Merrilee, look! Out upon Claw Moor! A great array comes!"

Merrilee looked to where the buccan pointed, and there, hammering across the wastes, came thousands of riders, but whether they were friend or foe, she could not say. "Hoy, Degan!" she called to the rider who led her steed. "Find King Galen!

Or Reachmarshal Ubrik! A great force rides toward us across Claw Moor!"

Degan spurred forward, leading Merrilee's mount behind, racing to find King or Marshal.

In the fore Lord Gildor's steed ran full tilt for the bridge. The Elf's eyes saw a small figure run forth upon the span, followed by a Troll. *Run, Waerling, run!* cried Gildor's mind, and yet the small mite turned to face his hulking adversary. Gildor urged his steed to even greater speed, but he knew he would not arrive in time to aid the tiny buccan.

Thuun! The sound of the great crank-bow came to the Elf's ears, and his eyes widened as he saw the mighty bolt flash down from the wall and strike the Troll in the back. And as the monstrous creature fell into the ravine, Gildor plunged onto the iron bridge, the Harlingar thundering after, the span booming and ringing as the strike force hurtled across, the black-oxen horns of Valon blowing wildly.

Past Patrel they ran headlong and through the open gate, hooves striking upon hard cobblestones within the fortress walls. Black-shafted arrows rained upon them from the ramparts, but the Vanadurin thundered inward like an iron wave, their lances piercing Rūcks and Hlōks in the courtyard before them. Gildor wheeled and gave a cry. Harlingar flocked to him, and they spurred toward a ramp leading up to the banquette above.

Outside, the Vanadurin pressed toward the bridge, a bottleneck to their invasion of Modru Kinstealer's holt. Here Degan searched among the milling press for Reachmarshal Ubrik or High King Galen, yet he found neither. But there was no need, for Ubrik's eyes had seen the oncoming force thundering out of the Shadowlight upon Claw Moor, and they were near enough to identify: Ghûls upon Hèlsteeds. Modru's Reavers had come to fall upon Galen's Host.

Black-oxen horns rang, and Ubrik's brigade wheeled to meet this new threat. Again the horns sounded, and lances were lowered and sabers raised. And at a third signal, first at a walk, then at a trot, Ubrik's Vanadurin set forth in a spreading line. Their pace quickened—now a canter, now a gallop— and at a fourth and last horn call it became a headlong run. The two forces raced pell-mell toward one another, leering Ghûls astride squealing Hèlsteeds, grim-faced Harlingar upon the fiery belling steeds of Valon.

Across the iron drawbridge the remaining Vanadurin pressed, yet they could not come into the Kinstealer's holt, for within the gateway and athwart the entry now stood a second Troll—the one that had guarded the Hèlsteed stables. The monster wielded a great iron War-bar and roared in pleasure as he smashed aside warrior and steed alike. Though he was dressed in nought but black leather breeks, still the swords and arrows of Men harmed him not, but glanced aside notched or shivered asunder against his scaled hide. And the black-shafted arrows of the *Rûpt* rained down, striking shield and horse and Man alike; and warriors and steeds fell screaming into the abyss below.

Lord Gildor, leading the Vanadurin already inside, fought his way through Rūcks and Hlōks and Ghûls toward the ramps leading up to the walls above the gate, for it was the mission of the strike force to secure the drawbridge winch and the portcullis hoist and to rescue the raiders, if any yet lived.

At last the horses burst through the *Spaunen* and came to the stone incline, and Lord Gildor leapt from his steed and raced up the pitch, Men charging upward in his wake. Rūcks ran down at them, but Red Bale clove through their ranks, as did the steel of Valon. And Spawn fell slain or tumbled to their deaths below. But still the weapons of the foe took their toll, as cudgel and iron pole, scimitar and tulwar, and hammer and pike slew the warriors of the Legion.

Yet Gildor's strike force won to the banquette and fought their way to the gate cap, where they found Brega and Igon and Flandrena and Dink in furious battle, still holding the gate area atop the wall.

And when the Vanadurin charged into the fray, *Rûpt* fell back. Igon flicked a brief smile at Lord Gildor, and Flandrena and Brega each gave a nod, while Dink took up his bow and loosed arrows upon the Spawn. And then the maggot-folk struck once more.

Up the steps from the gateway below came a wee buccan: Patrel. And his sword—the Atalar Blade—was asplash with black gore. He came onward, through the clash of steel upon steel and the shouts and screams of battle twisting and dodging, trying to win through the press and come unto Gildor.

"Lord Gildor! Lord Gildor! To me! To me!" cried Patrel. And Red Bale hewed through a Hlōk, felling the Spawn, and in two strides the Lian was at the Warrow's side.

"Quickly, Patrel, speak," barked Gildor, his eyes upon the swirling battle.

"An Ogru blocks the way and thwarts the Legion below," panted Patrel, but he said no more, for at that moment the combat came upon them, and buccan and Elf fought for their lives.

Yet toward the steps Gildor battled, and at last

he won free of the mêlée. Down the stairs the Lian warrior bounded, and now he could see the Troll at the gate. Scarlet fire blazed forth from the blade-jewel of Red Bale and leapt down its edge.

Chnk! Krch! The great Troll War-bar smashed into the fore of the Host, and horse and Man alike were slain. The mighty Ogru roared his laughter as steeds were reined back and the faces of Men blenched before this twelve-foot-high monster. And still the deadly arrows hissed down from the wall and into the milling warriors trapped upon the span.

Toward the hulking creature raced Lord Gildor, the lithe Elf running to come between the drooling Troll and the Ogru's victims. And as the Lian warrior finally came before the monster, so too did Galen King at last win his way through the press upon the bridge to push unto the fore of the Host. Galen raised Steel-heart and prepared to spur Wildwind forward, but Lord Gildor cried, "Nay, Galen King! This Troll is mine! For now I see his image through Vanidor's eyes!"

The Ogru blinked down at this *Dolh* before him, and a gaping leer spread o'er the monster's features, spittle dripping from yellowed tusks. Then he struck.

Clang! The great War-bar smashed upon the cobbles, but Lord Gildor darted aside, narrowly evading the blow.

Woosh! The bar slashed sideways through the air, driven by the massive thews of the twelve-foot-high creature. But the Elf fell flat, the iron pole lashing above him.

Chang! Once more the iron smashed to the stone, again barely missing as Gildor rolled away and sprang up and inward; and Bale flicked out to catch the twisting creature upon the thigh. Scarlet fire blazed out from the ruby blade-jewel as a great gash opened across the monster's leg and black blood gushed forth to fall smoking upon the cobblestone way.

The Ogru yawled in pain and fell back beyond Gildor's reach. And the moment the Troll gave way, Vanadurin surged forward, some to slip their steeds past the creature and into the fortress. Yet the monster moved once more to block the gate, lashing forth with the War-bar to smash aside warrior and mount. Yet again Red Bale flared up as it drank Troll blood, cleaving across the creature's fending wrist.

With a great bellow of rage, the Ogru struck at Gildor. *Krang!* The iron bar whelmed down upon empty stone, for the Elf was not there; he had leapt forward, under the blow. And impelled by all the force the Lian warrior could muster, Bale cut a great open swath across the Troll's abdomen. The Ogru roared in agony and stumbled to its knees as steaming entrails spilled forth amid a whelming gush of black blood. Gildor's sword lashed out, the blade-jewel blazing scarlet as Bale sliced through the Troll's throat, the Elf leaping aside as the huge Troll smashed facedown unto the cobbles, dead before striking the stone. And green fire blazed behind Gildor's eyes: Vanidor's killer had been slain.

King Galen spurred forward, Wildwind leaping over the great corpse. And with a glad shout, inward poured the Legion after.

And out upon Claw Moor, with a great juddering din of iron, Ubrik's brigade hurtled into the charging Swarm of Guula, lance thrusting against barbed spear, saber clashing against tulwar, horse lunging against Hèlsteed. And Men died, and corpse-foe fell slain, as the forces shocked through each

other, driving beyond one another's ranks. Ubrik
sounded his black-oxen horn, and the Vanadurin
wheeled to meet the turning Guula. And Ubrik
gave the call to mount a second charge, though he
knew that in the end the battle could have but one
outcome, for his fifteen hundred Harlingar rode
against six thousand reavers. Yet the Reachmarshal also knew that King Galen and the Legion
now pouring through the distant gate and into the
Kinstealer's holt needed time to disrupt Modru's
plan, and, by delaying the Guula that time could
be purchased. The price would be deadly, yet it
was a price Ubrik was willing to pay.

Back at the fortress, as King Galen and the Legion surged across the bridge and through the gate
and into the courtyards of the dark citadel, a shuddering blackness seemed to jolt across the darkling sky above as a spreading ebon tide surged
throughout the Shadowlight.

Lord Gildor raced back up the steps to the wall
above, where battle still raged. He looked upward
through the Dimmendark, though he knew what
he would see. Slowly the dim glow of the Sun was
fading away as the arc of the unseen Moon ate
across the last of the feeble disk above. And the
Elf's heart pounded as an ever-deepening gulf of
blackness rolled forth across the land. The deep
toll of a great Ruchen gong knelled through the
darkling air: *Doon!* . . . *Doon!* . . . *Doom!* And Gildor
despaired, for all about him *Spaunen* fought with
growing strength . . . their time had come at last.
Although the Men of Valon battled with fierce determination, still their eyes flicked to the dimming
sky, and their faces were grim, for the darkest
hour of the Darkest Day had come: it was the time
of the SunDeath.

South, in Grūwen Pass, Vidron and Talarin sur-

veyed the pitiful remnants of the Host that had
defied the Horde for *lo!* these many 'Darkdays.
Attack after attack had they fended off, delaying
the Swarm, buying time for King Galen. Yet the
Horde had hammered time and again into the
Men of Wellen and the Elves of Arden Vale, pounding them back with each strike. And now it was
the fifth 'Darkday since the Battle of Grüwen had
begun, and each 'Day more of the Wellenen had
fallen, more of the Lian had been slain. Still, hundreds upon hundreds of the *Rûpt* had been slaughtered as the combat raged by frigid 'Day and bitter
'Night upon the heights of the icy col. But slowly
the teeming Horde had battered the Host the full
length of the narrow pass. And now, no longer did
the sheer stone walls protect the Legion's flanks,
for at last they had been driven backwards across
the entire width of the Rigga Mountains; and exhausted Men and weary Elves and spent steeds
stood on the margins of Gron and watched as
Spawn poured through the notch and down into
the land to hem the allies against a great bluff.

"Aye, Lord Talarin, I deem you counted well,"
growled Fieldmarshal Vidron. "I, too, make our
number to be a scant six hundred or so. And though
we've left five thousand Wrg lying dead in our
wake, still there be another five thousand to come
against us this last time."

Talarin merely grunted and said no word in
reply as he watched the *Spaunen* continue to swarm
forth from Kregyn.

As the last of the *Rûpt* joined the iron ring surrounding the trapped allies, raucous calls blatted
forth from the brazen horns of the enemy, and
scimitar, tulwar, hammer, and cudgel were brandished. The foe readied themselves to destroy the
last of this stubborn Legion.

Vidron raised his black-oxen horn unto his lips, and its resonant call split the air, to be answered by the clarions of the surviving Wellenen. And four hundred or so weary Men, and half that number of worn Elves, mounted up onto exhausted steeds and made ready for one last battle.

Yet even as the allies girded themselves for the final charge, a great wave of blackness surged through the Dimmendark, and a loud wordless jeering shout rose up from the Horde. Talarin's eye caught that of Vidron. "It is the time of the Sun-Death, Hrosmarshal," said the Lian warrior, grimly. "It comes upon us even now, and I fear that Galen King's mission has failed."

Beyond the Grimwall and within the ring of the Rimmen Mountains in the Land of Riamon, furious battle raged before the gates of Mineholt North as Men and Elves and Dwarves alike fell upon the Swarm besieging the mountain where was delved the Dwarven Realm.

Swift horses bearing bright Elves shocked into the *Spaunen*, and the Men of Dael, on foot, struggled hand to hand with the foe. Forth from Mineholt North poured the black-armored Dwarves, hewing left and right with their double-bitted axes, cleaving a swath through the Squam.

Yet the Spawn, too, took their toll, as Free Folk fell slain by *Rûpt* weapon, and the vast numbers of the Horde pressed back in upon the allies.

Thrice had King Dorn joined his Men of Dael with the Elves of Coron Eiron to try to break this siege of Mineholt North and free the Dwarves of King Brek. Yet thrice had the Yrm hurled them back, leaving many dead in their wake.

Now this was their fourth attack, and its outcome teetered in the balance. The battle raged to

and fro, but at last the Men won unto the Dwarves'
side, splitting through the center of the ranks of
the Horde. A great glad shout rose up from the
allies, only to clog in their throats; for just as it
seemed that finally they had the advantage, a great
tide of darkness rolled throughout the Shadowlight
—and the hearts of Men and Elves and Dwarves
alike plummeted. And the Horde surged 'round
them, beringing them in an evil clutch as darkness
descended upon the land.

King Aranor of Valon sat upon his steed at the
fore of a great Host, and at his side sat Reggian,
Steward of Pendwyr. From concealment on the
slopes of the Brin Downs they looked forth upon
the vast throng marching into the plains of Jugo.
The Lakh of Hyree had come north, skirting the
Brin Downs, and now the swart Men of the south
marched past the Host.

And overhead the Sun was bright.

Now Aranor turned to survey the Legion, perhaps half the numbers of the Lakh. And the King
knew that the Host would be hard-pressed, yet
they would not quail from this fight.

Once more Aranor swung his gaze to the distant
enemy, and *lo!* they ground to a halt even as he
looked *and fell prostrate upon their faces upon the
ground . . . as if in worship!*

And a darkness commenced to fall upon the land.
Aranor glanced to the sky, and the hidden Moon
began to eat the Sun.

And south upon the waters of the Avagon Sea
the fleet of Arbalin came to stand across the mouth
of Hile Bay, where sat the ships of the Rovers of
Kistan; yet the enemy made no move to break the

blockade, for they moaned in ecstasy as an arc of darkness cut into the orb above.

Warrows wept as they fled back toward Littlefen. Rood was in flames, for once again the great Swann of maggot-folk had razed a Bosky town. Captain Alver's Thornwalkers had not been able to divert the Spawn from their march of destruction down Two Fords Road. And the raids of the Wellenen upon the Horde had been of little effect, for the Men were hopelessly outnumbered. No other allies had come unto the Severn Dells, though a herald had lately ridden to Captain Stohl bearing news that more Wellenen were on the way—but they had not yet arrived. And now the Warrows tramped toward the refuge of the marshes—though it was questionable how long the fens would remain safe, for they were iced over and even Rūck and Hlōk could walk across the frozen morass.

And as the Wee Folk trudged north and west, the hard-edged darkness of the Shadowlight began to deepen.

Reachmarshal Ubrik wheeled his outnumbered brigade once more to face the Guula. But the corpse-folk did not array themselves to whelm down on the surviving Men. Instead, Guula sat unmoving upon Hèlsteeds and gazed at the sky above Claw Moor. And while a distant gong tolled *Doom!* a vast darkness slowly descended upon the land.

Merrilee, Burt, Dill, Teddy, and Arch—Wee Folks all—mounted upon horses led by Vanadurin, were among the last to cross the bridge and come into Modru's dark citadel. Yet even as they thundered through the gate and clattered forth upon the fortress cobblestone and raced deep into the holt, a great spectral blackness flooded the very air. Men cried and rubbed at their eyes, and those upon steeds reined to a halt and dismounted. They groped forward with outstretched hands, or felt their way with extended sword or lance, for the Men could not see.

Yet the maggot-folk, too, were blinded by the cloaking blackness and stumbled unseeing, fumbling and feeling as they went.

But still the fighting continued: hand-to-hand grappling, dirk and longknife against kris and yataghan, blind warrior versus sightless Spawn, the Legionnaires crying *Adon!* as each came to grips with another being, striking swiftly if they received no answer, or the wrong reply.

Yet one warrior did not need to reply, for his weapon blazed forth his identity; Red Bale's blade-jewel still flared scarlet, and the ruby shafts of light drove through the darkness. And Elven eyes were not completely baffled by the ebon radiance, for Gildor and Flandrena both could dimly see those around them.

But it was the Warrows whose jewel-hued Utruni eyes fared best, for they could still see by the wrenching black light that streamed forth from Modru's Iron Tower, though their vision was greatly curtailed, as if looking through a dark glass.

"They can't see!" cried Teddy, leaping down from his steed and running forth to take the hand of the warrior who had led his horse.

Dismounting, all the Warrows stepped to the riders they had followed. "Stick with us," said Arch. "We can see."

"I thought I'd gone blind," croaked Degan, and Merrilee squeezed the Man's hand.

"What should we do?" asked Dill, peering through the blackness.

"We can pick off Rūcks and such," answered Burt, "or we can try to do something about *that*." The buccan stabbed a finger upward toward the tower whence the darkness streamed.

"You're right, Burt," agreed Merrilee, "we must invade that spike, for there, I think, lies the foul heart of this evil blackness ... and it must be destroyed. But I fear we cannot do it alone. Let us go forth, gathering more warriors along the way—and quickly, for the Sun-Death of the Darkest Day has come."

And so the Wee Folk moved swiftly into the dark fortress for an assault upon the tower, collecting allies as they went—Warrows leading Men. And among those mustered and led hand in hand toward the spire was the High King of Mithgar: Galen, son of Aurion.

And somewhere within the holt a great gong tolled: *Doon!* ... *Doon!* ... *Doom!*

Tuck groaned and rolled over, his mind struggling upward from darkness. Through the window came the blats of Rūcken brass and the resonant calls of black-oxen horns, the cries of Men and the snarls of Spawn in combat, and the din and clash of steel upon steel. *Got ... got to get up,* he muzzily thought, and tried to rise; but with a sharp hiss of air sucked in through clenched teeth, agony lancing upward from his broken foot, the buccan sank back to lie upon the cold stone floor, his legs drawn up, his entire being laced with pain. And then he remembered the looming black figure in the hideous mask. *Modru! That was Modru! The Evil One!* A chill dread raced through the Warrow's veins. *The Princess!*

"My Lady!" Tuck gasped, his mind now fully alert as he sat up with a start and stared wildly about. Laurelin was gone, as well as Modru. *The tower!* Tuck vaguely recalled the Evil One's hissing voice . . . something about taking the Lady Laurelin to the tower above . . . *to meet her fate.*

Tuck scrambled to his feet, anguish jolting up his leg. Taking up his bow and gritting his teeth, the Warrow hobbled to the door left standing ajar. A swift look down the length of the torch-lit hallway revealed no maggot-folk. And so, casting his hood over his head and adjusting his cloak, and closing the leaves of the silver locket—that had *somehow* sprung open—and tucking it under his torn jacket, the buccan limped the few strides to the near end of the hall, where steps mounted, and up these he struggled.

The steps came up to a wide circular stone floor, nearly sixty feet in diameter. Around him the walls of the tower reared upward into high darkness, and a torch-lit open stairwell clung to the side and spiralled up into the shadowed vault above.

Clamping his jaws together, bow in hand, Tuck started upward, step by torturous step, the *grinding* in his boot sending waves of sickening *hurt* through his very bones. Yet up the stairs he struggled, flight upon flight, past landing after landing, each with a window slit, and the great stone floor became lost in the blackness below. And sweating, grunting in pain, the wee Warrow slowly neared the top.

"Guttra!" a harsh voice suddenly snarled out, and Tuck gasped in startlement as the word echoed down the stairwell, for there, just one flight above upon a wide landing before a massive door, stood two scimitar-wielding Hlōks.

"Guttra!" Again came the harsh challenge, and Tuck thought to himself, *Do it right, bucco, for if you miss, and if there are any more of these Spawn behind that door, it's all over here and now.*

Swiftly the buccan plucked an arrow from his quiver and set it to string and drew, aimed, and loosed all in one motion. And ere that arrow struck, he was reaching for another. *Sssthock!* The first bolt struck one Hlōk full in the chest, and even as that Spawn pitched backwards . . . *Ssshthwock!* a second arrow pierced the other guard, this Hlōk to tumble down the flight of stairs and land with a sickening thud at the Warrow's feet as the scimitar spun down through the blackness toward the distant stone floor below.

Tuck paused, a third arrow set to string, the buccan listening, hearing only his own ragged breathing as he tried to determine if any foe behind the door above had detected the encounter . . . *ching* . . . The scimitar struck far below. As if that were a signal, Tuck began the ascent once more. And he painfully hobbled up the remaining steps to the landing and past the other dead Hlōk to come at last to the iron-banded door of Modru's chamber.

Tuck pressed his ear to the portal but could hear nought; the panel was too massive. Cautiously, the Warrow pushed at the door, and then shoved harder; but it did not budge, for it was barred on the inside. *I've got to get in there*, thought Tuck, *and see if this is where Modru has brought the Lady Laurelin.*

Hobbling past the dead Hlōk, Tuck painfully clambered upon a stone bench. Removing his quiver, he leaned out of the narrow window slit and peered along the outside tower wall. *There!* A short distance to the side and up was another, larger slit—and the eye-wrenching black radiance poured out through the opening. Tuck examined the stone. It was covered with ice and hoarfrost, yet projections outjutted from the wall just as they had on

the angles of the ramparts beringing the fortress—
and the buccan believed that he could reach the
wide slit. Tuck glanced below but quickly jerked
his eyes away, for the plumb drop down the sheer
tower wall was frightening. He could only hope
that he wouldn't fall, as he prepared to squeeze
through the narrow slit and out upon the vertical
height of the tower.

Tuck still had a short hank of Elven rope hanging from his belt. He tied one end 'round his waist
and the other end to his bow and quiver, and he
lowered the weapons out the window. Then he
levered his body up and squeezed through the slit.
Then, taking a deep breath and keeping his eyes
upon the wall before him, Tuck grasped a frost-
rimed stone and swung out upon the face of the
sheer drop, his boots finding purchase on the icy
juts, his left foot bearing weight in spite of the
pain. And the broken-footed Warrow clung to the
frozen stones on the side of the tower and began
edging over and up toward the wide slit, his bow
and quiver depending from a rope 'round his waist
and swinging pendulously. And as he clambered
across the sheer face, a great brass gong began dinning, the brazen sound pulsing throughout the holt:
Doon! . . . Doon! . . . Doom! And a deepening pall of
darkness descended upon the Iron Tower.

Laurelin yanked and twisted and pulled back in
vain as Modru dragged her up the long well of
steps and past two Lōkken guards and into the
chamber atop the tower, for the Evil One's grip
was like iron, and his wrenching strength was
overwhelming.

Boom! The iron-bound door slammed to behind
her.

Clang! The great bar fell into place.

And despite her struggles, Modru rent her cloak from her and hauled her past the ebon *blot* of the Myrkenstone and to a great dark lithic altar. He heaved her upon the raised slab and roughly locked her wrists and ankles into iron cuffs embedded in the stone.

The slab was canted, and Laurelin's head was lower than her feet. By arching her neck and tilting her face back, she could see the Myrkenstone looming nearby upon its pedestal. And her long flaxen hair lay in a channel that ran down from her shoulders to the edge of the stone. And Modru took up an iron knife and began hacking off her tresses, hissing, "We can't have these locks of yours soaking up the blood, for all of it will be needed: to *slake* my Master's thirst—upon His advent unto Mithgar—to invest Him with His full powers here in the Middle Plane; and to *quench* the Myrkenstone, closing the way behind, sealing forever the fate of all! *Tsss! sss, ssth!*"

Laurelin gasped, and again Modru's sissing laughter hissed forth as he sawed the blade through her hair. "*Ahh.* At last you know your purpose, *Princess.* Recall! Once you pledged that you would never serve me—I remind you of your foolish words now that it is time for the throne of Mithgar to be mine. Never serve me ... *tchaa!* It is *your* royal blood that my Master will quaff, *your* blood that will quench the 'Stone. I would have used the *Dolh's* —Vanidor's—but he was of Adonar; and here, the blood of one born to Mithgar is needed. Faugh! Any fool's would have done as well as yours, so long as he was of this world, but it *pleases* me to use the blood of a royal damosel. *Tsss, sssth, sss, ssss!*"

Tears brimmed in Laurelin's eyes as Modru stepped back to survey his handiwork. "*Sss.* Excellent. My Lord Gyphon will be pleased, for though your hair is cropped, still you are . . . unblemished. *Yesss,* pleased, for it has been long since He has sipped the blood of one so fair . . . and He *thirsts.*"

Modru turned and took up a stone basin and set it upon a stand at the edge of the altar where it would catch the blood flowing down the channel. And beside the basin he set an iron chalice. Then the Evil One brought forth a tray covered with black velvet, and he set it down on the altar slab and unfolded the cloth, revealing an ebon knife crudely shaped of the same hideous matter as the Myrkenstone. Lastly, Modru laid open a great tome on the slab and then consulted a chart.

And there came to the great turret the knell of a massive gong: *Doon! . . . Doon! . . . Doom!* And through the window slits an utter darkness could be seen descending upon the world.

Modru turned to Laurelin and hissed, "It is time, for the Sun-Death has come."

And the Evil One removed his black gauntlets, and his great clawlike hands took up the 'Stone knife and held it on high; and he began chanting, reading from the tome, the guttural obscene words of power rolling forth—vile, malignant, evil.

Still the gong tolled, and Merrilee's heart hammered in dread to hear the ominous *Doom!* Yet she and Burt, Dill, Teddy, and Arch each led hand in hand a small group of Sun-Death-blinded warriors, five Warrows guiding eighteen Men. And they veered between widespread groups of unseeing maggot-folk and struck for the tower.

At last they came to the great spire and made their way to a door. Whispered instructions were passed, and Men were cautioned to hold their places—to move not—and to be silent, for Spawn were near. And then, arrows nocked to bows, the chary Warrows slowly opened the door.

Torchlight streamed out, and the startled Men could see once more. *Har!* cried Rūcks to see the light streaming across the courtyard. Swiftly, sword in hand, Men rushed in after the Wee Ones and slammed the door behind.

Before them lay an empty hall.

"Quick now," commanded Galen, his voice low but urgent, "we must hurry. Spawn may be in these corridors, and surely those without come after. Let us to the top, for if the Wee Ones are right, the black heart of the Dimmendark lies in this pinnacle, and it must be destroyed."

Swiftly up the stairs they went, and no *Spaunen* did they see. One flight ... two flights ... and another and they came to the open stone floor above which reared the tower. They began the ascent up the long spiral staircase twisting upward inside the walls, King Galen in the fore with Steel-heart in his grip, and Men and Warrows coming after.

Landing after landing they crossed, each with a window slit looking upon the Sun-Death blackness outside, as upward they pressed. Now they neared the top, and they could see a door at the head of the stars. Another landing they came to, and a dead Hlōk lay in a pool of his own blood, a short-ened arrow through his heart.

As they hastened up the last flight of steps, Warrows looked questioningly at one another, for they knew the Hlōk below had been slain by a bolt from the bow of a Wee One: Yet who could it be?

They came to the last landing, and *lo!* another arrow-pierced Hlōk lay slain before the iron-bound door—this bolt, too, from buccan bow.

With her heart pounding in hope, Merrilee knelt

down to examine the quarrel, but ere she could do so—

The shrill scream of a Woman rang through the door, and a desperate anguished cry of words, their meaning muffled and lost.

Yet Galen recognized the voice. *"Laurelin!"* he shouted, and hurled himself at the door, to no avail. Wildly his eyes cast about. "The bench! The stone bench!" he cried, leaping for the massive seat below the window slit. "We'll use it as a ram to batter down the door!"

And as Vanadurin sprang to help him, *Ssss-thunk!* a black-shafted arrow chunked into the door. Merrilee and the buccen scrambled to the edge of the landing. There below, clattering up through the torch-lit shadows, swarmed a band of maggot-folk. *Shsss! . . . Shssh!* More black-shafted arrows hissed upward, to be answered in kind by deadly Warrow bolts flying downward.

And behind, as the Men heaved up the heavy stone slab to whelm the door, another piercing cry rang forth from Modru's chamber.

Doon! . . . Doon! . . . Doom! Still the toll of the gong knelled out as Tuck slowly hoisted himself up and across, his fingers clutching at the frost-rimed stone, his feet pressing into crevices. His teeth were gritted against the pain, and his eyes were locked upon the sheer wall before him to keep from looking down from the dizzying height to the courtyard far below.

A great darkness blotted the land, yet Tuck's jewel-hued eyes saw by a different light than those of other Folk—a light seen only by the Wee Ones. And up through this blackness he crawled, edging toward a wide window slit out of which poured an ebon radiance.

At last he came to the opening, and guttural obscene mouthings hissed forth from the window and fell upon his ears, and he shuddered in revulsion to hear such malediction voiced. Yet into this slot he would climb. He hauled up his dangling bow and quiver and slid them onto the wide sill before him, and then he hefted himself up after, clambering into the eye-wrenching blackness.

Squinting against the ebon radiance, through the turret wall he crawled, pushing his bow and arrows before him. He came out upon a raised stone catwalk that encircled the round room below. Yet Tuck saw little of the chamber, for his eyes were *trapped*—held by a great, dark *blot* resting upon a pedestal in the center of the room. And although Tuck did not know it, this was the very piece, the very fragment of the Dragon Star that had cloven the immense burning gash as it slashed over the Boskydells and beyond the Northwood, beyond Rian . . . even beyond Gron. It had smashed to Mithgar in the barren wastes where was exiled Modru, *just as Gyphon had planned four millennia agone.* This was the Comet Spawn, the Myrkenstone, the vile eater of light, the source of the ebon radiance that spread throughout the Dimmendark. And it trapped Tuck's eyes and seemed to draw the vision out of them, steadily replacing sight with darkness. And the Warrow could not tear his dimming gaze away from the hideous eye-wrenching *hole*, for its vile power held him locked.

Yet other powers, other energies, were at work within the chamber, too, as guttural obscene runewords rolled forth from the mouth of the Evil One to shock through the room.

And the very air began to *gather*, to *ripple*, as if it were become a dark liquid into which the words *fell* as would ebon stones fall into black waters.

And through the undulation, a dim figure began to appear, as if a distant dark portal had opened and an indistinct shape had stepped toward the room, drawing nearer with every hideous word uttered.

Closer it came, and closer; and with each syllable, each step, the form took on substance, and it *glowed* with a dark halo—as did the Myrkenstone. And now the figure could be seen more clearly, as if through a fluctuant glass: a Man, some would say; an Elf, would claim others; yet He was neither. Instead, it was He who once held Adon's trust, who once stood next to the High One's throne, who once wielded power exceeded only by The One, who once fell from grace and was forgiven, who fell again ... beyond the Spheres. It was Gyphon. And as He issued forth from the Great Abyss, the undulant air rippled less and less, for He came unto Mithgar, and finally His image took on a sharp definition and He could be seen clearly at last. And He was exquisitely beautiful, for He was the Great Evil.

It was Gyphon's darkly luminant form that pulled Tuck's eye from the Myrkenstone; and the buccan gasped, his spirit whelmed by the comeliness of the figure he saw; and he could but barely keep his eyes upon such fairness. The Warrow glanced away, and his heart lurched in horror, for there beyond the Myrkenstone was Laurelin, shackled upon an altar. Above her loomed evil Modru, chanting, foul words issuing forth from the hideous iron mask, his arms raised upon high, the vile 'Stone knife clutched in his left hand. And a stone basin and an iron chalice rested upon a stand at the end of a blood channel in the altar. *He's going to kill her!* Tuck's mind screamed.

His hands trembling in haste, the buccan untied

his bow from the Elven rope, and his eyes sought an arrow. And there before him, resting in his quiver, was the red quarrel from Othran's Crypt: an arrow no longer a dull ruddy color, but instead now flaring scarlet in the black light streaming from the Myrkenstone, an arrow made of a strange light metal and borne by the buccan on an epic journey from Challerain Keep to the Weiunwood and thence to Arden Vale, through Drimmen-deeve and the Larkenwald beyond, down the Argon and back to Gûnarring Gap, and thence up the Grimwall and through Grûwen Pass into Gron, and finally across Claw Moor and under the walls of the fortress and up to this very room atop the Iron Tower. And Tuck's hands, as if guided by another's will, snatched up the crimson bolt and set it to bowstring.

But even as Tuck nocked the arrow, the ripples in the air vanished entirely, and now Gyphon—the Great Evil—stood at last upon Mithgar, corporeal but powerless until the quaffing of sacrificial blood and the quenching of the Myrkenstone. The fate of the world teetered upon the brink of doom.

And Tuck stood and drew the red shaft to the full.

And Laurelin screamed, *"No!"*

For at the same moment Gyphon stepped forth into Mithgar, the Princess saw the Warrow rise up out of the shadows upon the catwalk. By his clawed face and silveron armor gleaming through his torn jacket she knew him to be Tuck, and she saw that he aimed at Modru.

"No!" she cried again, with all the force she could muster. "Slay Gyphon! Slay the Great Evil!"

The Great Evil? And then Tuck knew. And his aim shifted to the fair luminant figure. *Yet how can such beauty be evil? And even should I kill*

*Gyphon, Modru will murder Laurelin ere I can set
another arrow to bow.*

Again Tuck's aim fell upon Modru, but the Evil
One had spun around to see the Warrow, and
the 'Stone knife now threatened Laurelin's throat,
though the obscene chanting went on.

"*Gyphon!*" Laurelin's scream was rent from her
very soul. "Slay Gyphon!"

In that moment, *Boom! . . . Boom! . . . Boom!* the
iron-bound door shuddered from the impact of a
ram, and splinters flew as the heavy planking
cracked under the whelming blows, but the great
bar staying the door held fast.

Once more the buccan's aim swung to Gyphon,
but he could not bring himself to shoot, for if he
did, Laurelin would die. Again he sighted upon
Modru . . . yet Tuck realized that Modru was but a
servant of the Great Evil, and to slay the serf and
yet let *this* Master live would be the sheerest folly.
And, too, it then would be the Master who would
murder the Princess, perhaps to complete the rit-
ual ere Tuck could set another arrow to bow.

Boom! . . . Boom! . . . Boom!

And as the Warrow's aim wavered, two memories stirred deep within his mind.

From Othran's Tomb:

> *Loose not the Red Quarrel*
> *Ere appointed dark time.*

And Rael's Rede:

> "*Neither of two Evils must thy strike claim;*
> *Instead smite the Darkness between the same.*"

Suddenly the cryptic meaning of both of these
riddles became clear to the Warrow, resolving his

dilemma. And as the booming ram whelmed the door, and planks split and the bar cracked, Tuck swiftly aimed at the Myrkenstone, yet the ebon *blot* again wrenched at his Utruni eyes, and his remaining sight was gone: He could not see.

The voice of Old Barlo rang in his mind: *"The arrow as strays might well'er been throwed away."*

And Modru's chanting stopped!

And Tuck knew he had to shoot *now!*

Adon, guide my aim, fervently prayed 'Stone-blinded Tuck. *Red Quarrel, red arrow, fly true.* And he loosed the shaft.

Like a scarlet streak, the Red Quarrel hissed crimson across the room to strike the Myrkenstone square in the center, the strange metal arrow piercing deeply into the ebon *blot*. A blinding detonation shattered forth, dashing Tuck violently back against the window sill and blasting the batter-whelmed door into splinters and flying bolts of wood, hurling Galen and the others down upon the stair landing, their stone-bench ram smashing into shards as it fell ponderously to the deck and slid heavily down the steps. And a savagely intense glare flashed up to flood the room with a blazing incandescence so bright, so violent, that scrolls began to smolder and alembis filled with arcane liquids shattered.

For the Myrkenstone flared, radiance blasting forth, as if it yielded up the very sunlight it had stolen. And the ravening fulgor raged, blinding luminance blaring forth, great radiant beams blasting from the chamber.

And on the landing, amid the wrack of the iron-bound door, Galen and Merrilee and the Men and Warrows struggled up and shielded their eyes with up-flung arms and staggered toward the room. But they could not come into the glare, for it was too bright, and the wild light exploding through the door raged out like a furious gale ripping at weapons and armor and clothing and folk alike.

Blazing candescence lit up the interior of the tower, and stabbing beams shot through the window slits; and where the savage light touched, inside and out, Spawn were destroyed. Thus did some *Rûpt* perish upon the fortress walls, and so too died all the *Spaunen* upon the stairwell within the Iron Tower.

And in the fury-filled chamber atop the spire, raging light blasted forth from the Myrkenstone. And in this roaring fulmination, Tuck staggered to his feet, the unbearable brightness lancing into his 'Stone-blind eyes, *and the buccan could see once more!* Yet this 'Stone-light, too, ripped at Tuck's vision, hammering it toward oblivion. Still, the buccan's scathed sight saw Modru rise up from the altar where he had been flung over Laurelin. The Evil One stood and turned and held his clawlike hands out before him as if warding off an attack. Hoarse screams rang forth as he staggered back in horror against the stone slab, for the flesh on his taloned fingers was rent away by the savage light, and the very bones of his grotesque hands and wrists shone forth only to crumble into dust. His piercing screams chopped into silence as the flesh was rent from his throat. His chest and lungs were blasted away, his ribs collapsing into ruin. His desperate eyes *dissolved*, leaving empty sockets behind, which then disintegrated, too, as the remainder of his body pitched backwards onto the altar, destroyed ere he struck. And the hideous iron mask, now empty, fell to the floor with a hollow *Blang!*

And stricken by the scarlet bolt the Myrkenstone, too, fell toward ruin, its substance blazing away, perishing. And in the blasting glare as the 'Stone disintegrated, once more the air began to ripple. And a distant dark portal seemed to open, and Gyphon's features twisted into desperate rage; He screamed, yet no sound was heard. He began to recede, as if drawn back along the path whence He had come. And as the ripples became more intense, Gyphon's aspect began to *change:* His fairness, His comeliness, altered. His beauty fell away as if it were a mask removed, and a loathsome semblance stared forth. Yet this aspect, too, altered, shifting to a ghastliness beyond description as the figure of Gyphon rushed back toward oblivion. As the undulant air shuddered, once again Gyphon's features shifted, and Tuck could not face the hideous monster that fell down into the Great Abyss beyond the Spheres.

And the blinding flare died, for the Myrkenstone was destroyed, slain by a Red Quarrel loosed by one of the Wee Folk. And with its destruction, the Dimmendark collapsed.

Out in the courtyards and upon the walls of the fortress, hand-to-hand battle raged, and the passing of the Dimmendark was not then noted, for still the Moon hid the Sun, though a dim corona shone forth. But, of a sudden, beads of light sprang out from the rim of the unseen Moon, and slowly a fingernail-thin crescent of the Sun blazed forth. Rūcks, Hlōks, and Ghûls had time only to glance upward in horror ere the Withering Death struck; and they shrivelled to dust, arms and armor falling with a clatter to the stone.

On Claw Moor, Ubrik and his brigade waited grimly for the blackness to pass, knowing that

when the battle began once more, they would fall
to the tulwars and barbed spears of the Ghûls.

Yet when the darkness at last fell away, *lo!* the
flaring edge of the Sun gradually emerged from
behind the unseen Moon; and before the aston-
ished eyes of the Vanadurin, Ghûls and Hèlsteeds
collapsed into withered husks, and a chill wind
gnawed through their ashes.

In Grūwen Pass, Vidron, Talarin, and the surviving Men and Elves girded themselves for the last
charge, but suddenly the Dimmendark *vanished*,
and an arc of the Sun shone forth, partially eclipsed;
and the japing Spawn jeered no more, for they
were fallen into ruination.

In the Land of the Thorns, the Struggles came to
an end in a town called Rood—central to the
Boskydells—for there raged the Horde when the
Dimmendark collapsed and a curve of the Sun
burned down upon the Spawn.

Dwarf King Brek of Mineholt North, King Dorn
of Riamon, and Coron Eiron of Darda Galion came
together upon the battlefield before the slopes of
the Rimmen Mountains. They squinted upward at
the emerging Sun and then at the War-ground,
where Men and Dwarves and Elves wandered
awestruck among the slain and wounded. And of
the savage Horde there was no trace, except for
tattered clothes and empty armor and fallen weapons . . . and dregs stirring in the wind.

In Jugo the land had not fallen into total darkness, for there the Moon did not eat all of the Sun.
And Aranor and Reggian had watched as the Lakh
of Hyree had fallen down in worship at the begin-

ning of the fearful occultation. Slowly the hidden
Moon had eaten across the disk of the Sun while
Aranor and Reggian debated. The King of Valon
thought to launch an immediate attack upon the
prostrate Hyrania, while the Steward of Pendwyr
argued to wait until the depth of the obscuration.
Reggian prevailed, for he reasoned that the Lakh
would be in the thrall of their canting when that
moment came.

And so they waited, poised in the northern fringes
of the Brin Downs, ready to launch the attack. At
last the penumbral darkness reached its depth,
and the horns of Pellar and Valon blew wildly as
horsemen thundered across the plains.

Some among the Lakh looked up from their worship to see the Host charging down upon them,
and they leapt to their feet, crying in alarm. Up
swept the Hyrania, weapons in hand, ready to face
the outnumbered Legion. And the swart Men looked
to their Jemadars for orders, and the Jemadars in
turn looked to the vacant-eyed slack-jawed emissaries governing their battles. But at that moment,
the faces of the surrogates twisted in agony—eyes
rolling white, spittle frothing from grimacing,
clenched, shrieking mouths—and their muscles
spasmed. And then, as if strings had been cut from
puppets, the emissaries fell to the ground dead, as
if the malignant will driving them had been slain.

Yet even though they knew that something was
amiss in their vile chain of rule, perhaps in the
Iron Tower itself, still the Jemadars turned to command their Men, for they would fight against their
ancient enemies. And the Hyrani leaders shouted
orders as the horsemen of Valon and Pellar crashed
into their ranks. And a raging battle began, and
the Lakh of Hyree fought with the faith and strength

of zealots, for this was the day the long-held prophecy would be fulfilled.

Inward drove the Legion, spears and sabers meeting pikes and tulwars. And the Host sheered off, only to form and strike again.

And slowly the hidden Moon receded and the Sun grew toward fullness.

Again the Legion drove into the Hyrania, and once more steel skirled upon steel, and iron points pierced, and blades clove.

Men fell slain as the Sun crept from hiding.

Again the Host fell back to regroup, their ranks severely depleted. And Aranor and Reggian rode to one another to decide whether to press the fight once more or to withdraw.

And the Sun won free of the Moon.

And Gyphon did not appear among the files of the Hyrania: The prophecy was *false!* They had been *deceived!*

A moan of despair rose up from the Lakh, and many threw down their weapons and fled, while others went forth to the Legion and surrendered. Still others rent their hair and clothes and plunged knives into their own bosoms and fell dead, while a few—waving tulwars and screaming hoarsely—charged at the Host and fought to the death and were slain.

And the Battle of Jugo was finished.

In Hile Bay the fleeing Rovers of Kistan sailed upon the tide and into the blockade of the outnumbered ships of the Arbalina fleet. With ropes and timbers creaking, and canvass snapping in the wind, and waves *shsshing* upon hulls, the mighty armada of the south tacked and hauled toward the gap where lay the squadrons of the King's flotilla. And catapults flung burning fire—*thwack!*—and

timbers groaned against one another as argosy
met flotilla. Some Rover ships burned, but so did
craft of Arbalin, while others in each fleet sank,
holed by great underwater ram beaks. Some Kistania craft were grappled and boarded, and hand-
to-hand fighting ensued. Some brigand crews
surrendered. But for the most part, the ships of the
Rovers escaped, for their numbers were too many,
and they sailed beyond the line of the Kingsvessels
and away into the Avagon Sea.

Back at the Iron Tower, when the flare of the
Myrkenstone died, Merrilee and Galen and Men
and Warrows rushed through the sundered door
and into the evil sanctum. And there, near a great
scorched pedestal, they found Laurelin partially
covered by a black cloak and shackled to an altar.
And in the shimmering heat, Galen rent open the
bonds and fiercely swept the Princess up in his
arms.

And Merrilee glanced across the chamber and
upward, and there on a stone catwalk stood Tuck
swaying, his foot broken and his body bruised, his
face clawed ... and deeply seared, as if by the
Sun.

"Tuck!" cried the damman, and she raced past
the charred stand and to the far side of the room,
and scrambled up the ladder to him, and caught
him as he collapsed to his knees. And she wept and
would have kissed him but did not, for she was
afraid her touch would harm his burned face. "Oh
Tuck, my buccaran ... my buccaran." And she
sobbed uncontrollably as she held onto him.

"Merrilee?" Tuck's voice was questioning, hesi-
tant, and his seared hands fumbled out to touch
her face. "Oh my dammia, I cannot see you, for I
am blind."

* * *

At that moment out upon the ramparts a great glad shout rose up to greet the emerging Sun, for the foe was slain! The Shadowlight of Winternight was gone, the Winter War was ended; and here, as well as in all Mithgar, Free Folk rejoiced.

But there were those who did not join in the jubilation, for they stood among their slaughtered comrades and wept: in Riamon and Jugo, in Pellar and at Grūwen Pass, in the Boskydells, and upon Claw Moor in Gron.

And at the Iron Tower, atop the ramparts above the gate, stood five warriors, each of them wounded in some fashion—arm, wrist, forehead, side, leg— blood seeping unattended. They did not seek aid, but instead stood with heads bowed: a youth, a Man, Prince Igon; a buccan Warrow, Dink Weller; two Elves, Lian warriors, Flandrena and Gildor; and a Dwarf—bloody Drakkalan in hand, hood cast over his head—Brega. And they grieved. And before them sat a wee Warrow—Patrel Rushlock— weeping, keening, clasping the slain body of a black-armored buccan unto him.

CHAPTER 6

THE JOURNEY HOME

Tuck was led down from the tower to suitable quarters below where he was undressed and put to bed. A healer was summoned to treat his and the Lady Laurelin's wounds, for she too had been burned by the searing light of the flaring Myrkenstone, though not as severely as the buccan. Modru himself—though not by choice—had shielded the maiden from that initial, most violent blast, for he had been standing between the Princess and the 'Stone at the moment the Red Quarrel had struck. And when the Withering Death had smote him and he had pitched backwards onto the altar, his empty cloak had fallen across Laurelin in such a way that only her hands had been directly exposed to the unbearable glare; yet she had been closer to the 'Stone than Tuck, and her hands had been terribly seared.

Even so, at Laurelin's behest the healer treated Tuck's wounds first. Herbs were dissolved in water and daubed upon the Warrow's burns, the healer using a sunscald remedy; Tuck's broken foot was bound; and cold compresses were set upon his bruised arm and ribs. Then the healer carefully looked at the Warrow's eyes and said, "There's nought I can do about this. Perhaps Elven medicine can help, but . . ."

As the healer fell silent and turned to treat the Princess, Arch Hockley darted down the stairs and out the door to find Lord Gildor or Flandrena. The buccan called to several Men, but none knew the whereabouts of the Lian warriors until the Warrow came upon a soldier who said he'd last seen the Elves above the gate.

The buccan turned and trotted to the wall and up a set of steps to the ramparts over the portal. There he found the Lian warriors, as well as Prince Igon, Dink Weller, Patrel, and Brega staring grimly out across Claw Moor, where rolling clouds of a gathering storm could be seen from the northwest across the Claw Spur of the Gronfang Mountains.

"Lord Gildor," Arch panted, out of breath, "I've come to fetch you or Flandrena or both. Tuck's been blinded—"

"Tuck?" Patrel interrupted, his face haggard, his emerald eyes swollen. "He's alive? . . . Blinded? . . . How? Where?"

"Why, at the top of the tower, Captain," answered Arch. "He lost his sight when he destroyed the thing that made the Dimmendark, and light just exploded out of it—the Myrkenstone, the Lady Laurelin calls it—"

"Laurelin?" blurted Igon, cutting Arch's words short. "You . . . you've found Laurelin?"

"Oh aye," responded Arch. "The Lady is with the King and Tuck—though she's got a bit burned, too, 'cause when Tuck slew the 'Stone and killed Modru—"

"Modru slain . . . by Tuck?" Lord Gildor now asked, his green eyes wide.

"Look," said Arch, exasperated, "we could stand here all day telling tales about how Tuck slew the 'Stone and caused the Dimmendark to collapse, and how he killed Modru and rescued the Lady and sent Gyphon back beyond the Spheres—"

Gyphon! gasped several at once, but Arch was not to be deterred.

"Yes: Gyphon," snapped the buccan. "But I'm not here to tell stories. The plain fact is, Tuck needs your help, Lord Gildor, Flandrena—if you have any—and the sooner the better. And if you are interested in Tuck's adventure, I'll tell you all I know on the way to his room—yet little enough that is."

"You are right, Wee One," said Lord Gildor. "We should not stand here listening to tales when there are those in need. Lead us; we will follow."

Arch turned to go, but at that moment the gruff voic of Brega came from beneath his hood: "Patrel, you go, too."

"I can't." The words choked out of Patrel, and he vaguely gestured with one hand. Glancing to where Patrel had motioned, tears sprang to Arch's eyes, too, for there among the dead the Warrow could see the forms of three slain buccen, buccen whom he had come to know and love.

"You *must* go," growled Brega. "You all must. I will attend to things here." None could see the Dwarf's face beneath his cowl, yet they each knew that he grieved, too. They also knew that Brega was right: they needed to get away from the ramparts—away from the slain Warrows—to find peace . . . especially Patrel.

As Gildor and Flandrena, Igon and Dink, and Patrel all turned and followed Arch, hooded Brega stood upon the ramparts and watched the black clouds of the dark storm boil through the mountains and obscure the Sun, and a sudden blast of a frigid wind blew down upon the fortress.

Patrel was led weeping down the steps by Lord Gildor. And as they came to the bottom and crossed the cobbled way, behind them Reachmarshal Ubrik and his Men wearily rode across the iron drawbridge and in through the gate. It took long for the plodding horses to pass into the fortress, for their numbers were many; yet more than half the brigade had been left behind, slain upon Claw Moor.

In somber silence Arch led the five warriors across icy courtyards, and they followed the cobbled ways unto the central tower. They entered through a portal and mounted up a darkened stairwell and made their way along a torch-lit corridor to Tuck's door. Arch knocked softly, and then they all entered the room. There sat Laurelin wrapped in a blanket, and beside her sat King Galen, and Merrilee and the healer stood next to the bed where scalded Tuck lay.

Galen sprang to his feet, and he and Igon embraced one another, each glad to see that his brother lived. And then the Prince gently kissed Laurelin's bandaged hand. And she kissed Igon upon the cheek in her joy to see him once more; yet her happiness fled with quicksilver swiftness and tears brimmed in her eyes, for she had just moments before learned of Aurion's death, and it was as if her own father had died.

Merrilee turned to see Dink and Patrel, and she rushed across the room and gave both a hug and kissed Patrel. And she took Patrel by the hand and led him to the bedside, where Lord Gildor and Flandrena spoke quietly with the healer.

"Tuck," she said softly, and the burnt-faced buccan turned his head toward the sound of her voice. "Tuck, I've a good friend here: it's Paddy, Paddy's come." To her consternation Patrel began to weep, tears flowing down from his viridian eyes.

"Why, Patrel." Tuck reached out a bandaged hand, and Patrel took it gently. "This is a reunion, yet I hear you cry."

"Oh, Tuck ... Merrilee," Patrel reached forth with his other hand, gripping the damman's, too. "Danner ... Danner is dead."

A great blizzard raged forth out of the Boreal Sea to hurtle down upon Gron, shrieking wind wailing across the wastes, driving snow before it. The storm hammered upon the peaks and massifs of the Rigga and Gronfang mountains, whelming upon the Land. And its icy fist pounded at the walls and turrets of the dark fortress. Legionnaires huddled inside, none to venture forth—not even into the nearby courtyards—for Man, Elf, or Warrow could get lost but a few paces into the blinding fling.

Yet Gron was not the only place hammered by the great storm. It swept down along the Jillian Tors and across the Dalara Plains to strike into Rian and the Lands below: Wellen, the Boskydells, Harth, Rhone, Rell, Trellinath.

And it howled across the Steppes of Jord to vault the Grimwall, and there savage fury mauled: in Aven and Riamon, in Darda Erynian and Darda Galion, and in the Greatwood.

And to the south, torrents of freezing rain and sleet lashed down upon the Realms: Valon, Hoven, empty Gûnar, Jugo, Arbalin Isle, and Pellar.

It was as if the Dimmendark had been holding back the natural march of weather, for when the Myrkenstone had been destroyed and the 'Dark had collapsed, wind and snow and sleet and ice then had rushed in behind its fall—to the woe of those now trapped in the blasts.

In Grūwen Pass, Vidron and Talarin and the other survivors of that epic stand grimly fought their way southward through the shrieking blindness, pressing on for Arden Vale, for they knew that if they stopped they would perish.

In the Boskydells, Warrows huddled in the Dinglewood, and in Eastwood, and in Bigfen and Littlefen, and elsewhere, for the Ghûls had destroyed many homes, and the Swarm that had come after had levelled entire towns. Though no Spawn remained alive, still they had done great damage, and Wee Folk suffered for it, though the fens and the forests shielded them from the worst of the brunt.

In Riamon, the Men, Elves, and Dwarves entered through the great iron gates of Mineholt North and closed them fast behind to wait out the storm in the refuge of the carven halls of the Dwarvenholt under the Rimmen Mountains.

And all across Mithgar, wherever Free Folk dwelled, they took in friends and strangers caught in the blast and sheltered the homeless in bothy, cot, flet, burrow, lean-to, cavern, stone house, or whatever other haven they could offer. And whether it was meager or plentiful, food was shared. It was a time of great need, and few if any withheld their aid.

Though no one knew it at the time, the great storms were to rage without letup for nine days.

On the afternoon of the first day, Free Folk everywhere warily eyed the glowering skies and hurried toward shelter. In Gron, that shelter was in the dark fortress itself, where the Legion sought comfort and the wounded were treated. And one of those wounded was a blinded Warrow.

Lord Gildor, who was skilled in medicine, had examined Tuck's eyes; yet the Elf could not suggest any remedy to the healer concerning the buccan's sight, although Gildor did say that the Dara Rael in Arden perhaps could help, for she had more skill in healing than anyone else he knew. Gildor mixed a sleeping draught for Tuck to quaff later, for it could be seen that the buccan was in considerable pain and would need the potion to rest.

That night a fever came upon Tuck, and he alternately quaked with chills and burned with fire. His seared face and hands were ever hot to the touch, and his body at times was drenched in perspiration, while at other times it was parchment dry.

Warrows came to sit with him 'round the clock, and they daubed his face and hands with the solution of water and herbs.

Yet Tuck did not waken, though at times his eyes were wide open as he startled up in delirium to wildly cry out warnings and to call names and to implore that someone, *anyone*, give aid to those in need that only he could see—phantoms from other days, other places: Hob, Tarpy, Aurion, Danner.

And outside, the great storm hammered at the ramparts and towers, ravening at the stone and hurling snow and ice down upon the fortress.

The next day fluid-filled blisters rose up on Tuck's face and hands. At times when he seemed partially awake the attending Warrows tried to get him to eat; yet he retched even upon water and could keep nothing down.

And still the storm raged across the wasteland and rammed into the fortress, clawing at the citadel.

* * *

On the fourth day Tuck's fever broke, and he spoke with a saneness that had been missing from his voice. Dink was with him at the time and had been in the process of daubing the sunscald liquid on Tuck's face when the bedridden Warrow whispered quite clearly, "Who is with me?" For although he looked directly at Dink, Tuck's eyes could not see.

"It's me, Tuck . . . Dink Weller," said Dink, daubing more solution on Tuck's right hand.

"Hullo, Dink." Tuck's voice was raspy. "Would you have something to drink? My throat feels as if all the burning sands of Karoo were inside."

Quickly Dink poured water into a cup and propped Tuck up and held the cup to the buccan's lips, and Tuck drank greedily.

"Whoa now, Tucker," cautioned Dink. "The healer said to take it slow—little nips over a time."

Sipping, Tuck finished that cup and another and then sank back upon the bed. "Merrilee . . . where's Merrilee?"

"Ah, Tuck, she's sleeping," answered Dink. "Day and night she's been here. And she ran herself into the ground. Some of us finally dragged her off to a bed of her own, and she was dead to the world the moment she laid down."

A small smile played across Tuck's cracked lips, and he closed his eyes and said nought else. And Dink slipped from the room and ran to fetch Merrilee, but when they returned, Tuck had fallen into a deep natural slumber.

Dink insisted that Merrilee return to her bed, and she went without argument, for now she knew that her buccaran was going to be alright. And the damman crawled back under her blankets with her heart lightened, while outside the wind moaned and howled and snow hurtled across the 'scape.

The next morning, with the aid of Arch and Burt, Tuck tottered out of his bed to relieve himself, refusing to spend one more moment being cared for, as he put it, ". . . as if I am a helpless babe." Yet it was all the buccan could do to keep from swooning when he first stood upright.

The healer came and pronounced Tuck fit to take meals, and Merrilee brought him breakfast, meager though it was: gruel and bread and hot tea. Yet to Tuck it was a sumptuous banquet, but he could not eat it all.

And Tuck rested propped abed, while Merrilee sat. They quietly talked—whenever the buccan was awake, that is, for Tuck frequently fell asleep even as they conversed. At these times Merrilee would sit lost in her own thoughts, listening to the storm and waiting for Tuck to awaken again, and then they would talk on. And they spoke of many things, some more important than others.

"The King has come every day, Tuck," said Merrilee, softly. "He's been most worried about you. They say he smiled for the first time in days when he heard your fever had broken."

"He'll make a good King, Merrilee," responded Tuck. The buccan fell silent a moment, then: "How's the Lady Laurelin? And Prince Igon? And the others . . . how do they fare?"

"Well," answered Merrilee, "the Princess is wan, for she too has been ill from the sunscalding of the burning Myrkenstone, though not as gravely as you, Tuck. But she's been up and about for the last two days, and she spends much of her time visiting the wounded.

"As for Prince Igon, his wounds—shoulder and

wrist—are healing well. And he also has come to see you, as well as many others.

"Lord Gildor and Flandrena both are well, though Gildor was stabbed in the leg, and Flandrena took a cut across the cheek. He'll bear a scar the rest of his days . . ."

Merrilee fell silent as her words were drowned out by a rising howl of the blast hammering and clawing at the tower. And as the wind fell back to a sobbing moan, the damman stood and stepped to the fire, stirring up the blaze with an iron ere taking her seat once more.

"This storm is terrible, Tuck," she said, again pulling a blanket 'round her shoulders. "It has set everyone's teeth on edge, even the King's, for we've been trapped inside these squalid Rūcken quarters for five days now—the entire Legion—and all are restless and cross, nettled . . . everyone except Brega that is."

"Brega?" Tuck's voice was full of surprise, for he knew the Dwarf's bellicose nature, and if anyone were to have his hackles up, it would be Brega.

"Oh yes, Tuck," answered Merrilee. "Why, if it weren't for Brega no one could get between the buildings at all. I don't know how he manages to do it, but the storm doesn't seem to turn him around. Against all advice, he was the first to venture outside, and he's done it many times since. Yet Brega always seems to know how to get back safely. Why, they say he's even been outside the walls, through the gate and over the bridge and beyond. But why he went, what he did there, he will not speak of it.

"And he's guided King Galen, Prince Igon, and Princess Laurelin—as well as many others—between the buildings through that swirling white blast;

but they say that Brega moves as if he's on a well-trodden path.

"Why, I do believe that the horses would have starved had Brega not led some Men to the stables to care for the steeds. And the horses, well, they too are skittish and cross, living in that Hèlsteed stink the way they do. I pity them in those foul stables. But at least Brega took the Men there to feed and water the poor beasts."

Tuck listened to the juddering wind. "So Brega goes out into the storm," mused the buccan, shaking his head, "and to care for horses at that." The shriek of the blizzard climbed higher, and Tuck fell silent while his memories slipped back to recall the howling whiteness along the edges of the Dimmendark, where nothing could be seen in the hurtling fling; and he knew that if the blizzard raging now was anything like that, then it was indeed a wonder that Brega could fare in safety.

Merrilee stood once more and stepped to the window and peered out through the heavy drapes. With a shudder Tuck came out of his reverie at the sound of the curtains being thrust aside. "Is it gone, Merrilee?" he asked.

"Wha—what?" The damman turned. "I'm sorry, Tuck . . . the wind noise . . . I didn't hear what you said."

"The Dimmendark," responded Tuck. "Is it gone? Is it truly gone?"

"Yes, my buccaran, it is gone," answered Merrilee. "It is truly gone. The land is free of Shadowlight."

Tuck turned his sightless eyes toward his hands folded in his lap. "Oh . . . I would love to see that."

Merrilee faced once more toward the storm, and the sound of her weeping was lost in the wind.

* * *

Over the next two days, Tuck rapidly gained strength, and the sunscald diminished greatly. With the help of others to see for him, Tuck hobbled on crutches along the corridors. Too, he would sit in his room with his broken foot propped up and chat with visitors. And many came to see him: Galen, Igon, Laurelin, Brega, Gildor, Flandrena, Ubrik, numerous warriors of the Legion, and, of course, the Warrows. To all Tuck seemed of good cheer, and he spoke at length with each of them. Yet those who knew him best—Merrilee, Patrel, Galen, Gildor, Laurelin, even Brega—could see that Tuck was given to long lapses of deep introspection, and they spoke softly among themselves, voicing their concern for the Woody Hollow buccan; yet none knew of aught to do.

On the eighth day of the blizzard, the wind diminished somewhat, and the snow slackened to the point where dim shapes could be seen across the courtyards. Though the storm still raged, Legionnaires could now guide themselves without the aid of Brega. The spirits of many began to climb, for they speculated that the great angry tempest hammering upon the land out of the distant Boreal Sea was at last coming to an end. The crossness of the past few days began to melt away, and once again the talk was bright when Legionnaires grouped together.

All of the Warrows had gathered in Tuck's room, to sit and chat and speculate on how soon it would be ere the journey homeward would begin. Eventually the talk turned to the Winter War and the Struggles. And as is the wont of warriors everywhere, they began to tell stories of combat and danger, of heroism and hardship, and of feats both fearsome and foolish. And, too, as is also the wont of warriors, the Warrows laughed in one minute and grew sober the next and frequently talked all at once or fell into long silences. Yet at other times there were moments of unbearable poignancy.

"Ar . . . the worst part of being snowed in here," said Teddy Proudhand, "is the food—nothing but gruel, crue, hard bread, and tea."

There was a general murmur of agreement, but Tuck said, "Hold on there, at least we've now got the gruel, the bread, and the tea. When King Galen and I trekked from Weiunwood to Arden, all we had was crue and water."

Several Warrows groaned in sympathy, and a sharp laugh came from Patrel. "Hoi, you're right, Tucker. Let me tell you about the time in the abandoned town of Stonehill in the empty White Unicorn Inn when all that we had to eat was our crue with some leeks found by Danner . . ." Patrel's voice dropped into silence, and his green eyes clouded with tears. Without saying another word he arose and stepped to the fire and stood with his back to the others and stared into the depths of the flames.

For long moments silence reigned in the room, and then, to break the sad mood upon them all, Burt Arboran said, "Ar, Tuck, tell us about cuttin' the Gargon's leg. Be this the sword you used? What did you say as its name was?" Burt picked up the long-knife in its worn leather sheath.

"It is called Bane," responded Tuck, clearing his throat and wiping his cheeks with the heel of one hand.

Burt grasped the hilt and pulled the blade from the scabbard. "Oi!" exclaimed the buccan. "Does it always glow blue like this?" A cobalt flame flickered along the edges of the sword.

"Blue?" exclaimed Tuck. "Is it glowing? Does the blade jewel burn with an inner fire?"

Forgetting that Tuck could not see, Burt nodded, bobbing his head up and down, but Merrilee quickly said, "Yes, Tuck! The jewel is lit. The blade flames, too."

"Someone get Lord Gildor," snapped Tuck, "and King Galen. And hurry! Evil is about."

The voices of warriors and the rattle of arms and the jingle of armor sounded from the hall. Princess Laurelin and Merrilee stood as King Galen, Lord Gildor, and Brega came wearily into the room.

"Nought," said Galen, removing his gauntlets and dropping tiredly into a chair. "Though the Legion has searched high and low throughout this holt, still we've found nought." He turned a questioning eye toward Gildor.

"Evil is here, Galen King," said the Elf. "Both Bane and Bale whisper of it."

"Do they glimmer because this fortress itself is vile?" asked Tuck from his chair by the fire.

"Ah, nay, Wee One," answered Gildor. "Only to living evil will the blade-jewel glow, usually to creatures who are of the Untargarda—Ruch, Lok, Troll, Ghûlk, and the like—though now and again the gems will respond to a vile being of Mithgar . . . the Hèlarms, some Dragons . . ."

"Arr," growled Brega, sitting cross-legged on the floor, "no matter how long the list of foul things these blades can warn of, King Galen has said it: we found nought, though we searched high and low."

"The dungeons under the tower?" Laurelin's voice was strained. "When I was held within a cell there, a creature, a monster of the dark . . ." The Princess shuddered and stared into the fire.

Galen reached out and took her hand. "Aye, my Lady, we strode by torchlight through that most vile of pits. If ever a place could be said to be evil . . ." Galen's voice trailed off, and his lips pressed grimly into a thin line.

Silence reigned for a moment, then: "At the deepest level, the passages issue into a labyrinth of caverns," said Lord Gildor, "branching off in a myriad of directions. These we did not search, for they are dark and bodeful. I did not like their look, nor did I wish to tread them. Too, any mind mayhap would get lost in their twisting ways to never again come to the light of day."

"There you are not correct, Elf Gildor," objected Brega. "Neither I nor any Dwarf would get lost in any cavern. Even so, I agree with you on one point: I would not freely set foot in that foul place under, for it is a Squam grot. . . And now I know why it is said that the Utruni detest the Grg, for there below I saw how the Squam defile the living stone itself. But think you upon this thought: mayhap the blades glow because one or two Ukhs escaped and now hide in that abomination beneath."

Again silence fell upon the room, and about the dungeons no more was said, though the grim looks upon the faces of those who had been there spoke volumes.

Again there came from the hallway the sound of approaching soldiery, and Patrel, Igon, and Flandrena came into the room as other warriors of the Legion continued on down the passage.

Galen glanced up at Igon, and the Prince shook his head. "Fruitless," said the youth. "We found nought in the entire tower but this."

Laurelin gasped as Igon handed a hideous dark helm to Galen.

"What is it?" asked Tuck, unable to see.

"I don't—" Merrilee started to say, but she was interrupted by the Princess.

"It is Modru's iron mask, Tuck," said Laurelin, unable to tear her eyes away from the grotesque helm.

Galen drew his cloak over the iron vizard, concealing it from Laurelin's view. "Nothing else?" he asked.

Igon glanced from Flandrena to Patrel. "Nothing," said the Prince.

"But wait," spoke up Tuck. "What about Modru's 'Stone knife? Wasn't it there in the tower, too?"

"No, Tuck," answered Patrel. "And I especially looked for it, too, even though you warned me that it might draw at my vision. But it wasn't there."

"Perhaps it burned up with the Myrkenstone," suggested Flandrena. "The destruction of the one could have been the ruin of the other."

"You may be right, Elf Flandrena," rumbled Brega. "And you may be wrong. But it is in my mind that whatever creature it is that causes the swords to glow mayhap has taken the 'Stone knife."

At Brega's words Tuck's heart raced in his breast, for if the Dwarf was right, another feartoken was loose in Mithgar. Would it someday fulfill its evil destiny?

That night a double guard was posted, for none knew whether evil would strike in the dark. Bane and Bale were watched closely, yet their glimmers spoke only of a distant threat that came no closer in the night. And the talk among the Men was how fiercely the Warrows themselves guarded the blind one's room.

* * *

Throughout the ninth day the fury of the storm continued to abate. The howling shriek of the wind fell to a moan and then to a murmur, and by day's end only a gentle snow wafted lightly down upon the land.

Earlier in the afternoon, warriors had been put to work clearing a path from the stables to the gate, and scouts had been sent forth upon the moor. And as darkness fell they came riding in to report that huge drifts had accumulated near every great rock and tor and swale; but out upon the flats, the fierce blast had blown the snow across the moor and it had not foregathered to any significant depth—why, in some places the land had even been scrubbed bare by the wind.

Upon hearing this news, King Galen turned to Ubrik. "What say you, Reachmarshal? Should the waning storm come to an end tonight, as it seems likely, will the Legion be ready for travel on the morrow?"

"Aye, my King," replied Ubrik, with a fierce grin. "All are eager to leave this foul place and come once more to the wide lands and open skies of Valon, where the swift horses race free o'er the clean grass."

"Then so be it," responded Galen. "If the snow stops, on the morrow we ride."

Glad shouts rose up at such news, and all prepared for the long journey home. Litters had been made for those most severely wounded, and they would be drawn slowly southward upon travoises with healers and an escort in attendance. Yet it was incumbent upon the King to go swiftly to Pellar, for much needed doing to set the Kingdom right. And so he and the bulk of the Legion would ride ahead—though they would not fare south at the grueling pace that had borne them north.

And all of the Warrows would go with the King, for none of them bore major wounds, except perhaps Tuck, and neither his broken foot nor his blindness would significantly affect his riding.

That night guards again were posted against the distant vileness whispered of by Bane and Bale, yet no evil came to pass. And just after mid of night, the snow ceased to fall. The storm had ended.

The grey light of dawn found eight Warrows gathered around three cairns set upon the moor, out before the dark fortress. With them stood Brega, Bekki's son, Dwarf warrior of the Red Hills.

"I bore them here in the blizzard," said Brega his voice low, his hood cast over his head. "Harven, Rollo, and Danner. I could not leave them within the walls of that vile place, for they were my comrades in arms. And so I laid them here beneath these stones. Brave warriors were they all—brave as any Châkka—and they strode in honor. Nothing greater can I say of anyone."

Tears ran freely down the faces of all those gathered. Tuck knelt and reached forward with a hand, and Merrilee guided it to rest upon a stone of Danner's cairn. And Tuck spoke: "Once before—oh, it seems so long ago—I knelt beside a cairn like this. And I placed my hand upon a stone and swore an oath to avenge the comrade beneath it. And you, Danner, you swore that oath, too. And we kept it, you and I, and Patrel here . . . and all the rest. For the Evil that slew Hob and Tarpy and so many others is himself now dead. But oh, my friend, I would gladly give my own life if you could but have yours back . . ."

Tuck buried his face in his hands, and great sobs

shook his frame. Brega tenderly lifted him up as if he were but a babe and bore him back toward the bridge. And weeping and leading the horse that had carried Tuck out to the cairns, so went all the Warrows—except Patrel, for the tiny buccan remained behind as the others walked back toward the fortress. And as they crossed the bridge, there came to their ears a sweet singing; and they turned at the sound, pausing, seeing a small figure in the distance standing alone in the snow before Danner's cairn. And Patrel's voice rose up into the clear early sky, but he was too distant for any to catch the words of his song.

In midmorning the Legion entire at last rode out of the fortress. Five thousand had ridden north, and but thirty-five hundred now fared south, for hundreds had fallen in battle. And among the many Men that had survived rode a Princess, two Elves, eight Warrows, and a Dwarf.

South they hammered across the wind-swept snow, leaving behind the abandoned hulk of Modru Kinstealer's holt, the hideous iron mask nailed to the wall above the gate as a mute warning to all who would follow Evil's path.

Southward they fared, day after day, the white miles lengthening out behind them as they skirted 'round the edges of enormous drifts, keeping to the wind-scrubbed flats.

Down across Claw Moor they rode, and at the end of the second day they came to Claw Gap. The following morning they struggled through great drifts to pass across the Gap River valley, for there was no way around. And when they had won beyond that barrier, onward they pressed along the eastern margin of Gron. Past the great Gwasp

they rode to come to the long treeless barrens
wedged between the Rigga Mountains and the
Gronfangs.

Late on the eighth day they came to the north
end of Grūwen Pass, where they pitched camp.
And among the drifts they found scattered heaps
of Rūcken armor, as if a great battle had ended
here.

Dawn of the ninth day found the Legion pressing through Grūwen Col; and time and again they
rode past the frozen bodies of slain Men and Elves,
half buried in the snow, the blue and white of
Wellen and the Eld-Tree flags of Arden Vale proclaiming the identity of the dead. Here too lay a
cluttered splay of empty Rūcken armor and shattered scimitars and broken stags bearing a scarlet
ring of fire on an ebon field: the windtattered
standard of the Evil One, who was no more.

Past the rimed carnage and frigid litter of War
they rode, now and again breasting through icy
drifts; and it was late in the stary night when at
last they came down out of the frozen pass to
make camp in the Land of Rhone. Few, if any, spoke
of the bitter sights they'd seen this day. And neither
Lord Gildor nor Flandrena came to take a meal at
the fire; instead they stood at the edge of the night
and stared out across the bleak moonlit snow.

Just ere noon of the tenth day, as the weary
Legion wended along the northernmost flank of
Arden Bluff, one of the forward scouts galloped
back toward the Host, and *lo!* riding with him
came Elf Lord Talarin and Hrosmarshal Vidron.
And as the scout turned and again bore off to the
fore, the Lord and the Marshal reined their steeds
in a wide arc to come alongside Galen, matching
their pace to that of Wildwind.

"My King!" hailed Vidron, striking a clenched fist to his heart, a great smile beaming out from his silver beard. "Good news from the south: the War there is ended! We have won!"

Galen put his face in his hands, and long moments passed ere he looked up again.

"*Kel*, Galen King," said Talarin, his manner somber. "My eyes are glad to see you, yet my heart grieves for the dead."

"Aye," replied Galen, "many have fallen in this struggle against Evil. Yet it is finished at last."

At that moment Prince Igon thundered up on Rust, and in his wake rode Gildor and Flandrena and Reachmarshal Ubrik.

"Hai, Vidron!" cried the young Man, happy to see the warrior; and then, more gravely: "Hál, my Lord Talarin."

In response to the exuberance of youth, a brief smile flickered across the features of Talarin, and he nodded to the Prince; and the Elf's eyes sought those of Gildor and Flandrena as the Lian warriors and Ubrik joined the small foregathering. And they looked upon one another and were glad. And the talk turned to the ending of the War.

Yet Vidron raised in his stirrups and twisted to look back along the column bearing southward. But his searching gaze saw not what he sought, and, settling back into his saddle, he turned to Galen. "Sire, I must ask: the Lady Laurelin . . ."

"She is well, General Vidron," replied Galen. "She rides behind the vanguard in the company of Warrior Brega and the Wee Ones."

"Hai!" barked Vidron, a fierce grin upon his face. "And the Waldana how fare they?"

"Three were slain, and Tuck was blinded," answered Galen. "Your Danner was one who fell."

Vidron turned his eyes out over the snow, and

for long moments only the sound of hooves was heard. Then Talarin cleared his throat. "As you have said, Galen King, many have fallen in this struggle against Evil."

They rode along without speaking for a time, then again Talarin spoke, the Elf gesturing at the glittering brightness. "Once you pledged to bring the Sun back unto the world, and so you have, yet I pray that the price you paid to do so was not as heavy as the cost we bore in Kregyn."

"Our burden was most heavy—as was yours," responded Galen, his mind casting back beyond the trailing Legion and up into the frozen reaches of the mountains where lay Grūwen Pass, called Kregyn by the Elves. "We saw the signs of the brunt you bore."

"Long we held them," rumbled Vidron. "Yet each 'Darkday they hammered us deeper into the Pass. At last they drove us through, and we were trapped. As they mounted their final charge, a great blackness fell. But then, *whoosh!* the Dimmendark was gone! And they fell to Adon's Ban."

"But wait!" cried Galen in amaze. "That means you held them for . . ."

"Five 'Darkdays," interjected Vidron. "We held them five 'Days. Fifteen hundred Wellenen and five hundred Lian—"

"Against *ten thousand Spaunen!*" exclaimed Galen.

"Hai!" cried Igon. "This will be a saga the bards and tale-tellers will chant for ages to come."

Talarin nodded. "Aye, long will the harpers sing of Kingsgeneral Vidron, the Whelmer of Modru's Horde, for indeed it is a mighty tale. Yet let them not forget to sing of those heroes who did not ride away from the field when the battle was ended."

At last the fore of the long column of the Host

had ridden nearly to the concealed entrance to Arden Vale. "Come," said Talarin. "Lead your weary Legion down into the Hidden Refuge to spend some days of quiet and rest. We have warm shelter and hot food and drink. And as you pause, you can speak to us your tale, for we would hear how you brought about the downfall of the Dimmendark."

As Ubrik raised his black-oxen horn to his lips and signalled unto the column, Galen said, "Ah, but it was not I who vanquished the Shadowlight, Lord Talarin. Instead it was Tuck who loosed the shaft that slew the 'Stone and freed the light to destroy Modru and hurl Gyphon back beyond the Spheres. It was Tuck who caused the collapse of the Dimmendark and returned the Sun unto the world to whelm the Spawn. Aye, it was Tuck and none else who did this thing, and we did but help the Waerling along his fateful course."

And as Talain and Vidron listened in wonder to Galen's words, they led the Legion toward the bluff to ride through the hidden tunnel and down into Arden Vale.

Rael held a polished crystal in her fingers and peered through it and into Tuck's eyes. Behind her the light of a single candle shone over her shoulder, casting a dim glow within the darkened room. Long she looked, first into one eye and then into the other. And no one spoke. At last she stepped back and gave a sign, and window curtains were thrown open to let vivid sunlight stream through and fall upon the buccan sitting in the chair. As Rael continued her examination, watching the reaction of the Waerling's eyes to the brightness, Talarin continued a conversation he and Tuck had started earlier.

"And so," said the Elf Lord, "had Gyphon come

to rule in Mithgar, the power would have swung to Him."

"King Galen once told me that Mithgar was like the fulcrum of a teeter-totter," responded Tuck.

"Aye, Tuck," answered Talarin, "although I had never thought of it in that light, Galen is correct. And as it is with any teeter-totter, at the critical moment, when the powers are within balance, the slightest impulse one way or the other can shift the equipoise for good or for ill.

"Such was the case with you, Tuck, for you tipped the balance, but the force you used was by no means slight ... by any measure. For you see, although four thousand years apast Gyphon set into motion events none could stop, so too must have Adon started His own plan—and tokens of power were created upon Mithgar to find their way unto the Iron Tower for use at the critical moment.

"And you, Tuck, chose and were chosen to follow the course that would bring you to Modru's evil sanctum in that darkest moment of the darkest hour, where you could shift the balance away from Evil and toward Good, away from Gyphon and toward Adon."

Tuck seemed lost in thought. "Lord Talarin, this I have wanted to ask: Gyphon was so beautiful when I first saw Him, but then He changed to something ghastly. How can that be? How can it be that One so vile can be so fair to the eye?"

"Evil often comes with a fair face, Tuck," replied Talarin. "But beneath it all is a hideous monster."

Again Tuck seemed lost in thought. "There is something else that is puzzling me, Lord Talarin: In the moments just before I shot the Myrkenstone, Rael's rede and the inscription from the tomb of Othran the Seer came into my mind:

> *'Neither of two Evils must thy strike claim;*
> *Instead smite the Darkness between the same.'*

> *Loose not the Red Quarrel*
> *Ere appointed dark time.*

Now, in hindsight, the rede is clear: it told me to shoot the Myrkenstone instead of either Gyphon or Modru. But the tomb inscription still has me mystified. I thought it meant for me to shoot at *any* time during the Sun-Death, but I couldn't seem to loose that red arrow until Modru's chanting was ended. And I *knew*, as if someone compelled me so, that I had to shoot *then*. Why couldn't I shoot before? I mean, the Lady Laurelin was nearly slaughtered by my delay. Yet I did not, *could* not, shoot till the chanting stopped."

In the silence that followed, Rael stood and turned and stepped to the window and looked toward the distant pines. Merrilee, who had sat quietly during the examination, went to sit by Tuck's side, taking him by the hand. "Perhaps, Tuck," said the Elf Lord, then paused, "perhaps it was only *after* the incantation was completed that the Myrkenstone was vulnerable, open to attack. Mayhap *that* was the *appointed dark time* spoken of by Othran the Seer ages agone." Again silence fell.

Rael continued to gaze out o'er the sparkling snow, and in the stillness her voice spoke softly: "Tuck, say again how the Myrkenstone affected your vision."

"Well, when we first saw the black light streaming from the tower it *wrenched* at all of our eyes," responded Tuck, "all of the Warrow eyes, that is, for no other Folk could see it—not Man nor Dwarf nor even Elf. But the Wee Folk, we knew it was bad from the very beginning . . . yet none of us knew just how bad.

"When I first crawled into the room atop the tower where lay the Myrkenstone, it *trapped* my eyes: I couldn't look away from it. And my vision began to dim, to fade; and if Gyphon hadn't come, hadn't *pulled* my gaze to Him, I think I would have lost all my sight then and there.

"But He did come, and I looked away from the 'Stone, first to Him and then to Laurelin and Modru. And I took up the Red Quarrel and set it to my bow. When I looked back at the Myrkenstone to shoot it, well, it took away the last of my vision. I could see nothing at all: My sight had been devoured by that terrible maw.

"I must have been looking right at the 'Stone when I shot it. And only in the unbearable glare of its burning did I have vision once more.

"And when the glare was gone, I was blind."

Tuck fell silent a moment, then said in a low, halting voice, "My last sight . . . was of an unendurably hideous monster . . . falling . . . falling into a pit beyond conception. If one is to . . . to lose his sight, he should last see something of beauty . . . a flower, perhaps . . ."

Merrilee squeezed Tuck's hand as Rael turned from the window to face the buccan. "I do not know what caused the damage to your eyes, Tuck. Whether it was the strange black radiance of the Myrkenstone—as seems most likely—or whether it was the furious blare of the 'Stone's destruction, I cannot say. But this I do know: your affliction is not unlike that of snow blindness . . . but I fear it is permanent." Rael paused, her eyes filled with a great sadness. "You had brought the Sun back to Mithgar may never again see the light of day."

Merrilee drew in a great sob of air, and she wept

bitterly. Tuck drew her into his arms and stroked her hair and soothed, "Don't cry, my dammia. There's no need to cry. I may not live to see the Sun, but I can feel it on my face."

And Talarin and Rael quietly went from the room, leaving behind a blind buccan holding a weeping damman while sitting in a pool of golden sunlight.

A week fled quickly, and well the Legion rested, gaining in strength and haleness from the Elven provender. And in the quiet vale, spirits were renewed. Yet there was no celebration, for the Lian moved in a state of deep mourning. Although the number of their War-dead did not match that of the Men, still nearly half of the Elven warriors of Arden Vale had fallen in battle. And for a people said to be immortal, Death strikes an especially onerous blow. For with these Folk the Dark Reaper does not cut life short by a mere few years—instead an uncounted span of eras is lost.

On the seventh day the train of those wounded at the Iron Tower at last arrived from Gron, and they, too, were taken into the Hidden Refuge.

Their arrival seemed to be a signal to High King Galen: he would now fare south, and most of the Legion would go with him, for, as he told the council, "There is much to be done: The Realm is to be set aright, and I am needed in Pellar.

"Yet this also I say: I would that the Wellenen form an escort and return the Waerlinga unto the Land of the Thorns, for the Wee Ones have given more than any could ask, especially Tuckerby Underbank. None can ever repay him for the deeds he has done, for we owe him a debt beyond measure. Yet this is the way we will begin: Men shall come to help rebuild the Bosky, and Tuck's will be the first home restored. But that will not be all, for the Crown shall ever remember our obligation unto him, and he will want for nought.

"Now, if the Legion stands ready, we shall fare forth on the morrow."

Thus it was decided: Tuck and the other Warrows and the surviving Wellenen would strike west for the Boskydells while the Legion would fare south toward Valon, and beyond to Pellar.

But Brega—stubborn Brega—would not go with the Legion, for the Dwarf refused to mount a horse. "Hmph! Ride a horse? Nonsense!" grumbled Brega. "The War is over, and the only mount I will now sit astraddle is a pony. The Legion may ride south in haste upon their great beasts, but as for me, I will make my way back to the Red Hills at my own pace upon the back of a sensible steed—if any can be found. And if not, well then I will walk."

No amount of debate, no logic of argument, would sway the obstinate Dwarf from his decision: he would ride a pony or walk, nothing else would do. And the High King would not ask him to act otherwise, for although Galen did not know why Brega had taken this stand, still he respected the Dwarf's wishes.

In the end, a pony was located and given over to Brega. On the morrow the Dwarf would set out south for his beloved Red Hills, and with him would go Flandrena upon Swiftmane, keeping Brega company; for beginning with their mission to climb the walls of the dark fortress, the Dwarf and the Elf had become fast friends.

As for Lord Gildor, he would remain behind in Arden Vale for a while, for he too knew the healing art, and he would serve the wounded.

Thus were the Deevewalkers to be sundered, each

to answer a calling of his own. On the morrow they would bid their farewells.

The dawn came bright and clear. The Legion stood ready to depart. So, too, stood the Warrows in the company of the Wellenen. Brega held the reins of a small grey pony, and at the Dwarf's side was Flandrena. Talarin, Rael, and Gildor stood before an assembly of Lian, and they faced Tuck and Patrel and Merrilee, and Igon, Laurelin, and High King Galen. And behind the King stood Vidron and Ubrik.

And the three Elves—sire, dam, and son—stepped forward to say their farewells, clasping hands and embracing these most honored guests.

"Fare thee well, Lady Rael," said Laurelin as they embraced. "You came to me and gave me comfort in my gravest hour of need, and drew forth my spirit from a dark place where it had fled. Those days in Gron I shall strive to forget, but I shall always remember your gentle love."

The Lady Rael kissed Laurelin and held her at arm's length, and they smiled one upon the other, and it was like unto the Sun looking upon the Moon, so fair were they.

Gildor came to Tuck and knelt and embraced him. And when Tuck once agan tried to return Bane to the Elf Lord, Gildor said, "Nay, Tuck, it is for you and yours to keep forever."

Gildor then turned to Patrel. "When we were together in Challerain Keep, Wee One, and I heard you strum the lute, I knew that you could master the harp, too. And so I resolved that if we both survived the War, I would give you this." Gildor gave over to Patrel a finely wrought, black Elven harp with glistening argent strings. "It was mine when I was a youth, and I would that it be yours, now. Small it is, yet it will fit your reach, and the sound of its music is as sweet as the pure air."

Patrel took the gift and held it reverently, and a gentle vagrant zephyr caused a faint humming in the sheening web of silver. "Oh, my Lord Gildor, how can I ever take such a priceless gift? It deserves the sure hand of a master and not the clumsy fingers of a fumblewit."

Gildor laughed. "Fumblewit you are not, Patrel, else none of the Legion would have entered Modru's dark citadel. Yours was the quick wit that fooled the Troll at the portcullis, and caused him to use his own hand to fling up the grille. Nay, Patrel, take the harp—did I not say you could master it? I give you my word."

As Gildor and Patrel laughed together, Rael came to Merrilee, and the black-haired damman turned her sapphirine gaze up into the deep blue eyes of the Elfess. "Merrilee Holt," said Rael, smiling, "ever will I remember the 'Day I first met you, a gentle lady among warriors riding to battle. Tales will be told of your great courage and skill, long after the deeds of many of us are forgotten. Yours is a story most rare and beautiful—as are you yourself. Fare you well, Merrilee Holt, bright spirit."

A tear slid down Merrilee's cheek as she and Rael embraced; never again would the damman feel awkward in the company of anyone.

Talarin and Vidron gripped the forearms of one another in the clasp of Harlingar warriors. "We fought well together, you and I," said Vidron.

"An, yes," replied Talarin, "but I would that we never have to do so again."

Brega too, bade his farewells, brief to all but a few. Long did he speak to Tuck and Gildor and Galen, but what he said is not recorded. Yet when he came to Igon, these were his words: "My Prince, were it not for you, none of us would be standing here today. Yours was the strength that kept us from falling, there in that black ravine. And atop the walls, you were a mighty warrior. Should ever there come a time you are in need, send for Brega Bekki's son, and I will come to your side."

At last Talarin stood before all and held up his hands, and when quiet fell o'er the assembly, he spoke: "Galen King, now you prepare to leave our peaceful vale, for much needs doing to set the Realm right again. Yet hearken: when last you came to Arden, the world was plunged into darkness, and Evil beset us all. But now the days are bright once more, and yours was the Crown to bring this wonder about. Oh, aye, it is true that you did not do it alone, but no one ever does. And it is also true that there are many heroes here among this Company—and one special hero. Yet let us not forget those who fell upon distant battlefields, for they, too, heroes all, helped to achieve this victory—helped to return the miracle of light unto the world.

"We bid you farewell, Galen King, as well as those who set forth with you. May all who leave here find peace and happiness at journey's end."

Talarin fell silent, and now Galen took Tuck by the hand and led him to a dais, the buccan hobbling with the aid of a cane. And they stood together for all to see. And the High King spoke: "My Lord Talarin, all you have said is true: All of those who struggled against Evil are indeed heroes, and many fell in battle. Heed me: they shall not be forgotten.

"Too, this War was filled with the brave acts of many—some deeds of which we will never know.

"It is also true that none of us could have survived without the aid of others, many of whom now lie slain. And so I say that each of us who strove for Good can take great pride in our victory, no matter how large or how small our contribution.

"Yet there is one among us whose path led him straight to the destruction of Evil—and all of the rest of us but aided him along his way."

And now the High King of all Mithgar did an unprecedented thing: he knelt upon one knee in high homage to a Waerling of the Land of the Thorns. And so, too, did all the assembled warriors of the Legion, as well as the Lian. And the only ones left standing were the Warrows of the Boskydells.

And King Galen cried, "All hail Tuckerby Underbank, Hero of the Realm!"

And thrice a great shout burst forth from the assembled throng: *Hál! . . . Hál! . . . Hál!*

Tuck stood a long moment without speaking as the last echoes rang forth through the pines. His great blue eyes gazed unseeing out beyond the Men and Elves, the Warrows, and the Dwarf. At last Tuck spoke, and his voice was filled with emotion: "Cheer for yourselves, brave warriors, for had any of you been thrust along the path that I trod, you would have done as well or better than I." And Tuck raised his voice in praise, and he was joined by all: *Hál! . . . Hál! . . . Hál!*

And as the last shout cleft the air, Galen stood, and so did the throng. Merrilee rushed to Tuck and led him limping back to the waiting Warrows. And Brega was overheard to grumble, "I will not reach the Red Hills with my feet stuck here in Arden. Are you ready, Elf Flandrena?" At Flandrena's nod, Brega mounted his small grey pony, and Flandrena vaulted to the back of Swiftmane. And leading a packhorse, the two set out.

As if that were a signal to all, Galen signed to

Ubrik, and the Reachmarshal raised his black-oxen horn to his lips, and its resonant call pealed forth and was answered in kind by the horns of Valon.

So, too, sounded the calls of the clarions of the Wellenen. The Warrows were lifted to the backs of horses, and all of those departing mounted up as well.

And, amid the knells of horns and shouted good-byes, slowly the cavalcade went forth, the pace quickening as the warrior companies fell into a long column faring southward. Swiftly they over-took Brega's plodding pony, leaving the Dwarf and Flandrena in their wake. And onward rode the great long train, through the pines along the banks of the River Tumble down through the Vale of Arden.

And as they rode, a southerly breeze sprang up— redolent with an earthern smell, scented with the promise of new life. And the step of the horses grew light and spirited.

It was the first day of spring.

Two days the column fared south, and on the morning of the third day the travellers departed from their camp near the Lone Eld Tree and passed through the hidden way under the waterfall and out into the Land of Rell.

Soon they came to the Crossland Road, and here the Wellenen turned west to follow the road while the Harlingar continued south, striking for the old abandoned trade road through Rell, for they had reached the parting of the ways: the Warrows to be escorted to the Land of the Thorns, while the High King's entourage fared to Pellar.

Yet ere they parted, sad farewells were said as damman and buccan embraced Man and Woman, and they kissed one another, and then it was time to go. Yet Laurelin whispered into Galen's ear, and the High King turned to Tuck and Patrel.

"I am told that Aurion, my sire, commanded that until he personally recalled it, the Dwarf-made armor you now wear was to remain in your hands or in the possession of those you would trust." Galen's eyes turned to the west and north toward distant Rian, where lay Challerain Keep and his slain father. And he raised his voice so that all could hear: "Hearken unto me as I reaffirm the command of my sire: unless the shade of King Aurion recalls it, the armor is yours—silveron for Tuck, gilt for Patrel, and in the northern Wastes of Gron, black for Danner Bramblethron."

West went the Wellenen; south, the Harlingar. And as the columns parted and drew nearly beyond the sight of one another, Patrel took the argent Horn of the Reach from his saddlebag. He set the clarion to his lips, and a silver call split the air. And from the distant Harlingar came the answering sound of black-oxen horn. And then the two columns passed beyond the seeing of one another.

In midafternoon the Wellenen crossed the Tumble River at Arden Ford, passing from Rell into Rhone. The ford was still frozen, trapped under a sheet of ice, though here and there dark pools swirled where the chill grip of winter had begun to break.

That night the company camped within the eastern margin of the Drearwood. And Captain Falk set a double picket of Wellenen about the camp, saying, "We are in Drearwood, a place of ill repute of old. Here we will stand a double ward, for mayhap not all of the Spawn lie slain. Only those Wrg caught in the sunlight died the Withering Death. Those who perhaps were hidden in caverns and bolt-holes would not have fallen to Adon's Ban. And it is said that this dire wood harbors such places for the Spawn to escape the light of day. Hence, double guard, double caution, for I would deliver my charges safely unto their homes."

The next two days found the column pressing west through Rhone, spending the nights camped alongside the Crossland Road, still within the bounds of Drearwood. But early on the following day, the company crossed the Stone-arches Bridge over the River Caire to ride out of Rhone and into the Wilderland, caught between Rian to the north and Harth to the south; they had left the Drearwood behind.

Onward they rode, each day faring thirty miles or more, passing through the Wilderness Hills and across the open land north of the Wilder River, journeying through the Signal Mountains, where the Crossland Road skirted the northern flank of Beacontor.

The road then led them to the upper margins of the Bogland Bottoms, faring forty miles or so along its length, and here peat moss was gathered for the campfires.

On the eleventh day of travel, late in the evening, the column came to the rock wall surrounding Stonehill. Up to this bulwark rode the company, coming to a halt before the east gate. The barrier was closed.

"Who goes?" rang out a voice in sharp challenge.

"We are the Kingsmen of Wellen," called Captain Falk. "We escort the Heroes of the Iron Tower, and I ask that you give us shelter for the night—and hot food and drink for us all, if you can spare it."

"Don't you move none," called back the voice. "Just stand where you are till we fetch our Captain."

Minute after minute eked by, and the Men and horses grew restless, but at last a light could be seen atop the wall—a lantern held high in the grip of a Man, the yellow glow casting out to reveal the fore of the warrior column, the remainder of the Wellenen receding into the shadows before the gate and but dimly seen by the light of the half Moon.

"Here now," called down the Man, "just who did you say you were, and what's all this about Heroes of the Iron Tower?"

Although Tuck could see nought, still he recognized the voice of the speaker. "Hoy, Mr. Brewster!" called the buccan to the Captain of the Men of the Weiunwood Alliance. "It's me: Tuck . . . Tuckerby Underbank!"

Bockleman shielded his eyes from the lantern light as Tuck was led forward upon his steed. "Lor bless me!" cried the innkeeper. "Is it truly you, Master Tuck? . . . Well, so it is!" The Man turned to someone unseen by the escort. "Here now, Bill, open the gate straight away. These folks are alright if Master Tuck is with 'em."

As the heavy grind of the withdrawing gate bar grumbled forth, Bockleman turned back and called down to Tuck: "I did not expect you to come ridin' in with an escort of a couple hundred soldiers and all, Master Tuck. We can't be too careful hereabout these days. We're still on a War footing, you know, even though that awful Dimmendark and such seems to be gone. I mean, the Evil in Gron might be trying to fool us, I shouldn't wonder."

"Nay, Mr. Brewster," called back Tuck, "the Evil in Gron is no more: Modru is dead. The Winter War is ended."

Bockleman's eyes flew wide at these tidings. "Hoy! Now there's a good piece of news that I never thought to hear. Modru is dead! Well now, we'd got

the word that the War in the south was won, but
this is the first that we've heard of the Evil One.
And better tidings we couldn't have hoped for!"

The gate swung open, and Men with bows and
pikes could be seen, gathered to repel invaders if
need be. "Bring in your company, Master Tuck,"
called Bockleman. "I can't put you all up at the
Unicorn, but perhaps other folk in the 'Hill can
spare a bed or so, and stables . . . and even a warm
bite or two."

Slowly the column filed into the cobbled ways
of Stonehill, and as the last of the Wellenen rode
through, the gate was once again barred, for, as
Bockleman said, "Though the War is done, and
Adon's Ban rules the day, still it is night and we
can't be too careful of the Rūcks and such that
might be about."

The residents of Stonehill opened their hearts
and homes to the company. All of the Warrows
and many of the Men were put up at the White
Unicorn, and the stables were filled with their
steeds. The rest of the Wellenen were taken into
private dwellings. And all were fed.

At the White Unicorn the food was hot and the
ale was good, and stories of combat and War were
traded back and forth. And only Patrel seemed
withdrawn as he sat in a corner by the fire and
stared deeply into the flames. Merrilee quietly took
him a mug of ale and gently asked him if he felt
well, and the wee buccan replied, "I was just re-
membering the last time I was in the Unicorn."
And Merrilee reached out and took his hand and
squeezed it, a tear sliding down her cheek for lost
Danner.

All the next day the company rested in Stonehill,
but the dawn of the following day found the col-

umn once again ready to set forth upon the Crossland Road.

"Well, Master Tuck," said Bockleman as he stood beside the mounted buccan, "there's much you've told us that will live long in the hearthtales of the Stonehillers. And your name will stand at the top of the list of the Heroes of the Winter War.—Here now, don't you go gainsaying me, for without you we'd all be slaves of the Evil One, or some such thing I shouldn't wonder. And we're sorry that you had to lose so much—you bein' blind and all—but we're glad that folks like you stood up to Evil and won. And remember this: the hands of the Big Folk and the Wee Folk of Stonehill—and I'm sure of Arbagon's Wee Folk of the Weiunwood beyond—will always be open to you."

Tears glistened in Bockleman's eyes as he looked up at the blind buccan, and the innkeeper took out a great kerchief from his pocket and noisily blew his nose and wiped his eyes. Then he said, "Go on with you, now, Master Tuck. The Boskydells are waiting. And if you don't hurry and leave, I'm going to make a fool of myself crying before my Men."

Captain Falk signalled to one of the Wellenen, and the call of a clarion sounded. And slowly the column set forth, hooves ringing on hard cobblestones as the company rode toward the west gate; then out along the dirt dike they went, riding to the Crossland Road. And behind, Stonehillers cheered and waved. And Bockleman Brewster turned and went into the inn, and the sign of the White Unicorn squeaked in the breeze behind him.

Two days they fared, camping south of the Battle Downs the first night and then in the margins of Edgewood. And mid of morning of the third day they came to the great Spindlethorn Barrier. They rode through the thorn tunnel to come to the bridge over the Spindle River, where Thornwalker buccen opened the way to pass the column through.

West they journeyed, and in early afternoon they came to the town of Greenfields. Here Patrel with an escort of Wellenen was to turn south, heading for the East Ford, and Bryn, and beyond to his home near Midwood. Ere parting company, Patrel clasped hands with each of the buccen. He embraced Tuck and Merrilee, and the damman kissed him upon the cheek.

"I will come to Woody Hollow to visit you," said the wee buccan. "But not until my heart has rested from these grievous days—perhaps when the summer winds blow. Yet, today, be of good cheer, for after all is said and done, this is not a goodbye parting. And so I say, fare you well, until we meet once more."

In spite of Patrel's words, there were tears in Merrilee's eyes and a lump in Tuck's throat when Patrel and his escort fared forth down the Bryn Road. And just before he passed beyond seeing, the silver call of the Horn of the Reach drifted o'er the rolling hills.

And as the wondering citizens of Greenfields watched, the remaining Wellenen set out along the Crossland Road, striving for Raffin, where they spent the night.

The next day, westward fared the column, and at points along the way other buccen turned aside, one at a time, to journey with escort to their homes—Dink Weller, Arch Hockley, Burt Arboran, Dill Thorven, and Teddy Proudhand—some heading north and some south as the company rode west along the Crossland Road through Tillok and Willowdell and beyond. And everywhere the cavalcade passed, Wee Folk gathered and wondered who these Warrows were, and what they had done to ride high upon the backs of big horses and to be convoyed by a cavalry of Men.

It was late afternoon when the Wellenen turned north along Byroad Lane to ride through the burntout hamlet of Budgens. Still, the village was not abandoned, for tents were pitched alongside the charred remains as the citizenry prepared to rebuild their homes and places of trade. One tent even had a sign set before it—*The Blue Bull*—proclaiming the intentions of the owner of that Boskydell pub to reconstruct his tavern.

Beyond Budgens and along Woody Hollow Road they fared, plashing through Rill Ford and wending toward their goal. And as dusk fell, the escort crossed the bridge above the Dingle-rill to come into the town of Woody Hollow.

Up past the Commons they rode, Market Square and then Town Square on their left. And Warrows came forth to watch in silence as they passed. On up through the coomb they rode, soon to come to the wooded swale up at Hollow End. Yet they plodded beyond the curving lane to The Root—for Tuck's home, Tuck's burrow, had been burned by Modru's Reavers. Instead, the escort rode on to Merrilee's burrow, and there they stopped.

The two Wee Folk were helped down from their horses. And as the Wellenen turned to make camp in the End Field, Tuck and Merrilee moved slowly up the walk—the buccan hobbling with a cane and the damman leading him tenderly—and they went into the burrow and quietly closed the door behind. They were home at last.

And a soft warm wind blew gently from the south, and rills and streams sang with the sparkling waters of the snowmelt.

It was the fourth day of April.

CHAPTER 7

THE RAVEN BOOK

In the days following Tuck's return to Woody Hollow, winter loosed its chill grip, and spring grew into fullness and passed into summer. And free people everywhere came once more unto their homes, and the work of clearing away the rubble of War's destruction began.

And, too, across the reaches of Pellar, Valon, Jugo, and Hoven, and in Grūwen Pass and out upon the plains of Riamon, great turved mounds were raised as the dead were buried at last.

Dwarves led by Brega marched north from the Red Hills into Rell to tenderly place the slain forty upon a fitting pyre. And as the only survivor of that mighty battle with the vanguard of a Horde, Brega spoke the somber speech of the Châkka ere he fired the great bier.

Along the Battle Downs the slain of the last waggon train were laid to rest, while farther north at Challerain Keep great mounds were raised among the barrows. The Tomb of Othran the Seer was set aright, though the Atalar Blade and the Red Quarrel were now gone—yet these two tokens of power had only been held in the keep of the Seer until needed upon the face of Mithgar.

And Aurion Redeye was placed under the earth in a small barrow central to the mounds of those felled in that great opening battle of the Winter War. And above his grave a dolmen was raised bearing carven runes stating: *Aurion, who chose freedom.*

Far to the north in Gron, out before the dark citadel, a great mound was raised where the slain Harlingar were laid to rest. There too, in later years, a tomb was built above three cairns. Heavy was the stone, and dark, that made up the blocks of this monument. And three names were carven deeply in the rock. And under one of the names, another phrase was added so that the whole of it declared: *Danner Bramblethorn. King of the Rillrock.* Who built this tomb, and when, it is not told—though some say that it was the work of Dwarves.

And in the Bosky, in each of the Seven Dells, simple ceremonies were held as the fallen were returned to earth; yet many Warrow families grieved for their kith lost to War in strange and distant Lands.

And in that summer of the year two thousand and nineteen of the Fourth Era waggonloads of Men, sent by the King, came to the Bosky bearing lumber and tools and other goods to aid in the reconstruction. And true to Galen's word, the first place rebuilt was Tuckerby Underbank's Warren— The Root—made larger, more spacious, with rooms to house guests who might be Men, so high were the ceilings. And the walls were panelled with rich-grained woods: walnut, oak, cherry, and the like. Furniture, large and small, was brought in, some of it made by the wicker weavers of Bigfen and Littlefen. Tables came from Thimble and chairs from Weevin, and cloth for curtains from the village of Preece. Too, gifts were sent from Stonehill and Weiunwood, and from Wellen in the west.

And when they were finished with Tuckerby's Warren, the men went to help others rebuild houses and stores and mills and barns and other buildings destroyed in the ravage of War. All told, this work would take three years to complete, though none knew it at the outset.

On Year's Long Day—or as some would call it, Mid-Year's Day—during Fair Time, Tuckerby Underbank was married to Merrilee Holt. Fireworks filled the air, and there was great celebration, for not only was it their wedding day, but this was also the annual celebration for all who had had a birthday or an anniversary in the past year—which, of course' included everyone—especially those who had passed from one age-name to the next, as had Merrilee, going from her maiden years to those of a young damman.

In August of that year the newlyweds moved into The Root, for at long last the work was finished. There was a great home-warming party, and nearly everyone in Woody Hollow and Budgens came to see and to *ooh* and *ahh* over Tuckerby's Waren.

In September a Kingsman came to The Root, bearing a message from High King Galen, requesting the presence of Mr. and Mrs. Tuckerby Underbank at the wedding of Galen, son of Aurion, to Princess Laurelin of Riamon.

The wedding of the High King took place in the golden days of autumn. Caer Pendwyr had never before seen such pageantry and splendor. And every day in the last few weeks preceding the great event, it seemed as if some new and colorful retinue would come to the High King's holt in Pellar. Kingdoms from all corners of the world sent lavish gifts: from Gelen, Leut, Thol, Jute, Gothon, Vancha, Basq, Tugal, Alban, Hurn, and distant Lands unknown to most. And Kings, too, came by land and sea to attend the ceremonies. King Dorn of Riamon of course was there, for Laurelin was his daughter. King Aranor and Queen Alare of Valon came with a great entourage of Harlingar. Coron Eiron, sad-eyed Elf of Darda Galion, and Lord Talarin with his consort Rael came, as well as their son Gildor. And many looked on in wonder as the bright Elves and their escort came unto the castle. From Darda Erynian came Ural, a giant of a Man, Chieftain of the Baeron, and at his side was Lady Aska. Too, there came an unprepossessing Man from Stonehill, Bockleman Brewster, in the company of Elf Lord Inarion and one of the Wee Folk, Arbagon Fenner. Hrosmarshal Vidron and Reachmarshal Ubrik and other warriors too numerous to name were there. And Dwarves, too, marched into Caer Pendwyr: King Brek of Mineholt North and DelfLord Borta of the Red Hills. And in this company strode Brega Bekki's son. Additional guests came from Wellen and Trellinath and Rian and other places scattered o'er all Mithgar.

Yet it was one of the Wee Folk who drew a hush of reverent awe as he limped down the center aisle to take his place of honor, escorted on his right by a black-haired damman and on his left by a wee buccan in golden armor. Dressed in silveron mail he was, his sapphire-blue eyes staring sightlessly from a whip-scarred face. He was the Bearer of the

Red Quarrel, the 'Stone Slayer; he was Sir Tuckerby Underbank, Thornwalker, Hero of the Realm.

All that day the bells of Caer Pendwyr and of all Pellar pealed in glorious celebration, ringing in the changes, for Galen, son of Aurion, resplendent in scarlet and gold, had taken radiant Laurelin of Riamon to be his wife.

On this day, too, there came into being the Realmsmen, chosen of the High King, defenders of the Land, champions of Just Causes. For as Galen said to Tuck and Merrilee and Patrel, "Never again shall a threat such as Modru steal upon us unawares. These trusted guardians shall ward the Realms, quietly, without fanfare. Perhaps in some small measure this will give Danner's death meaning—and meaning to all those slain in the Winter War."

There was a grand ball that evening, and many came to bid their respects to Tuck. And it was only afterward that the buccan realized just how many stalwart comrades he had come to know during the War, for as he said to Merrilee that night, "I began this quest in the company of strangers, but now I find that they were my brethren all along."

Throughout that year storms had raged with unprecedented violence, as if the weather of the world had been terribly disrupted by the Dimmendark. And the winter of 4E2019 was no exception.

Yet the Winterfest of Yule was especially bright —in spite of the blizzard that raged over much of Mithgar in the north, and in spite of the freezing rain in the south. For this was to be a *special* Yuletide: The High King had decreed that Modru's downfall had marked the end of the Fourth Era, and that this Year's Start Day was the beginning of the Fifth. And everywhere, Free Folk rejoiced.

*   *   *

On January 15, 5E1, a monument was unveiled in Budgens, commemorating this village as the place where began the Struggles. It was set upon a knoll at the north end of the hamlet, and the names of the nineteen Warrows slain in the Battle of Budgens were engraved upon it. So too were Merrilee Holt's words set into the stone: *Let it be said now and for all the days hereafter that on this day the struggle began, and Evil met its match.*

The damman Thornwalker was there with Tuck, and she made a speech at the unveiling. Captain Patrel Rushlock had come all the way from his home near Midwood, and he blew a rousing call upon his silver horn, and all the gathered Warrows cheered.

A week later, before setting out from Tuckerby's Warren to return again unto his home, Patrel gave over the Horn of the Reach into Tuck's keeping, saying, "Hold it for me, my old friend, and blow it at least twice a year: Sound it on the ninth of November, for that was the day you and Hob, Tarpy and Danner, and I all set out from Woody Hollow on a quest that ended with Modru's downfall; and sound it again on the fifteenth of January, the day when we began the Struggles. Here now, I see protests springing to your lips, but heed me: there may come a time when the weather forbids travel, yet I would have this horn blown here in spite of it."

Patrel then turned to Merrilee, and she hugged him and kissed him on the cheek. "You know, Merrilee, I don't think I've ever told you this, but you were among the very best warriors in or out of the Bosky—bar none—yet you are the most gentle soul I have ever known."

With that, Patrel stepped through the studded oaken door of Tuckerby's Warren and mounted his pony and set off for his distant home.

On February the twenty-second there was a general celebration throughout the Boskydells, for that was the day that the Dimmendark had collapsed, marking the end of the Winter War. Yet in a solemn rite he would perform on this day for the rest of his life, blind Tuck was led by Merrilee down to the Rillstones, where the buccan placed a burrow-grown flower upon the center rock, the Rillrock. And there, too, upon the bank, stood Hanlo and Glory Bramblethorn, watching Tuck's quiet ceremony, for on this date their son Danner had died.

On October 12, 5E2, Merrilee Underbank was delivered of a wee damman. Black was her hair, dark as night, and when he was told of it, Tuck named her Raven. The celebration at the One-Eyed Crow lasted far into the wee hours.

Over the next few years a quiet change came over Tuck, and he seemed to slowly, gradually, withdraw from the world around him. He was not exactly embittered by his blindness, yet he seemed to feel as if he was useless—or, as Tuck put it, ". . . not pulling my weight." Only when he was playing with Raven did he seem happy—and then for but a little while. Yet even during those times he would become moody, for he could not see his own child.

Merrilee quietly, without telling Tuck, posted a letter to Galen, High King.

Three months later a special courier came to the Bosky, bearing a missive for Sir Tuckerby Underbank. With trembling hands, Merrilee took the letter from the Kingsman, and, breaking the elaborate waxed seal, she opened the crackling parchment. Taking a deep breath, this is what she read to Tuck:

Sir Tuckerby Underbank
Woody Hollow, The Boskydells

My Dear Cherished Waerling:

You have been much in my thoughts of late. My mind keeps returning to that long, grueling journey we made o'er the face of Mithgar. And I can still envision you scribing in that diary of yours by the light of the fires we kindled.

It is about your journal that I write you, for it holds the tale of the Winter War—or a part of it at least. It is a tale that needs recording, not only for scholars to study, but also for folk the world over to hear.

And that is why I am writing, for I recall a remark I once made as we spent a night in an abandoned house south of Challerain keep. There it was that I said that perhaps one day I would ask you to scribe your diary into a Waerling history of the Winter War—some day when the fighting was done.

Well, Tuck, that day has come, and I have a commission for you, if you will have it. I would that you write up your tale, and also tell the story of others who struggled in the Winter War. And when and if that work is ever done, I would have you gather other facts, other histories, other legends bearing upon Mithgar, and set them down, too.

Do not take on this task lightly, for it will take your lifetime and more, for it never will be finished since history itself is never done.

If you accept, then with the funds I have set aside I ask that you choose scholars to aid you with the gathering, reading, study, and scribing of the text.

But you, my cherished Waerling, must lead this endeavor, for I can think of no one more well-suited to the task.

> Galen, Son of Aurion,
> High King of Mithgar

Post Script: Laurelin is heavy with child, our first.

Merrilee's voice fell silent, and tears stood in the eyes of both Warrows; and it was long ere Tuck spoke: "Please pen a note to the King, my dammia. Tell him that I most graciously and humbly accept."

In the succeeding years, Raven grew from a youngling to a maiden and then to a young damman. And her hair was as black as ebony and her eyes as blue as the sea. And this beautiful damman spent her formative years in the company of scholars; and she herself worked tirelessly upon the great history of the Winter War.

Raven or one of the other scholars would read aloud to Tuck the terse handwriting from his journal, and the buccan would try to recall in full detail the events surrounding the entry, as scribes took down his words. And slowly a huge tome took form: *Sir Tuckerby Underbank's Unfinished Diary and His Accounting of the Winter War.*

Often the scholars would travel to other places, both within the Bosky and without, to speak to others concerning the events of the War. And many was the time that Tuck went on these journeys, to Stonehill and Vanar, to Challerain Keep and Arden Vale, and to Dael and Mineholt North, and to many other places. And everywhere he went, Merrilee and Raven went with him, and they were welcomed with open arms.

It was during a journey to the Cliffs in Westdell that Raven met Willen Greylock, and she knew that she'd lost her heart to this handsome buccan scholar. But a time was to pass ere she would see Willen again, for the Underbanks set forth for the Red Hills to seek out Brega who was now DelfLord of those Dwarven halls, to speak to him of the dark trek through Drimmen-deeve.

Yet Tuck, Merrilee, and Raven spent much time in Woody Hollow, too, where historians quartered in Tuckerby's Warren. And as they compiled the epic tale, often one scholar or another would marvel at how near to triumph Modru and Gyphon had come. In one of these moments, Tuck was heard to say, "Time and events are like a field of grain, each stalk producing seeds of chance that fall unto the earth. Some seeds lie fallow, while others take root and grow into reality and produce seeds of their own.

"General Vidron once said that a long string of chance had led him to rescue the Warrows during the Battle of Brackenboro. And I know that a long string of chance led me to the evil sanctum atop the Iron Tower.

"Think of how history might have differed had other events, other realities, taken root."

Willen Greylock came to The Root to work on the history, and Raven walked about with her heart singing. Soon it became apparent that Willen, too, was smitten to the core, for he and the raven-haired beauty spent long hours gazing at the stars together —and if it wasn't the stars, it was flowers, or the Moon, or ants, or an endless number of other totally fascinating things.

And Willen came to Tuck and asked for the hand

of Raven, and consent was granted. And one of the wedding gifts given to them was Tuck's original diary, and the first copy of the *Accounting of the Winter War*. As Tuck bestowed these precious books upon them, he said, "This account really ought to be called *The Raven Book*, for without Raven, it would not be what it is today."

After they were married, Willen and Raven Greylock moved to the Cliffs in Westdell.

Throughout the years, many a harper sang the deeds of the Heroes of the Winter War; yet sadly, the words and music of most of these songs never found their way onto paper. But in the Boskydells, Patrel Rushlock, a buccan bard playing a black Elven harp with silver strings, scribed two of the best-known lays:

The Loosing of the Red Quarrel

Loose not the Red Quarrel ere appointed dark time
When through the gate His beauty shines
As the portal of Evil's coming ope's
To crush the good and dash all hopes.
His beauty shields vile as Moon shields Sun.
Destiny asks, "Strike which one?"
An Evil so fair, and an Evil in iron,
High in the tower in the Wastes of Gron.
Neither of two Evils must thy strike claim;
Instead smite the Darkness between the same.
Loose then the Red Quarrel and free the light.
Loose then the Red Quarrel but lose thy sight.

The Lay of the Iron Tower

From frozen north
Comes Vile Power:

The Evil One in
The Cold Iron Tower.

His black Vulgs rave
Down through the Land;
Before their fangs
A bold few stand.

He calls the Hordes
Of evil kind;
By terror and fear
To him they bind.

The Swarms invade
To east and west.
The allies stand
To brave the test.

Dark Hordes come
Across the plains.
Many are felled;
Cold Death reigns.

Liege is slain
At the keep.
Few escape;
Many weep.

Challerain falls;
Winter is come;
Terror rules
The north Kingdom

The Hosts of the King
Are fettered in War,
As under the Mountains
Stride the Four.

The Horror is felled;
The Four win free;
To Larkenwald come:
The Land of Eld Tree.

South on the river
Ride the Four;
Then a swift gallop
To the Harlingar.

Vanadurin, Wellenen,
Fly toward the Wastes.
The Dakest Day comes;
Make all haste.

Wellenen and Elves,
Hold the way.
The Host races north
For the Darkest Day.

The Heroes come
To the Cold Iron Tower.
Nine are chosen
To assault the Power.

An arrow is loosed
With no chance at all,
Yet it fells the guard
Atop the wall.

The ravine is crossed,
The stone is climbed:
Eight go up;
One stays behind.

Under the wall
Crawls the one,

And wins to the tower
For the Death of the Sun.

The bridge is felled;
The iron teeth lift;
The strike force charges;
The horses are swift.

Swords are in
Among the Foe.
Brave friends die;
Sorrow and woe.

Darkness falls;
The Doom has come.
The Fate of the world
Depends on the one.

Through window slit
The Wee One tries;
Yet Myrkenstone
Traps Warrow eyes.

Evil chants fall
Upon his ears,
And Gyphon comes
From Beyond the Spheres.

Sped by the bow
Of the brave Wee One,
The Red Arrow is loosed
To strike the Myrkenstone.

The Myrkenstone dies
In a flare of light,
And the Wee One loses
His power of sight.

Yet Modru is slain,
And Gyphon cast below;
And the Dimmendark falls
To the Sun's bright glow.

The Hordes fall dead
By Adon's Ban.
And southward, too,
The War is won.

Many praised the victory;
Many mourned the slain;
Yet all prayed that nevermore
Would War come here again.

Yes once there was great Evil,
And darkling Shadowlight,
But thanks to many a brave one,
Outside the Sun shines bright.

These two ballads were ever popular in Mithgar, from King's halls to taverns, all across the Realm. And many a minstrel rendered them—but never so well as the wee buccan harper who always sang these lays with bright tears glistening in his viridian eyes.

In 5E35, Raven Greylock was delivered of a daughter, Robin; she was Tuck and Merrilee's first grandchild. The Underbanks travelled to the Cliffs to visit with the newest dammsel of the family. And Tuck was introduced to Willen Greylock's circle of historians, who called themselves the Raven-book Scholars. In the limestone holts of the Cliffs, these historians had begun to gather books and scrolls in what was to become one of the greatest libraries of all Mithgar ... but that would come

several years hence. At the time, the Ravenbook
Scholars were but a small circle of historians and
scribes, and their great work was to produce illu-
minated texts of Tuckerby's epic tale. Why, already they had sent a marvelous duplicate of *The
Raven Book* to the High King in Pellar, and he
cherished it.

The years fled by, and Tuck and Merrilee grace-
fully aged. Part of Tuckerby's Warren became a
museum, housing Merrilee's bow, Elven cloaks and
ropes, the silveron armor and Bane, as well as
Patrel's gilded armor and the Atalar Blade . . . and
the Horn of Valon that was still sounded regularly
on November the ninth in Woody Hollow, and on
January fifteenth in Budgens. Helms and trews,
arrows and quivers, flags and staffs, and other
accoutrements and arms and armor bedecked the
walls and rested in glass cases. Folks came from
miles around to see them.

And Tuck was content, his life a most peaceful
one—except for an occasional dream of terror from
which he would start awake in a cold sweat, his
blind eyes wide and again seeing the hideous monster Gyphon falling back into the Black Abyss
beyond the Spheres. At these times Merrilee would
hold him until the phantom of the past was dis-
pelled.

In 5E46 word came that King Galen had died
during a savage storm from the Avagon Sea that
whelmed upon the walls of Caer Pendwyr. Gareth,
eldest son of Galen and Laurelin, was now High
King. Tuck and Merrilee made the long pilgrimage
to far Pellar and stayed awhile with Laurelin, still
beautiful though she was nearing her sixty-fifth
birthday. And even though four and a half decades

had passed since the end of the Winter War, still the castle was abuzz with talk of this wee limping guest: Sir Tuckerby Underbank, the blind buccan with the whip-scarred face who had slain Modru and saved Mithgar.

At the end of the summer, the buccan and the damman journeyed back to the Boskydells. And except for an occasional trip to Stonehill, the days of their long journeys were ended.

It is told that after Galen's passing, Talarin, Rael, and Gildor rode the Twilight Ride unto Adonar. It is said that none of the three ever fully recovered from the death of Vanidor Silverbranch—especially Gildor Goldbranch, whose eyes always harbored a deep look of sadness.

It is also said that many other Lian passed unto Adonar, too, for their hearts had long held much grief for those slain in the War.

Yet whether or not these tales are true, none knows.

In the winter of 5E73, December seventeenth, to be exact, Tuck took to his bed with a cold. And as the days passed to become a week, and then another, the granther buccan sank deeper into his illness, regardless of all that could be done. He was ninety-seven at the time, and only he and Merrilee and Brega in the far Red Hills remained alive of all the mortals who had survived that epic day at the Iron Tower. Patrel, Igon, Laurelin, Ubrik, all were gone. One by one they had sailed upon the Darkling Sea to join Vidron, Aranor, Reggian, Arbagon, Bockleman, Dorn, and countless other loved ones on the endless journey 'neath the Silver Suns. And now, in spite of the healer's herbs and simples, in spite of Merrilee's tender ministrations, on this Year's End Day the flame of Tuck's life waned and flickered as his spirit was irresistibly drawn away. And though Merrilee held tightly to her buccaran's hand, she could feel the silver cord of his life slowly slipping from her frail grasp.

And as she gripped Tuck's precious hand, she did not see before her a fragile ancient Warrow; instead she looked beyond the pale translucent flesh and snow-white locks, and her eyes saw the handsome young buccan that she first had fallen in love with.

And she wept, for she knew she could not stay the hand of the Dark One.

Tuck's thready breath softly filled the room with the sound of dying, yet now and again he would murmur a few words—some in the ancient Warrow tongue.

And as the hour neared mid of night, and Merrilee laid her weary head down and wept bitter tears, she felt Tuck stroking her hair. "Do not weep, my dammia," he whispered, "I will wait for you."

Long moments passed, and his breathing grew faint, and the yellow candlelight guttered, the flame wavering, as if someone had come into the room.

Merrilee felt Tuck's grip tighten, and the buccan's sapphirine eyes flew wide. "Adon, oh Adon, you have made it so bright and beautiful," Tuck breathed. And then his voice was filled with the strength and vigor of youth, and he called out, "Hiyo! Hiyo, Danner! Wait for me!"

And then he was gone.

And Merrilee wept for her lost beloved, while down in the swale of Woody Hollow, out beneath the turning stars, horns sounded and people cheered and someone began ringing the fire gong, for it was the beginning of a new year.

The End

"But if for no other reason, Evil must be destroyed so that we can once more guide our own destinies."

Rael of Arden
January 10, 4E2019

APPENDICES

A Word About Warrows

Common among the many races of Man throughout the world are the persistent legends of Little People: Wee Folk, pixies, leprechauns, sidhe, pwcas, gremlins, cluricaunes, peris, and so forth. There is little doubt that many of these tales come from Man's true memories of the Eld Days ... memories of Dwarves, Elves, and others, hearking back to the ancient times before The Separation. Yet, some of these legends *must* spring from Man's memory of a small Folk called Warrows.

Supporting this thesis, a few fragmentary records are unearthed once in a great age, records that give us glimpses of the truth behind the legends. But to the unending loss of Mankind, some of these records have been destroyed, while others languish unrecognized—even if stumbled across—for they require tedious examination by a scholar versed in strange tongues—tongues such as Pellarion—ere a glimmering of their true significance is seen.

One such record that has survived—and was stumbled across by an appropriately versed scholar

—is *The Raven Book*; another is *The Fairhill Journal*. From these two chronicles, as well as from a meager few other sources, a factual picture of the Wee Folk can be pieced together, and deductions then can be made concerning Warrows:

They are a small Folk, the adults ranging in height from three to four feet. Some scholars argue that there seems to be little doubt that their root stock is Man, since Warrows are human in all respects—that is, no wings, horns, tails, or the like—and they come in all the assorted shapes and colors that the Big Folk, the Men, do, only on a smaller scale. However, to the contrary, other scholars argue that the shape of Warrow ears—pointed —the tilt of their bright strange eyes, and their longer life span indicate that some Elven blood is mingled in their veins. Yet their eyes do set them apart from Elvenkind: canted they are, and in that the two Folk are alike; but Warrow eyes are bright and liquescent, and the iris is large and strangely colored: amber like gold, the deep blue of sapphire, or pale emerald green.

In any case, Warrows are deft and quick in their smallness, and their mode of living makes them wood-crafty and nature wise. And they are wary, tending to slip aside when an *Outsider* comes near, until the stranger's intentions can be ascertained. Yet they do not always yield to intruders: Should one of the Big Folk come unannounced upon a group of Warrows—such as a large family gathering of Othens splashing noisily in the waters of the fen—the *Outsider* would note that suddenly all the Warrows were silently watching him, the dammen (females) and oldsters quietly drifting to the rear with the younglings clinging to them or peering around from behind, and the buccen (males) in the fore facing the stranger in the abrupt quiet. But it is not often that Warrows are taken by surprise, and so they are seldom seen in the forests and fens and wilds unless they choose to be; yet in their hamlets and dwellings they are little different from "commonplace" Folk, for they treat with *Outsiders* in a friendly manner, unless given reason to do otherwise.

Because of their wary nature, Warrows usually tend to dress in clothing that blends into the background: greys, greens, browns. And the shoes, boots, and slippers they wear are soft and quiet upon the land. Yet, during Fair Time, or at other Celebrations, they dress in bright splashes of gay, gaudy colors—scarlets, oranges, yellows, blues, purples— and they love to blow horns and strike drum, gong, and cymbal, and in general be raucous.

Some of the gayest times, the most raucous, are those which celebrate the passing from one Warrow age to another, not only the "ordinary" birthday parties, but in particular those when an "age-name" changes: Children, both male and female, up to the age of ten are called "younglings." From age ten to twenty, the males are called "striplings" and the females "maidens." From age twenty to thirty, males and females are called respectively "young buccen" and "young dammen." It is at age thirty that Warrows reach majority—come of age, as it were—and until sixty are then called "buccen" or "dammen," which are also the general names for male or female Warrows. (The terms "buccen" and "dammen" are plurals; by changing the *e* to an *a*, "buccan" and "damman" refer to just one male or female Warrow.) After sixty, Warrows become "eld buccen" and "eld dammen," and beyond the age eighty-five they are called, respectively, "granthers" and "grandams." And at each of these "special" birthday parties, drums tattoo, horns blare, cymbals clash, and bells ring; gaudy colors adorn the celebrants; and annually, on Year's Long Day, during Fair Time, bright fireworks light up the sky for all who have had a birthday or birthday anniversary in the past year—which, of course, includes everyone—but especially for those who have passed from one age-name to the next.

Once past their youth, Warrows tend to roundness, for ordinarily they eat four meals a day, and on feast days, five. As the elders tell it: "Warrows are small, and small things take a heap of food to keep 'em going. Look at your birds and mice, and look especially at your shrews: They're all busy gulping down food most of the time that they're awake. So us Wee Folk need at least four meals a day just to keep a body alive!"

Warrow home and village life is one of pastoral calm. The Wee Folk often come together to pass the day: The dammen klatch at sewings or cannings; the buccen and dammen gather at the field plantings and harvests, or at the raising or digging of a dwelling, or at picnics and reunions—noisy affairs, for Warrows typically have large families.

Within the home, at "normal" mealtimes all members of a household—be they master, mistress, brood, or servantry—flock 'round the table in one large gathering to share the food and drink, and to speak upon the events of the day. But at "guest" meals, customarily only the holtmaster, his family, and the guests come to the master's table to share the repast; rarely are other members of the holt included at that board, and then only when specifically invited by the head of the house. At meal's end, especially when "official business" is to be discussed, the younger offspring politely excuse themselves, leaving the elders alone with the visitors to deal with their "weighty matters."

Concerning the "hub" of village life, every hamlet has at least one inn, usually with good beer—some inns have the reputation of having better beer than the average—and here gather the buccen, especially the granthers, some daily, others weekly, and still others less frequently; and they mull over old news, and listen to new happenings, and speculate upon the High King's doings down in Pellar, and talk about the state that things have come to.

There are four strains of northern Warrows: Siven, Othen, Quiren, and Paren, dwelling, respectively, in burrows, fen stilt-houses, tree flets, and stone field-houses. (Perhaps the enduring legends concerning intelligent badgers, otters, squirrels, and hares, as well as other animals, come from the lodging habits of the Wee Folk.) And Warrows live, or have lived, in practically every country in the world, though at any given time some Lands host many Warrows while other Lands host few or none. The Wee Folk seem to have a history of migration, yet in those days of the *Wanderjahre* many other Folk also drifted across the face of the world.

In the time of the writing of both *The Raven Book* and *The Fairhill Journal*, most northern Warrows resided in one of two places: in the Weiunwood, a shaggy forest in the Wilderland north of Harth and south of Rian; or in the Boskydells, a Land of fens, forests, and fields west of the Spindle River and north of the Wenden.

The Boskydells, by and far the larger of these two Warrowlands, is protected from *Outsiders* by a formidable barrier of thorns—Spindlethorns—growing in the river valleys around the Land. This maze of living stilettoes forms an effective shield surrounding the Boskydells, turning aside all but the most determined. There are a few roads within long thorn tunnels passing through the barrier, and in generally peaceful times these ways are left unguarded, and any who want to enter may do so. During times of crisis, however, along the roads within the barrier Warrow archers stand guard behind movable barricades made of the Spindle-thorn, to keep ruffians and other unsavory characters outside while permitting ingress to those with legitimate business.

In that cold November of 4E2018, when this tale began, it was a time of crisis.

Calendar of the Iron Tower

Events of the Second Era

In the final days of the Second Era, the Great War of the Ban was fought. On the High Plane, Adon prevailed over the Great Evil, Gyphon; on the Middle Plane, by an unexpected stroke the Grand Alliance won and vile Modru was defeated upon Mithgar. Adon set His Ban upon the creatures of the Untargarda who aided Gyphon in the War: they were forever banished from the light of Mithgar's Sun, and those who would defy the Ban suffer the Withering Death. Gyphon, swearing vengeance, was exiled beyond the Spheres. Thus did the Second Era end and the Third Era begin ... and so matters stood for some four thousand years, until the Fourth Era.

Events of the Fourth Era

4E1992: Patrel Rushlock born near Midwood, Eastdell, the Boskydells.

4E1995: Tuckerby Underbank born in Woody Hollow, Eastdell, the Boskydells.

4E1996: Danner Bramblethorn born in Woody Hollow, Eastdell, the Boskydells.

4E1999: Merrilee Holt born in Woody Hollow, Eastdell, the Boskydells.

4E2013: Comet Dragon Star flashes through the heavens of Mithgar, nearly striking the world. Great flaming gouting chunks score the night skies, some pieces hurtling to earth. Many see this hairy star as a harbinger of doom.

The Winter War
4E2018

August: A cold month. Wolves sighted in Northdell, the Boskydells. Gammer Alderbuc begins organizing the Thornwalker Wolf Patrols. Some days of frost in late August.

September: Gammer Alderbuc appoints Captain Alver as head of the Thornwalkers. Snow falls on the seventh of the month. Old Barlo begins archery classes in Woody Hollow, training a group of Thornwalker recruits; Tuck and Danner are students. Rumors come to the Boskydells of some dark Evil up north, reputed to be Modru.

October: Several Boskydell families disappear; none can say where. Cold grips the Land. Snow.

November 2: Old Barlo's archery class graduates. As Thornwalker recruits, Tuck, Danner, Hob Banderel, and Tarpy Wiggens are to join the Eastdell Fourth, guarding Spindle Ford.

November 9: With Patrel as their guide, Tuck, Danner, Hob, and Tarpy set out for Spindle Ford.

November 10: The five Warrows stop at the Huggs' farm, but the owners have disappeared. The Warrows discover evidence of evil Wolf-like Vulgs who apparently have slain the Huggs.

November 11: Vulgs attack the Warrows at Rooks' Roost. Hob is slain.

November 13–December 5: Tuck, Danner, Tarpy take up their Thornwalker duties in Patrel's com-

pany, standing Beyonder Guard at the Ford and
riding Wolf Patrol. On December 3, a waggon train
of refugees passes through bearing news that High
King Aurion prepares for War at Challerain Keep.
On December 4, a Kingsman arrives calling the
muster at Challerain Keep. A Vulg attack upon the
herald results in the drowning of the Man, the
horse, and Tarpy. Tuck survives, rescued by Danner.
On December 5, Tuck, Danner, Patrel, and forty
other Warrows volunteer to answer the King's call.
December 6–13: The Warrows travel to Challerain
Keep. On December 13, Tuck, Danner, and Patrel
meet Prince Igon, Princess Laurelin, Elf Lord Gildor,
Kingsgeneral Vidron, and High King Aurion. The
Warrows learn of the Dimmendark, a spectral
Shadowlight to the north where the Sun shines
not and Adon's Ban does not rule, hence vile creatures roam free.
December 14–20: Warrows take up duties as members of the Castle-ward. Tuck becomes friends with
Princess Laurelin, learning that she is betrothed to
Prince Galen, who even now rides with a company
of Men within the Dimmendark, scouting for evidence that Modru is gathering his evil Hordes of
old.

Tuck, Danner, and Patrel attend the Princess's
birthday eve feast, and as the celebration rises to
its height, a wounded warrior comes bearing news
that the dreadful pall of the Dimmendark has
started moving south. The Winter War has begun.
December 21: First Yule: Princess Laurelin departs
Challerain Keep on the last waggon train of refugees, escorted by Prince Igon, who is sent to hasten the King's Host from Pellar to Challerain Keep.
December 22: Second Yule: The Dimmendark
sweeps over the Keep and beyond. The spectral
Shadowlight baffles eyesight: Men see at most two

miles over open plains, and even less in forests and hill country; Elves see perhaps twice as far as Men; Warrows, as if seeing by a new color, see farthest of all, as much as five miles.

December 23: Third Yule: The Warrow company is disbanded, and the buccen are posted among the King's Companies to use their Warrow eyes to see for the Men.

On this day the Horde, thirty thousand strong, lays siege to the Keep.

December 24: Fourth Yule: In the distance north of the Keep, Galen's Men set fire to a siege tower, yet other siege engines arrive to be used by the Horde. Catapults fling fire over the walls, and the city burns.

December 25: Fifth Yule: Challerain Keep continues to burn.

Laurelin's waggon train is attacked by Ghûls; Prince Igon is felled; Princess Laurelin, her arm broken, is taken captive; all others are slain.

December 26: Sixth Yule: The Horde attacks. The first and second walls of Challerain Keep fall.

Prince Igon, sorely wounded, takes up pursuit of Laurelin's captors.

December 27: Seventh Yule: The third and fourth walls of Challerain Keep fall.

The Battle of Weiunwood begins. Here, in this shaggy forest, the Weiunwood Alliance of Men, Warrows, and Elves fends off another of Modru's Hordes.

December 28: Eighth Yule: Challerain Keep is abandoned. The King's forces attempt to break free of the Horde. King Aurion is slain. Separated from the others, Tuck flees, taking refuge in an ancient tomb where he discovers the Red Quarrel and the Atalar Blade. By happenstance, Prince Galen comes to the same tomb. Together they flee southward, riding for a rendezvous in Stonehill with any others who might have survived.

Danner and Patrel, also cut off from the others, begin their own trek for Stonehill.

General Vidron and Lord Gildor, along with the pitiful remnants of the Kingsmen, break free and ride east toward the Signal Mountains.

The Battle of Weiunwood enters its second 'Day.
December 29: Ninth Yule: The Battle of Weiunwood enters its third 'Day. The Horde breaks off and marches east and south, skirting the borders of the shaggy forest.
December 30: Tenth Yule: Year's End Eve: Tuck and Galen discover the slaughtered waggon train and begin the long pursuit of Laurelin's captors.
December 31: Eleventh Yule: Year's End Day: Danner and Patrel come upon the slaughtered waggon train. Knowing that ponies are too slow to overtake the Ghûls, the pair decides to continue on to Stonehill and the rendezvous.

4E2019

January 1: Twelfth Yule: Last Yule: Year's Start Day: Snow covers the track of Laurelin's captors. Tuck and Galen arrive at the Weiunwood; they are given food and a place to sleep and are warded by members of the Weiunwood Alliance.
January 2–3: Seeking information about Laurelin's captors, Tuck and Galen travel through Weiunwood to meet the Alliance leaders: Arbagon Fenner (Warrow), Bockleman Brewster (Man), and Lord Inarion (Elf). Galen is told that the Ghûls passed by, heading eastward, perhaps riding for Drearwood. Tuck and Galen strike out for that dire forest.

Vidron and Gildor and the remnants of the Kingsmen of Challerain Keep come to the Weiunwood. Gildor turns aside to confer with his kith while

Vidron continues on toward Stonehill. Gildor learns that Galen passed through the Weiunwood, and the Elf sets out in pursuit, one day behind.

January 4: The captive Princess Laurelin is borne through Grūwen Pass and into Gron. She knows now that she is bound for the Iron Tower, Modru's mighty fortress upon Claw Moor.

In her wake, Prince Igon, suffering dreadfully from his wound, collapses in the snow. He is discovered by a patrol of Elves who bear him to the Hidden Refuge of Arden Vale, where he is tended.

January 5–7: Tuck and Galen continue the long pursuit, crossing Drear Ford on the sixth and picking up the track of Laurelin's captors as it runs through Drearwood.

Danner and Patrel come to Stonehill; the town is deserted. They decide to wait two days, and if no one else comes, they will go west to the Boskydells and gather more Warrows and then fare south to Pellar to join the Host and be their eyes in the Dimmendark.

January 8: Tuck and Galen enter Arden Vale, where they meet Lord Talarin and Lady Rael, Elven leaders of the Hidden Refuge. Lord Talarin takes them to see the wounded Man the Elves found lying in the snow. It is Prince Igon, abed and delirious from his wound. At last Galen confirms that Laurelin is indeed a captive. Lord Gildor finally catches up to Galen and informs him that King Aurion is slain and that Galen is now High King. Galen must choose between love and duty: to pursue the captive Princess, or to rally the Host to War.

Danner and Patrel leave Stonehill for the Boskydells. Just as they ride out through the west gate, General Vidron and his force ride in through the east gate; they do not see one another.

January 9: Galen finds he has no choice; he must ride south and rally the Host to fight the enemy. With heavy hearts, he, Tuck, and Lord Gildor begin the long journey toward Pellar.

Vanidor, Gildor's twin brother, with three comrades—Varion, Duorn, and Flandrena—sets off north into Gron to spy out Modru's strength and, if fortune favors them, to rescue the Princess.

An ex-soldier named Jarek comes to Stonehill and tells Vidron that Gûnarring Gap, the key pass to the south, is held by the foe. Vidron decides to ride west to Wellen and muster troops to break the grasp of the enemy upon the Gap.

January 10: Danner and Patrel enter the Boskydells and discover that Modru's Reavers have laid waste to the village of Greenfields. During the night, General Vidron and his company gallop through Greenfields on their way to Wellen. Again, the two Warrows just miss encountering Vidron.

January 11: Princess Laurelin arrives at last at the Iron Tower. Modru imprisons her in a lightless, filthy cell.

January 12: Danner and Patrel arrive at Woody Hollow; Ghûls have set the hamlet aflame. Merrilee Holt saves Danner and Patrel from a reaver. Danner and Patrel learn that Tuck's parents as well as Merrilee's were slain by the raiding Ghûls.

January 13: Warrow archers meet in Whitby's barn to make plans to strike back at the Ghûls.

January 14: Tuck, Galen, and Gildor, riding south along the Grimwall Mountains, come upon Brega, Dwarf warrior, the only survivor of a great battle between a Dwarven company and the vanguard of a Rücken Horde. Brega joins the trio and south they ride.

January 15: Battle of Budgens: Warrows ambush Ghûl reavers in Budgens, Eastdell, the Boskydells.

January 16: Fleeing before Ghûls, Tuck, Galen, Gildor, and Brega are forced to the Dusk-Door of Drimmen-deeve. There they are attacked by the Krakenward and flee into the dark, Gargon-ruled halls of the ancient Dwarven Realm.

Laurelin is taken from her cell and led to a high tower, where she finds Vanidor captive. Modru gloats over the Myrkenstone, a chunk of the Dragon Star used to create the Dimmendark. Laurelin is forced to witness Vanidor's murder. By an unknown Elven power, in the moment of his death Vanidor thrusts a Death Rede upon his twin, Gildor, who is far to the south at the Dusk-Door.

In the Boskydells, Budgens is burned.

January 17–18: Tuck, Galen, Gildor, and Brega trek through Drimmen-deeve, heading for the Dawn-Gate and freedom. The Gargon, a fear caster, discovers that they are in the caverns and pursues them, aided in the hunt by a Horde of maggot-folk. The four Heroes manage to slay the Gargon and escape.

January 19–20: Travelling south, Tuck, Galen, Glldor, and Brega at last win free of the Dimmendark.

In the Boskydells, the Company of Whitby's Barn joins with the Eastwood Company, and on the twentieth they ambush a great gang of Ghûls in the Battle of Brackenboro. Danner, Patrel, and Merrilee are rescued by Vidron and warriors from Wellen who are on their way to free Gûnarring Gap from the Lakh of Hyree.

January 21: Tuck, Galen, Gildor, and Brega come to Darda Galion, Land of Eld Trees, Land of the Silverlarks.

Danner, Patrel, Merrilee, and seven more Warrows join Vidron to act as eyes for the Men as they set off for Gûnarring Gap.

January 23: Tuck, Galen, Gildor, and Brega speak with Coron Eiron in Wood's-Heart, Darda Galion. Plans are made to fare by boat to the Argon Ferry where, if the ferry is in friendly hands, they can find aid to lead them to the Host.

Vidron's Legion leaves the Boskydells, riding for Gûnarring Gap.

The vanguard of the Horde from Challerain Keep enters the Boskydells by the old abandoned Northwood tunnel.

January 24: Tuck, Galen, Gildor, and Brega set out by Elven boat for the Argon Ferry.

The main body of the Horde from Challerain Keep enters the Boskydells.

January 25: Whlle speaking of an eclipse, Gildor at last remembers Vanidor's Death Rede: "The Darkest Day, The Greatest Evil . . ." Gildor surmises that during the eclipse coming February 22, Modru will attempt to bring Gyphon to Mithgar from beyond the Spheres.

January 28: Tuck, Galen, Gildor, and Brega arrive at the Argon Ferry.

January 29–31: Tuck, Galen, Gildor, and Brega, accompanied by Reachmarshal Ubrik, ride for Gûnarring Gap.

At the Gap itself a great battle rages between the Harlingar of Valon and the Lakh of Hyree. After three days, the Harlingar prevail.

February 1: Tuck, Galen, Gildor, Brega and Ubrik arrive at Gûnarring Gap. King Aranor of Valon commits five thousand Vanadurin warriors to ride north with High King Galen to the Iron Tower to attempt to disrupt Modru's plans on the Darkest Day, the 'Day of the eclipse.

Vidron at last comes to the Gap, and, believing it to be enemy-held, plans an attack.

February 2: Vidron, not realizing that the Gap is

now in friendly hands, unknowingly launches an attack upon the Vanadurin. In the last moment both sides see that neither is the foe of the other, and each sheers off the attack.

Vidron's Legion joins High King Galen's quest.

Tuck is reunited with Merrilee, Danner, and Patrel.

At the pace of a Valanreach long-ride, the Host starts north for Gron in a race to arrive at the Iron Tower ere the coming of the Darkest Day.

February 5: Galen's Host comes to Gûnar Slot.

February 7: Galen's Host comes to the edge of the Dimmendark.

February 8: Galen's Host passes Ragad Vale.

The Horde attacking Weiunwood breaks off the assault and starts east from Stonehill to intercept Galen's Host.

February 9: The Host passes the road to Quadran Pass.

The Horde is at Beacontor.

February 10: The Host crosses Rhone Ford. The horses of Vidron's Legion are weary, for they have come all the way from Wellen, and they begin to have difficulty maintaining the hard pace.

The Horde continues east at a forced march.

Elf Lord Inarion sets out from Beacontor to warn Lord Talarin in Arden Vale of the Horde's eastward march.

February 11: The Host camps south of Drearwood. The horses of Vidron's Legion continue to grow weary.

The Horde nears the Wilderness Hills.

February 12: The Host comes to the Crossland Road near Arden Ford.

The Horde comes to the Stone-arches Bridge.

Lord Inarion arrives in Arden Vale.

February 13: The Host camps alongside Arden Bluff.

Prince Igon, Elf Lord Talarin, Elf Lord Inarion, and Elf Flandrena come to High King Galen's camp. Inarion speaks of the Horde. Flandrena, the only survivor of Vanidor's ill-fated mission into Gron, tells of the strength of the Iron Tower. Galen asks Vidron and the Wellenen to delay the Horde at Grūwen Pass. Talarin and the Elves of Arden join Vidron's force of Wellenen. Prince Igon, recovered from his wound, joins Galen on the mission to the Iron Tower.

February 14: The Host passes through Grūwen Pass to come into Gron.

Vidron's Legion and the Elves of Arden take up positions to defend Grūwen Pass.

The Horde comes to Arden Ford.

February 15: The Host continues north.

The cast is removed from Princess Laurelin's arm, now healed. Laurelin continues to seek a means of escape.

February 17: The Host comes to the south edge of the Gwasp.

The Horde arrives at Grūwen Pass.

February 18: The Host comes to the north edge of the Gwasp.

The Horde attacks the defenders of Grūwen Pass.

February 19: The Host comes to Claw Moor.

Second 'Day of the Battle of Grūwen Pass.

February 20: The Host arrives at the Iron Tower.

Third 'Day of the Battle of Grūwen Pass.

February 21: Galen and his War-council plan the assault of the Iron Tower.

Fourth 'Day of the Battle of Grūwen Pass.

February 22: The Darkest Day: The Host begins the assault on the Iron Tower. Brega leads a raid across a chasm and up the fortress walls to lower the drawbridge and open the gate. Injured, Tuck crawls through a drain under the rampart and slowly makes his way to Laurelin's prison chamber. Modru stuns Tuck and drags Laurelin to the top of the tower to sacrifice her and bring Gyphon to Mithgar. Brega's raiders drop the drawbridge. Patrel tricks a Troll into opening the gate. The Host invades the fortress. Danner is slain in the battle atop the gate. Tuck wins to the tower and slays the Myrkenstone, killing Modru and sending Gyphon back beyond the Spheres. Tuck is blinded. The Dimmendark collapses; Adon's Ban is restored and the Withering Death strikes down the maggot-folk. The Lakh of Hyree are defeated. The Rovers of Kistan flee across the Avagon Sea. The Winter War is ended.

February 23–March 3: Great storms hammer Mithgar. A blizzard traps the Host in the Iron Tower.

March 4: The Host leaves the Iron Tower and begins the trek homeward.

March 13: The Host arrives in Arden Vale.

March 20: First Day of Spring: After a week's rest, the Host again resumes the journey homeward.

March 22: King Galen, Princess Laurelin, Prince Igon, General Vidron, and the Men of Valon continue south for Pellar, while Tuck, Merrilee, Patrel, and the surviving Warrows, escorted by the Men of Wellen, turn westward along the Crossland Road heading for the Boskydells.

March 30: The Warrows and their escort arrive at Stonehill.

April 1: The Warrows and their escort leave Stonehill.

April 3: The Warrows and their escort enter the Boskydells. Patrel Rushlock turns aside to journey to Midwood, Eastdell, the Boskydells.

April 4: Tuck and Merrilee arrive in Woody Hollow, Eastdell, the Boskydells.

June 21: Year's Long-Day: Mid-Year's Day: Tuckerby Underbank marries Merrilee Holt.

August: The Underbanks move into The Root.

Autumn: High King Galen marries Laurelin of Riamon.

The Order of the Realmsmen is founded.

December 31: Eleventh Yule: Year's End Day: Last day of the Fourth Era.

Events of Later Years

January 1, 5E1: Twelfth Yule: Last Yule: Year's Start Day: First day of the Fifth Era (5E).

January 15, 5E1: A monument is unveiled in Budgens on the anniversary of the Battle of Budgens commemorating the village as the place where began the Struggles.

October 15, 5E2: Raven Underbank is born in Woody Hollow, Eastdell, the Boskydells.

Circa 5E7: Tuckerby Underbank is commissioned by the High King to gather and record the history of the Winter War, a work that is to take his lifetime and will be called *Sir Tuckerby Underbank's Unfinished Diary and His Accounting of the Winter War*. In the work Tuck will be assisted by many scholars and scribes, but mainly by his daughter, Raven. In later years Tuck will refer to the work as *The Raven Book*.

5E31: Raven Underbank marries Willen Greylock. They move to the Cliffs, Westdell, the Boskydells, where Willen founds the Ravenbook Scholars.

5E35: Robin Greylock born, the Cliffs, Westdell, the Boskydells.

Circa 5E40: Tuckerby's Warren, The Root, becomes a museum housing artifacts of the Winter War.

5E46: High King Galen dies at Caer Pendwyr, Pellar, during a raging storm. His and Laurelin's eldest son, Gareth, becomes High King.

Circa 5E47: Rumors abound of many Elves passing to Adonar upon the High Plane, leaving Mithgar behind.

December 17, 5E73: Tuck falls ill.

December 31, 5E73: Eleventh Yule: Year's End Day: Tuckerby Underbank, Bearer of the Red Quarrel, 'Stone Slayer, Hero of the Realm, dies at the age of 97.

5E91: Merrilee Holt Underbank dies.

5E193: Brega Bekki's son, DelfLord of the Red Hills, dies at the age of 242. Thus passes away the last of the mortal Heroes of the Winter War.

The Long Journeys

In the course of the Winter War, several extraordinary, long, hard journeys were undertaken. Ravenbook Scholars summarize these journeys as follows:

The pony ride of the Company of the King from Spindle Ford to Challerain Keep: 175 miles in 7½ days (December 6–13, 4E2018).

The Hèlsteed ride of the Kinstealers from the Battle Downs to the Iron Tower: 600 miles in 18 days (December 25, 4E2018–January 11, 4E2019).

The pony ride of Danner and Patrel from Challerain Keep to Stonehill: 250 miles in 10 days (December 28, 4E2018–January 6, 4E2019).

The ride (on Jet) of Tuck and Galen from Challerain Keep to the Battle Downs and thence to Arden Vale: 400 miles in 11½ days (December 28, 4E2018–January 8, 4E2019).

The ride (on Fleetfoot) of Gildor from Challerain Keep to the Signal Mountains and then to the Weiunwood and thence to Arden Vale: 350 miles in 11½ days (December 28, 4E2018–January 8, 4E2019).

The ride of Vidron (and Men) from Challerain Keep to the Signal Mountains and then to the Weiunwood and thence to the Battle Downs and on to Stonehill: 300 miles in 11½ days (December 28, 4E2O18–January 8, 4E2019).

The ride of Jarek from Gûnarring Gap to Stonehill: 565 miles in 12¼ days (December 28, 4E2018–January 9, 4E2019).

The pony ride of Danner and Patrel from Stonehill to Woody Hollow: 125 miles in 5 days (January 8–12, 4E2019).

The ride of Vidron (and Men) from Stonehill to Wellen: 300 miles in 6 days (January 9–15, 4E2019).

The ride of Tuck, Galen, and Gildor from Arden Vale to the Dusk-Door of Drimmen-deeve (Brega joined the trio for the final 3 days): 325 miles in 8 days, the final 20 miles while being pursued by Ghûls on Hèlsteeds (January 9–16, 4E2019).

The ride of Vanidor, Varion, Duorn, and Flandrena from Arden Vale to the Iron Tower: 275 miles in 6 days (January 9–14, 4E2019).

The ride (on Swiftmane) of Flandrena from the Iron Tower to Arden Vale: 275 miles in 3½ days (January 16–19, 4E2019).

The ride of Vidron's Legion from Wellen to Brackenboro: 175 miles in 4 days (January 17–20, 4E2019).

The ride of Vidron's Legion from Brackenboro to Gûnarring Gap: 575 miles in 12 days (January 21–February 1, 4E2019).

The Elven boat ride of Tuck, Galen, Gildor, and Brega down the River Argon from Bellon Falls to the Argon Ferry: 750 miles over 4 days (January 25–28, 4E2019).

The ride of Tuck, Galen, Gildor, Brega and Ubrik from the Argon Ferry to Gûnarring Gap: 400 miles in 4 days riding horses with trailing remounts and obtaining fresh mounts at the Red Hills Garrison (January 29–February 1, 4E2019).

The ride of Vidron's Legion from Gûnarring Gap to Grūwen Pass: 635 miles in 13 days (February 2–14, 4E2019).

[Note: Perhaps the three rides of Vidron's Wellenan Legion are the most remarkable of all. The horses of Wellen, bearing Warriors, arms, and armor, covered a combined total of 1,385 miles in 29 days (January 17–February 14, 4E2019) in an unremitting Valanreach long-ride from Wellen to Brackenboro to Gûnarring Gap to Grūwen Pass. It is little wonder that this grueling trek took its toll upon the steeds such that they at last could no longer keep up the pace.]

The ride of the Host from Gûnarring Gap to the Iron Tower: 900 miles in 18½ days (February 2–20, 4E2019).

The forced march of one of Modru's Hordes from Stonehill to Arden Ford and thence to Grūwen Pass: 350 miles in 9½ days (February 8–17, 4E2019).

The ride (upon Wingfoot and Wildwind) of Inarion from Beacontor to Arden Vale: 215 miles in 3 days (February 10–12, 4E2019).

The ride of the Host from the Iron Tower to Arden Vale: 275 miles in 9½ days (March 4–13, 4E2019).

The ride of the Warrows and Wellenen from Arden Vale to Stonehill: 375 miles in 11 days (March 20–30, 4E2019).

The ride of the Warrows and Wellenen from Stonehill to Woody Hollow: 125 miles in 4 days (April 1–4, 4E2019).

Thus were the remarkable journeys of both friend and foe during the Winter War, as recorded in *The Raven Book.*

The Eclipse of the Darkest Day

The Raven Book makes it clear that the solar eclipse of February 22, 4E2019, was a total one at the Iron Tower. Further, from the context it can be inferred that the duration was lengthy. But the text may be misleading, for if we assume that the celestial mechanics of the earth-Moon-Sun system of Mithgar of yore are the same as those of the earth-moon-sun system of today, then the duration of the totality at the Iron Tower could not have exceeded seven minutes thirty-three seconds (the maximum possible duration of totality at any given point on the earth's surface along the path of the umbra). And if a few simple assumptions are made about the probable latitude and longitude of Modru Kinstealer's holt, then it is more likely that the duration of the totality would fall somewhat short of this maximum time. Finally, if the eclipse was "typical," a totality time of two to four minutes seems reasonable.

Yet, two or four or even seven minutes does not seem to be enough time to carry out the actions known to have occurred during the totality at the

Iron Tower. For example, after the darkness fell, could Merrilee and the Warrows have gathered together a force of warriors in the courtyards and then gotten to the top of the tower . . . all in seven minutes or less? It does not seem likely.

Three immediate hypotheses spring to mind: (1) the actions described actually took place in a very brief time; (2) the motions of the earth-Moon-Sun system of Mithgar of yore were not the same as those of our system today; or (3) the darkness fell within the Dimmendark prior to total occlusion.

Of these three hypotheses, the last one seems most likely: that is, somewhat prior to totality, the Sun's rays were eclipsed to the point that the remaining light simply was too feeble to significantly illuminate the Dimmendark. At this point the Men could no longer see, and the Elves, but dimly. This theory is supported by the fact that approximately two hundred miles southward in the Dimmendark, at Grūwen Pass—and for that matter, at Mineholt North in Riamon, as well as even further south in the Boskydells—where the eclipse was not total, darkness fell upon the combatants, and they, too, could not see. (Except, of course, wherever Warrows were, the Wee Folk saw by the "black" light of the Myrkenstone.)

Hence, it can be surmised that although the time of the totality at the Iron Tower was but two to four minutes in duration, the actual span of time that only the Warrows could see was perhaps fifteen or more minutes—certainly time enough for the described actions to have taken place.

Two other items of interest: (1) Based on *The Raven Book*, it can be surmised that the path of totality swept from the west across Rian, over The Rigga Mountains and into Gron, across Claw Spur and over the Iron Tower, past the Gronfang Mountains and into Jord, and thence over the Grimwall Mountains and through Aven and beyond. In Grūwen Pass, Arden, the Boskydells, Riamon, Valon, Jugo, Pellar, and the like, the eclipse was only partial. (2) The "beads of light" spoken of in *The Raven Book* that sprang forth from the rim of the unseen Moon as the eclipse was lifting were, no doubt, Baily's beads, which are described elsewhere in astronomical literature.

Finally, the latitude and longitude of the Iron Tower only can be speculated upon, and many scholars have tried to deduce its location (some have suggested that it was situated near Leningrad [30° east, 60° north], while others have selected a site near Warsaw [21° east, 52° north], and yet others have their reasons for selecting a diverse number of even different locales). Again, the reader is cautioned that it is sheer speculation as to the location of Modru Kinstealer's holt. *The Raven Book* states that Gron was in the north and was a cold barren Land; hence, any location above perhaps 50° north is suitable grist for scholars' mills. It would seem that astronomers specializing in solar eclipses are more likely to isolate the probable location of the Iron Tower than are historians and linguists.

The Effect of the Myrkenstone on Tuck's Eyes

Although the Ravenbook Scholars of Tuckerby's time speculated long over the cause of Tuck's blindness, they came to no firm conclusion. In the Sixth Era however, Warrow Historian Burmly Gribbs proposed that Tuck's sightlessness came about as follows:

It seems clear (postulated Burmly) that the Myrkenstone emitted a radiance beyond the usual range of vision, a radiance seen only by Warrow and not by Man, Elf, Dwarf, or even by Spawn. Hence, when Tuck confronted the 'Stone—standing but a few feet from it—his eyes were whelmed by the dark "glare" just as if he were staring at an extremely bright source of nearby ordinary light, a source so brilliant that close-by torches emitting normal light were lost to his sight in the darkling blare of the Myrkenstone. Tuck's "special" Warrow vision was blasted by this black radiance, rending him of his ability to see in the dark luminance. Yet, there is good evidence that he would have been able to see by normal light had he at that time been taken away from the vicinity of the 'Stone.

Instead, he loosed the Red Quarrel, and when it struck the Myrkenstone a raging flare blasted forth. Now, in truth, Tuck was staring through a glare so bright, so intense, that his "normal" sight was destroyed, too. Hence (concluded Burmly), what vision the harsh black radiance did not sunder, the blaring bright radiance did, and Tuck was totally blinded as a result. No scholar since Burmly's time has set forth a more convincing explanation.

Songs, Inscriptions, and Redes

(Listed by: type; title; first line; books[s] and chapter[s] of appearance)

Old Barlo's Admonition: The arrow as strays might well'er been throwed away (Book One, Chapters 1, 5; Book Two, Chapter 3; Book Three, Chapter 5)

Warrow Song: *The Thornwalkers' Song:* We are Thornwalkers (Book One, Chapter 2)

Warrow Dirge: *Sail the Endless Sea:* The Shadow Tide doth run (Book One, Chapter 2)

Othran's Tomb Inscription: Loose not the Red Quarrel (Book One, Chapter 4; Book Two, Chapter 6; Book Three, Chapters 5, 6, 7)

Warrow Song: *The Merry Man in Boskledee:* Oh—Fiddle-dee hi, fiddle-dee ho (Book One, Chapter 4)

Rael's Rede: Neither of two Evils must thy strike claim (Book Two, Chapter 2; Book Three, Chapters 5, 6, 7)

Warrow Dirge: *The Four Seasons:* In Winter's glade now cold and bare (Book Two, Chapter 3)

Budgens Monument Inscription: Let it be said now and for all the days hereafter that on this day the struggle began, and Evil met its match (Book Two, Chapter 3; Book Three, Chapter 7)

Rael's Sooth: Bright Silverlarks and Silver Sword (Book Two, Chapter 6)

Vanidor's Death Rede: The Darkest Day (Book Two, Chapter 6; Book Three, Chapter 3)

Warrow Lay: *The Loosing of the Red Quarrel:* Loose not the Red Quarrel ere appointed dark time (Book Three, Chapter 7)

Warrow Lay: *The Lay of the Iron Tower:* From frozen north (Book Three, Chapter 7)

Translations of Words and Phrases

Throughout *The Raven Book* appear many words and phrases in languages other than the Common Tongue, Pellarion. For scholars interested in such things, these words and phrases are collected together in this appendix. A number of tongues are involved:

Châkur = Dwarven tongue
OHR = Old High tongue of Riamon
OP = Old tongue of Pellar
OR = Old tongue of Rian
Slûk = Spawn tongue
Sylva = Elven tongue
Twyll = ancient Warrow tongue
Valur = ancient War-tongue of Valon

The table on the following page is a cross-check listing of the most common terms found in various tongues in *The Raven Book*.

——————Man——————

Warrow (Twyll)	Valon Valur)	Pellar (Pellarion)	Elf (Sylva)	Dwarf (Châkur)
Rûck	Rutch	Rukh	Ruch	Ûkh
Rûcks	Rutcha	Rukha	Rucha	Ûkhs
Rûcken	Rutchen	Rukken	Ruchen	Ûkken
Hlôk	Drôkn	Lôkh	Lok	Hrôk
Hlôks	Drôkha	Lôkha	Loka	Hrôks
Hlôken	Drôken	Lôkken	Loken	Hrôken
Ghû	Guul	Ghol	Ghûlk	Khôl
Ghûls	Guula	Ghola	Ghûlka	Khôls
Ghûlen	Guulen	Gholen	Ghûlken	Khôlen
Dread Gargon	Dread Gargon	Dread Gargon	Dread Gargon	Dread Ghath
Gargons	Gargons	Gargons	Gargoni	Ghaths
Ogru	Ogru	Troll	Troll	Troll
Kraken	Kraken	Kraken	Hèlarmûs	Madûk
maggot-folk	Wrg	Yrm	*Rûpt*	Grg
Spawn	Spawn	Spawn; *Spaunen*	*Spaunen*	Squam
Dwarf	Dwarf	Dwarf	Drimm	Cnâk
Dwarves	Dwarves	Dwarves	Drimma	Châkka
Dwarven	Dwarven	Dwarven	Drimmen	Châkka
Elf	Deva	Elf	Lian;* Dylvan	Elf
Elves	Deva'a	Elves	Lian; Dylvana	Elves

————————Man————————

Warrow (Twyll)	Valon Valur)	Pellar (Pellarion)	Elf (Sylva)	Dwarf (Châkur)
Elven	Deven	Elven	Lianen; Dylvanen	Elven
Giant Giants	Giant Giants	Utrun Utruni	Utrun Utruni	Utrun Utruni
Warrow Warrows Wee Folk	Waldan Waldana *Waldfolc*	Waerling Waerlinga Wee Folk	Waerling Waerlinga —	Waeran Waerans —

*The Elves consist of two strains: (1) the Lian, the First Elves, and (2) the Dylvana, the Wood Elves.

In the following text, words and phrases are listed under the tongue of origin. Where possible, direct translations () are provided; in the other cases, the translation is inferred from the context {} of *The Raven Book*. Also listed is the name of the speaker [], if known.

Châkur
(Dwarven tongue)

Aggarath (untranslated) [Brega] {Grimspire}
Baralan (Sloping land = the Pitch)
Châkka djalk aggar theck! (Dwarven————!) [Brega]
Châkka shok! Châkka cor! (Dwarven axes! Dwarven might!) [Brega]
Ctor (Shouter) [Brega]
Dēop (Deep) [Brega]
Drakkalan (Dark Shedder) [Brega]
Gaard! (untranslated) [Brega] {a Wizard word perhaps meaning Move!; Act!)

Ghatan (untranslated) [Brega] {Loftcrag}

Hyranee (Hyrani) [Brega] {one or more Men of Hyree}

Jarak (Courser) [Brega]

Khana (Breakdeath) [Brega]

Kistanee (Kistani) [Brega] {one or more Men of Kistan}

Kraggen-cor (Mountain-might) [Brega] {Drimmen-deeve}

Kruk! (untranslated expletive) [Brega]

Mountain (Living stone) [Brega]

Rávenor (untranslated) [Brega] {Stormhelm}

Uchan (untranslated) [Brega] {Greytower}

Vorvor (untranslated name of a whirlpool) [Brega]

OHR
(Old High tongue of Riamon)

Zūo Hělm widar iu! (To Hèl with you!) [Laurelin]

OR
(Old tongue of Rian)

Ahn! (horn call meaning, Ready!) [Jarriel]

Ahn! Hahn! (horn call meaning, Assemble!) [Jarriel]

Hál! Aurion ūre cynig! (Hail! Aurion our King!) [Captains of Challera Keep]

Hál! Hēah Adoni cnāwen ūre weg! (Hail! High Adon knows our way!) [Aurion]

Rahn! (horn call meaning, Prepare!) [Hogarth]

OP
(Old tongue of Pellar)

Cepān wyllan, Lian; wir gān bringan thē Sunna! (Keep well, Lian; we go to bring the Sun!) [Galen]

Hál ūre allience! Hál ūre bond! (Hail our alliance! Hail our bond!) [Galen]

Hōhgarda (High Worlds) [Galen]

Jagga, Rust! Jagga! (Hide, Rust! Hide!) [Laurelin]

Larkenwald (Lark Wood = Wood of the Larks)
Maeg Adoni laenan strengthu to ūre earms! (May Adon lend strength to our arms!) [Aurion]
Mittegarda (Middle Worlds) [Galen]
Poeir bē in thyne earms! (Power be in thine arms!) [Galen]
Rach! (untranslated expletive)
Untargarda (Under Worlds) [Galen]

Slûk
(Span tongue)

Arg tla! Shugg du! (untranslated) [Hlōk gate captain] {You there! Name yourself!}
Dolh (Elf/Elves) [Modru]
Dolh schluu gogger! (Elf——————!) [Modru] {Elf on rack!}
Dubh (Dwarf/Dwarves) [Modru]
Garja ush! (untranslated) [Modru] {Raise her up!}
Ghun (untranslated) [Ghol] {Gone}
Glâr! Glâr! (Fire! Fire!) [Drimmnen-deeve Horde]
Gluktu! (untranslated) [Modru/Hyrani emissary] {Attack!}
Glu shtom! (untranslated) [rebellious Ghûl] {I would stay!}
Guk klur gog bleagh. (untranslated) [Rūck] {Eating is better than fighting.}
Gulgok! (untranslated) [Ghûl emissary] {Master!}
Guttra! (untranslated) [Hlōk door guard] {Halt!}
Khakt! (untranslated) [Modru] {Here!}
Nabba thek! (untranslated) [Modru/Naudron] {Dead search! = Search the dead!}
Nabbu gla oth. (untranslated) [Modru/Naudron] {Death take you.}
Negus (Lord/King) [Modru] {Negus of Terror = Lord of Terror = the Gargon}
Rul durg! (untranslated) [Modru/Naudron] {Ready her!}

Schtuga! (untranslated) [Hlōk jailor] {Fool!}

Shabba Dūl! (untranslated) [Modru] {To the Pit!}

Shuul! (untranslated) [Modru] {Guard!}

Slath! (untranslated) [Modru] {Stop!}

Theck dral, guth! (untranslated) [Hlōk overseer] {Get to work, sluggard!}

Thuggon oog. Laug glog raktu! (untranslated) [Modru/Naudron] {Split in two. Half join the Horde!}

Urb schla! Drek! (untranslated) [Modru/Naudron] {All go! Ride!}

Ush (untranslated) [Modru/Naudron] {Up!}

Vhuul! (untranslated) [Modru] {Troll!}

Vulpen (Vulgs) [Modru]

Sylva
(Elven tongue)

Aevor (untranslated) [Gildor] {Grimspire}

Alor (Lord)

Aro! (untranslated exclamation) [Gildor]

Chagor (untranslated) [Gildor] {Loftcrag}

Cianin Andele (Shining Nomad) [Gildor]

Cianin taegi! (Shining days!) [Gildor; Vanidor]

Coron (Ruler/King) [Gildor] {Stormhelm}

Coron Eiron, va Draedan sa nond! (King Eiron, the Gargon is dead!) [Gildor]

Dara (Lady) [Elven healer]

Darda Erynian (Leaf-tree Hall-of-green = Greenhall Forest)

Darda Galion (Leaf-tree Land-of-larks = Forest of the Silverlarks)

dele (porridge)

Draedan (Dread One/Gargon)

Drimm (Dwarf) [Gildor]

Drimmen-deeve (Dwarven-delvings) [Gildor]

Ealle hál va Deevestrīdena, slēanra a va Draedm!

(All hail the Deevewalkers, slayers of the Gargon!) [Eiron]

Eborane (Dark Reaver) [Eiron]

Eryn (Green: e.g., Eryn Ford = Green Ford) [Eiron]

Falanith (Valley Rising = the Pitch)

Fian nath dairia! (May your path be ever straight!) [Inarion]

Gralon (untranslated) [Gildor] {Greytower}

Hal, valagalana! (Hail, valiant warriors!) [Havor; Eiron and Lian escort]

Kel! (untranslated greeting) [Talarin]

Kest! (Stop!) [Duorn; Tuon]

Kregyn (untranslated) {Grūwen Pass}

Lianion (First Land) [Talarin].

mian (waybread)

Nond? Va Draedan sa nond? (Dead? The Gargon is dead?) [Eiron]

Talarn (Steel-heart) [Eiron]

Va Draedan sa nond . . . (The Gargon is dead . . .) [Gildor]

Vanil (silvery)

Vani-lērihha (Silverlarks)

Vio Gildor! (I am Goldbranch!) [Gildor]

Vio ivon Arden. (I am come from Arden.) [Gildor]

wela (mead)

Twyll
(ancient Warrow tongue)

Chelga! (Stand still and speak your name!) [Baskin]

Ellil! (Friend!) [Tuck]

faer sylva (fair forest)

Hai roi! (untranslated exclamation, probably Valur in origin) (buccen of the Eastdell Fourth]

Hanlo's Reya (Hanlo's Foxes) [Danner]

Hlafor Galen, tuon nid legan mi hinda! (Lord Galen, do not leave me behind!) [Tuck]

Hyranan (Hyrani) [Tuck] {a Man of Hyree}

Mandrak (Man-Dragon)
Skut! (untranslated expletive) [Danner; Luth]
So ho! (untranslated ancient hunting call, perhaps meaning, Here!) [Tuck]
Taa-tahn! Taa-tahn! (Warrow horn call meaning, Rally! Rally!) [Patrel]
Ta, tahn! Ta, tahn! Ta, tahn! (Warrow horn call meaning, Attack! Attack! Attack!) [Patrel]
Thuna glath, Fral Wilrow. (Go in peace, Friend Wilrow.) [Tuck]
Wanderjahre (Wandering Days)

Valur
(ancient battle-tongue of Valon)
daemon (demon) [Borel]
Garn! (untranslated expletive) [Vidron]
Hahn, taa-roo! (Valon horn call meaning, Return!) [Vidron]
Hai roi! (untranslated exclamation) [Borel]
Hál, Deva Talarin! Vanada al tro da halka! (Hail, Elf Talarin! Together we shall be mighty!) [Vidron]
Hrosmarshal (Horse Marshal)
Waldfolc (Wood Folk = Folk of the woods)
Zlye pozhiratelly koneny! (Vile gluttons of horse-flesh!) [Vidron]

About the Author

Dennis L. McKiernan was born April 4, 1932, in Moberly, Missouri, where he lived until age eighteen, when he joined the U.S. Air Force, serving four years during the Korean War. He received a BS in electrical engineering from the University of Missouri in 1958 and an MS in the same field from Duke University in 1964. Employed by a leading research and development laboratory, he lives with his family in Westerville, Ohio. Though he has free-lanced articles for magazines, the Iron Tower Trilogy—*The Dark Tide, Shadows of Doom* and *The Darkest Day*—marks his debut as a novelist.